"We've a
sword-po...
or another."

"I did not love you before."

He held his breath. "Do you…love me…now?"

She shivered and her voice caught on a sigh. "Yes."

She loved him? But how could she? He'd flaunted her as
a courtesan, warned her she could not trust him. But he'd
never told her that she had taken his breath away the first
time he'd ever seen her.

"Dianthe," he said, his voice cracking over the force of
his emotions. "I…not a single one of your relatives would
thank me for loving you, and a few would call me out.
And they'd be right. I want nothing more than to despoil
you." He held her closer, burying his face in her hair and
breathing in her scent.

"Do not try to be noble," she said. "Finish what you've
begun…!"

* * *

The Courtesan's Courtship
Harlequin Historical #783—January 2006

THE COURTESAN'S COURTSHIP

GAIL RANSTROM

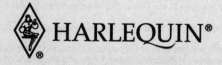

HARLEQUIN®

TORONTO • NEW YORK • LONDON
AMSTERDAM • PARIS • SYDNEY • HAMBURG
STOCKHOLM • ATHENS • TOKYO • MILAN • MADRID
PRAGUE • WARSAW • BUDAPEST • AUCKLAND

ISBN 0-373-29383-6

THE COURTESAN'S COURTSHIP

Copyright © 2006 by Gail Ranstrom

www.eHarlequin.com

Printed in U.S.A.

Please address questions and book requests to:
Harlequin Reader Service
U.S.: 3010 Walden Ave., P.O. Box 1325, Buffalo, NY 14269
Canadian: P.O. Box 609, Fort Erie, Ont. L2A 5X3

Once again, with love, to my family.
Thank you for all the years of love, laughter
and friendship. I couldn't ask for more.

My gratitude and love to Rosanne, Margaret, Cynthia,
Lisa, Eileen and Suzi, who always tell me the truth,
even if I don't like it. And especially to Sandi F.,
through thick and thin.

Chapter One

August 18, 1820

Fragmented shadows skittered across the dark pebbled pathway in Vauxhall Gardens, confusing in their quickly changing patterns. A sigh. A moan. The wind? Even the shadows menaced. Dianthe was not timid, but she had never liked being alone in the dark. Objects seen or imagined disappeared with the next shift of the wind. She stumbled, certain her friends had come this way to watch the fireworks over the river just moments ago. Had she made a wrong turn in the dark?

The bushes nearby rustled and a prickle of fear raced up her spine. Was it the breeze off the river, or were Hortense and Harriett doubling back for her? Or could it be that strange man shrouded in a scarlet cloak who'd run into her earlier? She hadn't been able to see his face, but he'd seemed surprised when she'd turned to glare at his hand on her arm, as if he had thought she was someone else.

She stubbed her toe again and seized the trunk of a tree to keep her balance. Eerie dappled moonlight filtering through the leaves and branches cast another kaleidoscopic mix of shadows and light, but this time there was no mistake. The object she'd stumbled upon was a woman. She looked like a forgotten doll lying facedown and partially hidden beneath a fragrant honeysuckle bush.

Dianthe recognized her—the girl's white dress, actually. It was almost identical to her own, right down to the pink satin ribbon that trimmed the neckline and hem. She'd seen the young woman earlier in the evening, near the entrance.

Hortense, who had been returning from the privy, had stopped and stared. "My goodness, Dianthe, she could be your twin. Even her hair is your light blond," she'd said. That had been hours ago.

Dianthe knelt beside the girl and touched her shoulder. "Miss? Are you ill? Do you need help?" she asked, fighting rising alarm.

"Miss?" she asked again, shaking the girl's shoulder gently. A faint moan sped Dianthe's heartbeat. She tugged at the woman's shoulder and turned her over, her hands coming away wet and sticky. A dark gleaming stain spread in a ragged pattern over the bodice of the young woman's gown. Dianthe was shocked by the look of panic and despair on the girl's face.

"Oh…'tis you. S-stop…him," she whispered in a faint, wavering voice. "Don't let…him get away with…this. Promise me."

"What?" Dianthe asked. "Get away with what, miss?"

"M-murder. Promise…." The woman was agitated, though her voice was growing weaker by the moment. "Be careful, Dianthe…he saw you and will come for you next."

"Do I know you, miss? Who will come? And who was murdered?" she asked.

"The others…and…me," she said with a soft sigh. "Stop him…before…"

A chill of fear and dread raced along Dianthe's nerves. No, that didn't make sense. The girl expelled another sigh and seemed to settle into her arms.

Dianthe shook her again, and her head lolled to one side. "Miss!" she said, her voice tight with anxiety. "I promise, miss! I promise! Just say something. Please!"

The girl's eyes were open. Why wouldn't she answer? "Miss?" Dianthe asked again, louder this time, and fighting the onrushing panic.

She leaned forward, her hair tangling on the branches of the honeysuckle bush and coming loose from her coiffure. An object lay on the ground beside her and, without thinking, she picked it up. Moonlight flashed off the edge. A knife!

Aghast, she recoiled and fell back on her bottom, growing dizzy with disbelief. No, it wasn't true. The young woman's eyes were still open—she couldn't be dead!

Dianthe gulped in a lungful of air, then another, fearing she was about to faint. She couldn't gather her wits or comprehend the horror of what lay before her. Still dizzy, still holding the knife, she drew her knees up and placed her forehead on them, breathing deeply and fighting her rising nausea.

"What the deuce—"

She looked up to find a stranger staring down at her in horror. "Someone bring a lantern!" he shouted.

A moment later, the small clearing sprang to life and a sea of faces surrounded her. Hortense and Harriett pushed forward, staring down at her with mouths agape. Their father knelt on the other side of the dead girl and felt for a pulse.

"What happened, Miss Lovejoy?" Mr. Thayer asked.

"I don't know," she squeaked. "Miss Banks went home and left me to search for you alone. I was trying to catch up for the fireworks and I tripped over..." She swallowed hard, bile rising in her throat. Blood. There was blood on her gown and her hands. And on the knife she still held.

A gentleman dressed in sober black pressed forward and appraised the scene. She recalled meeting Dr. Worley at parties and soirees, and had even danced with him once or twice. Surely now that he was here everything would begin to make sense.

He looked across the body at her. "Why, 'tis Nell Brookes. What is *she* doing here? And what are you doing with her, Miss Lovejoy? She's hardly the sort I would expect to see you with."

What could he mean? What sort? "I found her here," she said, pushing her tangled hair out of her face.

The doctor knelt beside Mr. Thayer, touched the dead girl's neck and shook his head. "She's only been dead a few minutes," he said. "The knife punctured her heart. That's why there's so much blood. Her killer will be covered in it." He looked back at Dianthe and frowned. "What happened, Miss Lovejoy?"

Uncomprehending, she glanced from the girl to Dr. Worley and back again. "She... I found her..." She glanced around at the growing crowd surrounding her. They were looking at her in fascinated horror. Good heavens! Could the murderer be among them? Could he be staring at her even now? Would she be next, as the girl had warned? "I...I fell over her," she said weakly.

"The weapon?" he asked, gesturing at the knife in her hand. "Where did you get it?"

"On the ground. B-beside her."

"How did you come to have so much blood on you, Miss Lovejoy?"

"Here now!" Mr. Thayer interceded. "What are you suggesting? Miss Lovejoy is a proper lady. She does not get herself into trouble."

Hortense and Harriett nodded in agreement.

Mr. Thayer calmed himself and spoke again. "Miss Lovejoy has not been out of our sight more than ten minutes."

Dr. Worley looked sympathetic. "Miss Brookes has been dead less than five," he said. "Was there anyone else about, Miss Lovejoy? Anyone who can verify your story?"

She shook her head. She couldn't even recall her own name. She could only remember a feeling of dread and disquiet.

The crowd was pressing forward in morbid curiosity, and Dr. Worley turned to them. "Did any of you see someone fleeing down any of the paths?"

No one spoke. A number of cautious glances passed from person to person. Surely they couldn't believe she would murder a complete stranger for no particular reason? Dianthe sought a friendly face, someone who had witnessed the event and who could solve the mystery. But they were all strangers to her.

Oh, dear! Not all strangers, curse the luck.

One man, taller than the rest, and absurdly good-looking, edged through the crowd and quickly scanned the scene. He took in the dead girl, the people crowding into the tiny clearing, the shrubbery around them, and then his gaze settled on her. Only the quickest blink of his hard hazel eyes betrayed that he recognized her.

Lord Geoffrey Morgan! Oh, of all the people she'd not have wanted to find her in such a state, he was at the top of her list. How he must be relishing this moment after her set-down in her aunt's drawing room months ago.

But why was he here? For all that he was a baron and from a respectable family, he had fallen low. He should be in some Covent Garden hell, bilking some poor green lad of his fortune. He was a devil—a notorious, ruthless and unscrupulous gambler. And it was ridiculous to think that he might have a life as mundane as to include visits to a pleasure garden.

Edging past the front row of spectators, he knelt beside Dr. Worley and looked at the body. "Nell Brookes," he muttered, his frown forming creases between his eyes. He passed one graceful, elegant hand over the girl's face to close her eyes. "What happened, Worley?"

"Stabbed in the heart. She cannot be dead five minutes. Miss Lovejoy, here, was…found her."

Morgan looked up at her, a flicker of surprise lifting his eyebrows. "What were you doing here, Miss Lovejoy?"

"I was going to the river to meet the Thayers. I tripped over her as I came down this path." She looked around at the faces again. If the murderer knew the girl had spoken to her—had made her promise to find him—would he come after her? No, she had to keep the dead girl's words a secret. "She…she was already dead," she finished, horrified to hear her voice rise with hysteria.

Lord Morgan reached across the distance, gently opened her fingers and pried the knife from her grip. She suddenly realized that she must look very suspicious, indeed—with blood on her hands and gown, her hair tumbling loose from its pins and the knife in her hand. A sinking feeling caused her to go suddenly cold, and she shivered.

The frown lines between Lord Geoffrey's hazel eyes deepened, but she took heart from the strength that poured into her from him. He lowered his voice to a whisper. "This is no time for missish vapors, Miss Lovejoy. Keep your wits about you."

She clamped her mouth shut and hugged herself tightly, fighting back tears.

He smiled with satisfaction. "There's a good girl." He turned to the crowd. "Back away please. You are trampling evidence. Someone fetch the constabulary. And someone bring a blanket."

Dianthe could not take her eyes off the girl. "She is so young," she said.

"In years," Lord Morgan agreed.

"Should…should someone fetch her parents?" The tears she'd been fighting welled in Dianthe's eyes as she thought of how deeply they would mourn. She looked down, not wanting Lord Morgan to witness her weakness.

"I do not believe she has parents," he said.

"You knew her?"

"We had met," he commented in an even tone.

"Then who is her guardian?"

"She was without a guardian. A woman of…independent means."

Dianthe felt a blush steal up her cheeks as she met his eyes. Independent means. She suspected she knew what that meant. "Even so, Lord Morgan, someone must care for her. Someone must have brought her here. They should be told."

Mr. Thayer interceded with an angry glance at Lord Morgan. "You ought not to be carrying on such a conversation with Miss Lovejoy. 'Tisn't fit for innocent ears."

"She's shown more sense than the rest of you," Lord Morgan said, his appraising gaze sweeping the crowd. "Someone see if you can find Miss Brookes's escort." He turned to Dianthe and asked, "Did you come here with Mr. Thayer?"

"Yes," she breathed.

"Then leave with him. You will not want to be here for the rest of this, and it will be better if you are not too available. Where is your aunt?"

"She and Mr. Hawthorne have gone to Italy on their wedding trip. They will not be home for another month, I think."

"Where will you be if the police need to speak with you?"

"The Thayers'."

"Then I'd advise you to remain quietly with the Thayers until your aunt returns. Do you think that is possible for you, Miss Lovejoy?"

Was he insinuating that she was a rowdy chit who had difficulty behaving? She stood and lifted her chin in the air as she swept her skirts away from him, then went to stand beside the Thayers. Harriett and Hortense each took one of her arms and led her away from the scene. When she looked over her shoulder, she saw Lord Morgan watching her, a speculative gleam in his eyes. Could he actually suspect her of murder?

The seedy Whitefriars tavern in a back street was the sort of place few people would even notice. Geoffrey could have bought the whole damn tavern for the sum he'd paid in rent over the last four years. Ah, but it was good to have a safe den in unexpected areas if one needed to go to ground quickly. Or needed to meet with people one would rather not be seen with.

He climbed the back stairs, drew his dagger from his boot, unlocked the door and stepped into the room, ready for whatever was waiting. In this part of town, break-ins were commonplace. But all was well tonight. He slipped the dagger back in his boot, took kindling from a basket, lit the fire and then the oil lantern on the table. A whiskey bottle and two glasses completed his preparations. Nothing fancy here.

Sir Henry Richardson's knock was right on time. The man was nothing if not prompt. Geoff let him in and locked the door behind him.

"What's so damn urgent to pull me from Polly's bed?"

Geoff shook his head. Sir Harry, as the man was widely known, was a true ladies' man. Tall and lanky, with bright blue eyes and dark hair, he never lacked for female attention, though he was wise enough to confine his amorous attentions to the demimonde. It would never do to have the angry father or brother of some innocent debutante looking for him.

Harry sat and Geoff poured him a stiff glass of whiskey. "Nell Brookes is dead."

Harry choked midswallow. "Nell? Son of a… What the hell happened?"

"Murdered."

"Not you?"

Geoff sighed. "I confess the thought entered my mind more than once, but no. If she had made some connection to Mustafa el-Daibul, well, she could have been the best lead we've had since the bastard entrenched himself in Tangier years ago. Nell knew women were missing, but I warned her to keep out of it. The stubborn minx did not tell me she was determined to see if she could get to the bottom of it. She knew I'd stop her."

"A great pity. Nell was an excellent toss in the sheets. Knew all the tricks of the trade," Sir Harry mused, and lifted his glass in a silent toast. When he'd finished the contents, he slammed it down on the table. "So we're set back a bit. What's next?"

"I'm still trying to sort that out," Geoff told him. "There are…complications."

"And what might those be?"

Geoff envisioned Miss Dianthe Lovejoy, bent over Nell's body, holding the knife and smeared with blood. Dr. Worley had said the killer would be covered in blood, and Geoff had watched the gates until damn near dawn. No one had exited with any trace of blood on his or her clothing—except Miss Lovejoy. Surely, despite mounting evidence to the contrary, she had nothing to do with Nell's death. What could her motive possibly be?

Geoff's other thought—less likely but more troubling—was that Miss Lovejoy and not Nell Brookes had been the killer's target. She looked enough like the courtesan to have confused a hired killer, and their gowns were startlingly similar. If that were the case, Miss Lovejoy would need a warning.

"Geoff?" Harry asked.

"Just thinking," he said, pouring them both another glass of whiskey.

He went back to the table and sat. Lowering his voice, he said, "A young woman who is associated with friends of mine was found bending over Nell's body. The doctor thought she might have been searching Nell."

Harry smiled. "But you don't think so, do you?"

Geoff shrugged. What, really, did he know about Miss Lovejoy, except that she detested him—and not entirely without reason? He had nearly gotten her cousin killed three months ago. "I cannot imagine why she would," he said truthfully. "She looks to be the same age as Nell, but years more innocent. I would think a young woman of her sheltered upbringing would be too shocked to find a dead body to think of searching it. But after she left with the

Thayers, we found a note in Nell's reticule. It had notations detailing Miss Lovejoy's address at the Thayers', and that she would be at Vauxhall Gardens tonight. This gives rise to the question of whether Nell was seeking her out for some other purpose."

"Could the Lovejoy chit actually have been Nell's killer?" Harry ventured.

"Again, why?"

Harry shrugged.

"Even more curious, Miss Lovejoy could be Nell's twin."

Harry's eyebrows shot up. "There's a coincidence! And a rather intriguing possibility. Could Miss Lovejoy and Nell be siblings?"

"Unlikely. Miss Lovejoy has an older sister and a younger brother. The family was country-bound. That wouldn't leave room for her father to beget a child on a mistress, nor for her mother to stray."

A slow smile lit Harry's face. "If Miss Lovejoy is as comely as our fair Nell, she's bound to be a real stunner. Yes, might have to arrange an introduction."

"She's better looking than Nell, fresher and more inno-cent. But stay away from her, Harry. She's trouble or my name isn't Geoffrey Morgan."

Harry looked speculative. "Are there any suspects?"

"Just Miss Lovejoy, it seems. No one saw anyone else coming along the paths afterward, or reported seeing any-one following Nell. Miss Lovejoy may not have a motive, but that doesn't seem to bother the authorities. She's all they've got at the moment. I would not want to be in her shoes."

"She won't be arrested, will she?"

That thought gave Geoff pause. Although he didn't ac-tually care what happened to the haughty little chit, he would not want her cousin caused distress. The man had saved his life, after all. "I hope not, Harry, but that's not our business. Her family will look out for her. We need to focus on el-Daibul. Damn! I thought we were onto something with Nell. Now we're going to have to scramble for information again. I fear I'm making a career out of this case."

"Where do you suggest we go from here?"

"Back to the hells."

Harry grinned. "And back to the demimonde, for me."

Dianthe perched on the edge of her chair in Lady Annica's private sitting room, studying the faces around her. Lady Annica, Charity MacGregor and Lady Sarah Travis were staring at her in horror, and even worse, they were speechless! This was bad. She'd never seen them speechless before. These ladies, masquerading as the Wednesday League, a bluestocking group, secretly obtained justice for wronged women. They had seen and heard things worse than Dianthe's story, but only one had involved one of their own members. Until today.

At last Lady Annica blinked and closed her mouth. She cleared her throat before she spoke, as if she were afraid she'd lost her voice. "Dianthe, dear, that is appalling!"

"There's more." She clasped her hands tightly in her lap to keep them from trembling. "Somehow, Miss Brookes knew my name. She called me Dianthe. How could that be?"

"You said you had the same dress?" Lady Annica asked. "Perhaps she asked someone who you were."

Dianthe shivered, recalling the horror of the scene last night. "Too many coincidences. It defies logic."

"This entire event defies logic," Charity declared.

"There is worse. Before I could even leave Vauxhall, the police found a note in Miss Brookes's reticule with my name and address on it. They stopped me and asked extensive questions and said they would come by the Thayers' today for a sample of my handwriting." Dianthe's stomach clenched with anxiety. "They told Mr. Thayer not to let me out of his sight until they'd had a chance to verify my story, but I slipped away because I knew you all would be frantic once you heard the news. Does that not sound as if they suspect me of something?"

Lady Sarah frowned. "But that is completely absurd. You would not harm a fly."

"No," she agreed, "but they don't know that. All they know is what they saw."

"Lord Geoffrey Morgan was there?" Sarah asked.

"He advised me to go home and stay there until this was over. Can you imagine?"

"That is good advice, Dianthe," Sarah said. "But rather than go back to the Thayers', I think you should come stay with me."

"Or me," Annica said.

"Or me." Charity nodded. "You should be with one of us. I fear Mr. Thayer would not understand what we are about to do."

"What are we about to do?" Dianthe asked.

"Why, investigate Miss Brookes's death, of course. Once we prove you innocent, the police will have to leave you alone," Lady Annica announced with confidence. "And they would not dare to bother you if you are with me and Auberville. He would never permit it."

Dianthe warmed with the knowledge of how much these ladies would sacrifice for her. But, of course, she could never permit it. She did not like putting the ladies at risk when it was her problem and her future hanging in the balance. Nor could she tell them about Nell's last words—that she would be next. Or that she'd promised to stop Nell's killer. They would never let her out of their sight if they knew that little piece of information.

She shook her head. "Auberville is rising in government and I would not do anything to jeopardize that. And Sarah, I know your brother is being considered for Lord Barrington's vacant post, so I would not have my scandal attached to your name. Likewise for you, Charity."

Annica frowned, little lines forming between her dark eyebrows. "I appreciate your sensitivity to the matter, Dianthe, but your safety is paramount. We shall write to your sister at once. She and McHugh will return from the Highlands to take charge of this. But that will take two or three weeks. It is possible that Grace and Mr. Hawthorne will return in the interim, but we cannot count on that. Meantime, we must find a safe place for you. And I frankly do not think Mr. Thayer has the necessary connections to provide that. You belong with one of us."

Dianthe clasped her hands together to keep them from trembling. Oh, how she wished she could accept Lady Annica's invitation. But as terrified as she was, these women had been far too good to her family to taint them with her scandal. She took a deep breath and launched her carefully prepared lie. "I have my own plan. I have already packed a small valise and left a note for the Thayers saying that I shall find lodgings elsewhere. No—" she held up one hand to silence their questions "—I shall not tell you with whom. I do not want you to have to lie should the authorities ask. The arrangements are quite proper and I could not be safer."

"What will you do?"

Dianthe fought back her encroaching fear. She took a deep breath and lied as if she'd been born to it. "I will keep out of sight until the matter is resolved. Please, there is no need to worry."

Lady Annica sighed. "We shall begin making inquiries, Dianthe. Now the Wednesday League is fighting for one of our own. Someone is bound to find out something."

"Do you have the funds you will need?" Lady Sarah asked.

"I believe so." Dianthe hedged. She had little more than ten pounds, but if they knew her plan to investigate the murder herself, they'd take her in, tie her to her chair and keep her locked up until her family came for her.

Lady Annica frowned. "When, Dianthe? When shall we see you again?"

"Heavens! There may be no need of even a week. The police may find the murderer today and I shall be safely back with the Thayers by tomorrow."

"Do you promise to meet with us every other day?"

That was a small price to pay for their peace of mind. "Promise. But if the police are looking for me, they will watch your houses. Shall we meet at La Meilleure Robe?"

Charity nodded. "Madame Marie will accommodate us, and we shall put Mr. Renquist on this case at once. A Bow Street runner will be just the thing to hurry this along. Should you need anything—money, shelter or assistance— you know we stand ready to assist you."

"Yes," she said, "I know."

"I fear for you, Dianthe. The streets of London are fraught with danger," Lady Sarah warned. "All sorts of unscrupulous people are waiting to take advantage of an unwary woman."

Dianthe stood and smoothed the skirts of her gown. "I shall be wary, Lady Sarah, and quite safe withering away in hiding. If you must be concerned, be concerned over my utter boredom," she said with a wisp of inspiration.

Chapter Two

"I am sorry, Miss Smith, but I cannot let you a room," the clerk at the desk of Emery's Hostel for Women told Dianthe. "It is not our policy to rent to unchaperoned young ladies."

She glanced around the spotless lobby, which was nearly deserted in the late afternoon, and fumbled with her reticule, wondering how one went about bribing a clerk. "I assure you, sir, that my aunt will be arriving later this evening. I…I will pay extra if that will ease your mind."

The clerk's bushy eyebrows lifted at that. "Later? You traveled to town alone?"

"She…ah, sent me ahead."

"That is most unseemly, Miss Smith. Perhaps you and your…aunt would be more comfortable at Desmond's?"

He didn't believe her! He thought she was a woman of questionable virtue. She'd never been refused admittance anywhere, and this was an insult she could scarcely suffer in silence. She'd give the man a set-down if necessity didn't require discretion. Her cheeks burning, she lifted her valise and walked into the street.

In truth, she'd already tried Desmond's Hostel and had been refused there, too, and another three hostels besides. She would go back to Aunt Grace's home on Bloomsbury Square, but returning there would be tantamount to walking into the Bow Street office and announcing her name.

Fighting frustrated tears, she found a vacant bench in the square across from the hostel and sat dejectedly, despairing of finding a safe place to spend the night. Her empty stomach growled. She'd never had to provide for herself or depend on her wits for survival before, and she fought the creeping fear that she was doomed to failure.

After a brief rest, she stood and retrieved her valise. Her last chance for shelter tonight was just around the corner. She prayed the little flat above Madame Marie's shop was still vacant. If she could stay there for a few days, surely this mess would be straightened out.

She arrived at La Meilleure Robe just as Madame Marie was locking up for the night. The modiste opened the door and admitted her before locking it and pulling the shade over the window. Dianthe glanced around the dimly lit foyer and dropped her valise on a chair to remove her gloves.

Madame Marie peeked out at the street from behind the shade before turning to her. "*Chérie!* Where 'ave you been? My 'usband 'as been looking for you all day."

"Mr. Renquist is looking for me? Whatever for?"

"The ladies 'ave told 'im what is afoot. But 'e already knew. Orders 'ave come down from Bow Street that all runners are to appre'end you on sight and bring you to the Bow Street station for questioning."

"Drat," she muttered under her breath. "Now I shall truly have to stay out of sight. Is the room upstairs still vacant, *Madame?*"

"No, *chérie*. It was let months ago."

"Then I must leave at once." Dianthe fought tears of frustration as she began pulling her gloves back on.

"But wait! François will not turn you in. You shall stay with us, eh?"

She could no more allow Mr. Renquist to risk his job, family and reputation than she could have her other friends. "Thank you, *Madame,* but I cannot. I have just thought of a nice solution," she lied. She was dismayed by how easy that was becoming.

"Will you not stay and speak with François?"

"Tell him I will come day after tomorrow. I am meeting the ladies here in the afternoon. Once I am settled I shall be able to think about how to proceed."

Geoff crossed Leicester Square at an angle, heading for Green Street. With dusk settling over the city, traffic was thinning. He would be home in a few minutes. Or, at least, the place he called home. He preferred the moderate home on Salisbury Street just off The Strand to his new mansion on Curzon Street.

Yes, on Salisbury Street, his footsteps did not echo on marble floors, reminding him how alone he was. Still, even there he was haunted by the memory of Constance Bennington. Constance, the first woman he'd ever loved. Her death weighed on his conscience every day. Every night. He knew he could never put her memory to rest until he found the man responsible for her death.

Four years ago, when he'd first begun hunting the white slaver, el-Daibul, to put an end to his kidnapping of Englishwomen, he hadn't realized the price he'd pay—the price *she'd* pay—for his efforts. Before they'd put an end to el-Daibul's scheme, more women had died. Women who

could have been saved if only…what? He'd been more dil-
igent? Uncovered el-Daibul's henchmen sooner? But he
hadn't. And now the memory of what might have been was
a constant reproach. And the memory of the others who'd
died… Oh, God, he couldn't even think about the others.

Now he could add Nell Brookes to his growing list of
regrets. He should have been more insistent with her when
he realized she was sticking her nose into the business of
the missing women. Locked her up until the danger was
past. If he'd known for certain that she was delving into
matters that didn't concern her…

He shook off his brooding mood. No profit in that. Only
pain and remorse. He picked up his pace across the square
and stopped to buy an apple from a cart. He used the moment to look around. In his experience, it was always good
to take stock of one's surroundings frequently. Less chance
of being surprised that way.

Men were bustling home from their work, women hurrying back from the greengrocer with provisions, children
skipping as they hurried to keep up with their governesses.
And there, on a bench with a valise at her feet, trying her
best to look inconspicuous, sat someone who looked very
much like Miss Dianthe Lovejoy. Enjoying her last hours
of freedom, no doubt.

He took a bite of the crisp red apple and watched her
for a moment. Yes, it was Miss Lovejoy. There could not
be two in London like her. God fashioned only one of
those a generation—perhaps a millennium. Even Nell had
been a pale copy.

He strolled toward her, wondering if he should speak.
When he was near enough, he noted the pinched look be-
tween her eyes and the slightly reddened rims of her eyes.
Had she been crying?

"Trouble, Miss Lovejoy?" he asked. Her chin snapped upward, indicating that he'd startled her. For once, it seemed, he had the advantage in their meeting.

She crumpled her handkerchief and pushed it into the sleeve of her bishop's-blue spencer. Shrugging, she assumed a haughty mien. "I do not see how that is your concern, Lord Morgan."

He grinned, finding her continued dislike of him more amusing than aggravating. He almost liked the chit, for no other reason than her dead reckoning of his character. He lifted his foot and planted one of his boots on the bench beside her yellow skirt. "It isn't my concern. I was merely curious. You. A valise. Alone. You must admit the circumstances are rife with possibility."

She narrowed her eyes and turned away to study the apple cart.

"Going somewhere?" he persisted.

"As you know, Lord Morgan, I am in somewhat of a pickle. I do not want my scandal attached to my friends' names."

"Ah, then you're going home? Back to Bloomsbury Square?"

She sighed deeply and glanced sideways at him. "It is locked up until the Hawthornes' return."

"That places you in a rather awkward position, does it not? No family, no friends?"

"Thank you for stating the obvious, my lord."

He chuckled. "Where *are* you going, Miss Lovejoy?"

"I intended to let a room at a ladies' hostel."

"Were there no vacancies?"

She hesitated, then murmured, "None, I fear."

"So you are going back to the Thayers?"

"Of course not," she snapped.

Although he already knew the answer, Geoff raised an eyebrow. "Are the authorities after you, Miss Lovejoy?"

"I…I imagine they are."

Pity. The girl was in over her head and had no one to help her. His conscience tweaked him and he did his best to ignore it. Miss Lovejoy was just the sort of empty-headed little ingenue he avoided at all costs. "Then what are you doing here in the open? Shouldn't you be looking for a hiding place?"

"Did I not tell you that I do not want my friends inconvenienced by my problems?"

The first uneasy stirrings of guilt prickled the hair on the back of Geoff's neck. Adam Hawthorne had been one of the few men to give him the benefit of the doubt. For that reason alone, he owed the man. And then Adam had taken a bullet meant for him, which had compounded the debt. Now that Adam had married Dianthe's Aunt Grace, could he leave Adam's gently reared cousin alone on a bench at dusk? Not likely. But he avoided involvement in other people's lives like the plague. Maybe it was a simple matter of money. Yes, he could give her money and be done with her.

"Vacancies can be found with enough money, Miss Lovejoy. I shall be happy to—"

"Keep your ill-gotten gains, Lord Morgan. They cannot buy me what I need."

How like the high-minded little brat to bite the hand that fed her. "Damn it, Miss Lovejoy, they will buy you a room."

"No, my lord, they will not." She took a deep breath and raised her chin in proud disdain. "No one will rent me a room, because I am alone and unchaperoned."

"I shall hire you a chaperone," he offered.

She rolled her eyes so comically he nearly laughed. "Your money will not buy you everything."

"It buys enough to pass for everything."

"No doubt it is why you get away with so much. But your money will not buy me, Lord Morgan, so scoot away, if you please." She made a sweeping motion with one hand.

"Even if I don't please?"

"Even then," she confirmed.

He removed his foot from the bench and crossed his arms over his chest. What was he to do with this prickly little baggage? He could find her a room easily enough, but it wouldn't be in a part of town suitable for her, or in an establishment even remotely acceptable.

"Well, go!" she said.

He turned to do just that. But then Adam Hawthorne's face, white from loss of blood, rose to his mind, and another idea occurred to him. Miss Lovejoy would be an excellent way for him to repay his debt to Adam. Besides, she would be child's play to manage.

"Do you care about *my* name or reputation, Miss Lovejoy?"

"Yours are beyond redemption," she declared.

True, but he didn't like hearing it from Dianthe Lovejoy. He took a deep breath and reined in his temper. "Excellent. Then you should have no objections to accepting *my* hospitality."

His statement so surprised her that she coughed. "You cannot be serious!"

"Completely," he confirmed, surprising even himself. "I have a home in the West End that is presently unoccupied. There is only a small staff, but I could hire more if needed."

"But you—"

"I prefer my house in Covent Garden. We would not be sharing the same quarters. My housekeeper would vouch for your…ah, reputation, until I can find a more suitable chaperone for you."

"I do not like owing you, Lord Morgan."

"I do not like owing your cousin, Miss Lovejoy, but things are what they are. Your present circumstances place you in a position to benefit from the debt I owe him, although I rather think he will owe *me* after this. It is a simple proposition and will not require you to be courteous to me—or even speak with me, which would be preferable, given your general lack of civility. I'd advise you to take the offer before I think better of it."

She blinked those gorgeous blue eyes and gave him a slightly confused look. A moment passed while she seemed to consider her options. Or lack of them. He offered his hand.

Hesitantly, she took it. Her hand was warm and strong, and it looked insignificant resting in his palm. He grinned. Miss Lovejoy made it clear how much she detested him and any necessity of dealing with him. She was a bit of a snob and considered him socially beneath her. Only his title had kept him near her social circle. Still, she had no reasonable alternative, and they both knew it.

She stood. "This…this is one of the most remarkable mésalliances I have ever heard of, Lord Morgan."

"I could not agree more, Miss Lovejoy, but do not mistake this for an alliance of any sort. I am repaying a debt, and with very little inconvenience to myself." He picked up her valise. "This, in fact, may be the last time we are required to speak to one another."

A *home* on the West End? This was a mansion! On Curzon Street just around the corner from Half Moon Street, it boasted one of the best Mayfair addresses. Berkeley Square was a stone's throw away and Green Park just a fraction farther. Heavens! It must have cost Lord Morgan an entire fortune—if he hadn't won the place from some poor unwary gambler!

He opened the front door, entered unannounced, and dropped her valise with a sharp slap on the polished marble floor. The central hall, as large as a chapel, contained two curved staircases that met at the second floor landing. The doors to the right and left of the foyer were taller than any she'd seen outside a palace or a church. A balding servant scurried from a hidden hallway behind the stairs at the first sounds of Lord Morgan's entry.

"My lord! We did not expect you this evening." The man—a butler, Dianthe assumed—bowed and darted a glance in her direction. "Will you be staying for dinner?"

"I haven't decided, Pemberton. I've brought Miss Lovejoy to stay with you. She's, ah, just come to town and neglected to secure a room in advance. I assume you will not have trouble accommodating her?"

"No, my lord."

Pemberton turned to her and bowed deeply from his waist. He must think her someone of importance. She smiled and nodded as regally as she could manage, given her state of surprise.

Lord Morgan moved behind her, lifted her spencer from her shoulders and held it while she freed her arms of the sleeves. He handed the wrap to Pemberton and indicated one of the tall doors with a sweep of his hand. "I believe Miss Lovejoy would like a cup of tea, Pemberton. Could you ask Mrs. Mason to bring it to the library, please?"

"As you wish, my lord." Pemberton bowed and hurried back down the hallway.

Following the sweep of her host's hand, Dianthe went toward the room she assumed to be the library. When he opened the door, she stopped short. A bank of windows directly across the room admitted the last pinkish rays of the sun, sparkling through the crystal glasses and decanters on a long sideboard. Large, and with a high ceiling, the room contained three walls of bookshelves filled with leather-bound tomes of varying sizes and thicknesses. A massive polished desk took up most of one corner. A grouping of leather club chairs before a fireplace, unlit in the summer heat, was on the opposite side of the room. Lush Turkish carpets in red, gold and deep brown tones muffled their footsteps as they went forward.

Lord Morgan indicated the chairs with another sweep of his hand. A tea cart to one side and a low table in the center of the grouping waited to hold refreshments. "Make yourself comfortable, Miss Lovejoy. Tea will be along presently."

She ignored him and turned to look at the titles of some of the books, running her finger along the spines.

"Are you a reader, Miss Lovejoy?" he asked.

She glanced at him. He was pouring a draft of deep amber liquid into a crystal glass. As she watched, he replaced a stopper and lifted the glass to his lips. With the sun behind him and the grace of his movements made so obvious by the light, she suddenly realized he could very easily be a charming man if he chose.

"Not as much as I'd like to be," she admitted, turning back to the books. "I haven't had much time until just recently."

She heard the soft pad of his footsteps on the carpet as he came toward her. She could feel the heat of his body behind her when he reached over her shoulder, ran his index finger along the row of books until he found what he was looking for, and pulled the volume from the shelf.

"Since you will have time while you await your cousin's

return from the Continent, may I recommend this one? You may actually learn something from it."

She took the slender volume from his hand and read the gold embossed title: *The Taming of the Shrew,* by William Shakespeare. Anger bubbled upward. She turned to find Lord Morgan mere inches away, blocking her path. Narrowing her eyes, she recalled that scarcely seconds ago she had been thinking he had a rough sort of charm! She would have to guard herself against such ridiculous notions in the future.

"Stand aside please," she said in a cold voice.

He made no move to do so. Her temper snapped and she lifted her hands to push him away. He caught them and held them to his broad chest as he turned around with her, giving her the freedom she sought. She could have sworn a smile played at the corners of his mouth, and that infuriated her further.

A soft knock at the door drew her attention away from the insufferable lord. He released her hands and stepped back.

"Come in, Pemberton," he called.

Clutching the volume she'd been tempted to throw at him, Dianthe went to the circle of chairs near the fireplace. Pemberton brought a silver tray laden with a tea service and plates of little sandwiches and sweets. Her stomach growled again and her mouth watered. Food! At least she would not starve.

"Mrs. Mason has instructed the staff to ready the blue room for Miss Lovejoy, my lord, and Sally is unpacking her valise. Cook is preparing partridge and vegetables for dinner."

"I won't be staying, after all," Lord Morgan said with a glance in Dianthe's direction. "Business requires my attention."

"As you wish, my lord." With a bow, the butler left and closed the library doors behind him.

"Help yourself," Morgan told her with a wave at the tea service.

Oh, how she wished she could turn her nose up, but she was famished. She hadn't eaten since leaving the ladies at Lady Annica's earlier. She poured herself a cup of tea and, with a pair of silver tongs, placed a watercress sandwich on a fine china plate. When she glanced up from her task, Morgan was watching her, all signs of mockery gone.

"Do not hesitate to ask for anything you want or need. The servants will accommodate you. And, if you like, do avail yourself of the library."

"Thank you. I expect to be very busy, though."

"Busy? What have you to do but wait for your cousin's return?"

"I am not quite so shallow as you think me, Lord Morgan. I have interests beyond reading and sitting all day."

"What might they be, pray tell?"

"It is none of your concern. You are only affording me shelter, remember, and have no interest in my doings."

"True, but you'd be wise to stay hidden from the authorities. That would mean staying home with your embroidery or knitting."

Lord! The man was an absolute dunce! "I have business to tend to, Lord Geoffrey." She couldn't tell him about Nell's last words. Like all the others, he'd try to stop her. But she could not help but respond to his arrogance. "I...I intend to investigate. I shall endeavor to do whatever is necessary to clear my reputation."

Morgan's hazel eyes narrowed. "You cannot do that, Miss Lovejoy. It could prove dangerous."

She gave a short laugh. "More dangerous than hanging for a crime I did not commit?"

"If you simply lie low, the authorities are bound to discover the truth of the matter."

"I had the distinct impression they'd made up their minds and would do little else but make a case against me. And the longer they waste their time chasing me, the less likely they are to find the real villain."

Lord Morgan seemed to be struggling with the effort to remain silent. That was likely a first for the man. Finally, he stated, "If you will remain quietly here, either your cousin or your sister will arrive in a week or so, and by then the case will be resolved."

"It is far too important a matter to remain sitting on my hands and doing nothing. If you cannot accept that, and wish to withdraw your hospitality, I shall understand." Dianthe studied his face, waiting for his response.

"I make it my policy, Miss Lovejoy, never to interfere in the personal matters of others, nor to question their actions or motives."

She gritted her teeth and gained control over her temper before she responded. "Excellent! As you have reminded me that you do not involve yourself in the affairs of others, I'm certain that you will wish to keep to your custom and leave me to my own devices."

His jaw tightened. "As you please."

The echo of the slamming door still rang in Geoff's ears as he crossed the street and hailed a hackney. The annoying little fool! She was hell-bent on landing herself in trouble. Well, she could do as she damn well pleased. He refused to become involved. He knew from bitter experience that he could not change the way people thought or the decisions they made. He'd given up long ago.

The most irksome part of this scheme was that he was forced to acknowledge that he was just like every other man in little Miss Lovejoy's sphere. She smiled, and his body, if not his mind, responded in the most primal way. She'd looked hungry and vulnerable, and he'd wanted to slay her dragons. *Physical. It was merely physical.*

He'd restricted his amorous activities to members of the demimonde for the past five years. They'd been seductive and skilled, and some had even managed to teach *him* a few tricks. And the last thing he needed or wanted—now or ever—was an insipid, spoiled, smugly superior debutante complicating his life. But were she anyone other than Adam Hawthorne's cousin…

Well, she might be naively innocent, but she was right about the police. They would not look an inch farther for Nell's killer than Dianthe Lovejoy's door. And, as much as he wanted to, he could not prevent her from investigating Nell's death. He doubted anyone would take her seriously, or that she'd have the least little success. It was more likely she'd get herself arrested.

And he wouldn't care as long as she did not get in the way of *his* investigation. But she wasn't going up against el-Daibul, so that was unlikely. He couldn't stop her from asking useless questions, so he may as well prepare for the consequences.

Yes, he'd just look in on the troublesome miss daily and leave her to her own devices the rest of the time. Her cousin would be back from the Continent soon and take her off his hands. Geoff prayed that would happen before Miss Lovejoy embroiled herself in another scandal or got truly under his skin.

Chapter Three

The truth is, Dianthe mused as she sank into the huge copper tub of steaming, jasmine-scented water, *I could become very used to this sort of life.* She'd never known decadent luxury and rather thought it suited her. She'd mentioned to Mrs. Mason in passing her desire for a hot bath, and found it waiting for her when she'd come up to her room. A maid had even been sent to help her undress and pin up her hair.

Dianthe squeezed the huge porous sponge over her bare shoulders, loosening a stream of warm water. *Heaven! This was heaven.* She hadn't been terrified once since coming here. She was safely isolated from the rest of the world.

Lord Geoffrey Morgan was obscenely rich, but she'd never dreamed what that would entail. It was whispered that he was as rich as Croesus. And why not? He'd won several of the country's largest fortunes in games of chance. The money was not really his, so she should not feel in the least bit guilty for accepting his hospitality while she sought out Miss Brookes's killer.

She needed to make a list. The task had seemed so simple before she actually had to think of the details, but now that she was faced with the execution of her plan, she was puzzled by the daunting task.

First, she would need to find out where Miss Brookes's family was and who her friends were. The only way she knew to accomplish that task was to attend the girl's funeral. Certainly her friends and family would be there, and surely the girl had confided in someone about an enemy so dangerous he might want to kill her.

Madame Marie would lend her a dark gown and bonnet. Dianthe had had room for only a few gowns in her valise, and she'd never anticipated the need for a mourning gown. Since the bluestocking ladies had enlisted Mr. Renquist to begin investigating, she suspected he, too, would be at the funeral.

Stepping out of the tub, she dried herself quickly and wrapped the towel around her. She glanced over at her simple lawn nightgown draped across her bed. She hadn't even had room to bring her dressing gown, so Mrs. Mason had brought her one of Lord Morgan's robes to use during her stay. It was made of rich, midnight-blue brocade with matching satin lapels and cuffs, and she couldn't wait to wrap the lush fabric around her.

Having the warmth of Morgan's robe around her was oddly like an embrace. His scent enveloped her. The clash of her bath oil and his French milled soap reminded her that, even in such little things, they were at odds. The robe engulfed her and she had to roll the sleeves back several turns.

Seeking a distraction, Dianthe went to curl up in a chair by the fire to sip tea from the delicate blue-and-white porcelain cup. The *Times,* folded on the tray, was open to the death notices. Two narrow lines reported Nell's name and the place and date of her funeral. Tomorrow. Heavens! So soon?

She glanced toward the bed uncertainly. Hung with deep

blue curtains, the white velvet coverlet strewn with blue-and-gold pillows, it held the promise of comfort. Sleeping in Geoffrey Morgan's bed didn't seem right, somehow. Well, in Geoffrey Morgan's house, at any rate. It could be a very dangerous thing to be in his debt. But Lord Geoffrey had less in the way of reputation to lose than her friends, and it wasn't as if she were living under the same roof.

She shook off her brooding and put her teacup down. Tomorrow, then, she would borrow a somber gown from Madame Marie and attend Miss Brookes's funeral. Dianthe would learn what those closest to Nell knew about the murder and, with a touch of luck, she and Mr. Renquist would conclude the matter.

The weather had turned gloomy and a steady drizzle kept traffic on the thoroughfares to a minimum. Dianthe took a shortcut through Duke's Court to St. Martin's Church, heedless of the sodden hem of her charcoal-gray skirts. She had draped a black veil over her gray bonnet to obscure her face, and kept her black umbrella low over her head.

A few carriages were drawn up outside the church, but no mourners milled on the steps. Had she made a mistake? Were the services later? She was about to turn and retrace her steps when she saw Mr. Renquist, without the usual red waistcoat of the Bow Street runner, enter the church. She took a deep breath, climbed the steps and closed her umbrella before passing through the vestibule into the nave and taking a seat in the back.

Only one other woman was in attendance, sitting in the back pew on the opposite side of the aisle, and perhaps a dozen men sitting separately near the front. Were these Miss Brookes's clients? Protectors? Her family?

The men turned to watch her. Dianthe bowed her head

and kept her veil in place. She could feel their eyes boring through her, and she prayed she would not be recognized.

A few moments later, the minister entered and faced the meager congregation. She had never attended actual funeral services before, as Aunt Henrietta believed that gently reared females were too delicate for such disturbing events. In her entire life, Dianthe had only visited her father's and mother's graves in Wiltshire once, and gone to her aunt's grave. That was the extent of her experience with death rituals, so she watched the proceedings carefully.

Prayers were said, then a short, impersonal eulogy that revealed little about the woman they were about to bury. The cleric alluded to Nell's profession only when he made the point that "even those who had fallen were beloved of Christ." Then an actual rite for the dead was read. Though the men bowed their heads at prayers, she could not detect any sign of genuine grief from their posture or bearing. Except Lord Geoffrey Morgan.

He had entered late and taken a seat near the front. His face was tense though composed. Dianthe knew him well enough to recognize the way he registered distress. His lips were drawn thin and his complexion was pale. She thought a little better of him for being here and for feeling grief or compassion for Nell Brookes.

Dianthe, too, was deeply touched, and wiped impatiently at the hot tears seeping down her face. She could not forget the beautiful young woman lying forever still inside the narrow coffin. Did no one but she lament the dreadful circumstances that had brought Nell to such a pass? Then the other woman began weeping, too, and Dianthe wondered if she could be Nell's mother or sister.

After a shockingly brief time, the funeral was over. The woman stood and hurried out of the church, and Dianthe followed, hoping Mr. Renquist would at least learn the names of the men in attendance.

"Miss!" she called as the woman reached the street.

The dark-cloaked form missed a step but did not turn or stop.

Dianthe hurried after her, raising her umbrella against the steady drizzle. "Miss! Please, spare me a minute!"

This time the woman stopped but did not turn. When Dianthe came abreast of her and raised her veil, the woman gasped. "You must be Miss Lovejoy. Everyone is talking. You *do* look like Nell." She resumed walking and spoke in a soft voice. "What do you want?"

"I want to talk about Miss Brookes," she answered.

"Walk with me, then. I do not wish to be seen here—or with you."

"Why?"

"For the same reason there are so few people at Nell's funeral. We cannot afford to be associated with murders, nor to be questioned by the authorities. Were our names, or those of our clients, made public…well, you can imagine the scandal."

Dianthe matched her stride. "Are you Miss Brookes's sister?"

"Nell had no family. Or none that she spoke of."

"A friend, then?"

There was a hesitation, then she murmured, "Yes."

Dianthe's curiosity spiked. The woman was lovely, despite the drab colors she wore, and she used cosmetics— something Dianthe and her friends would never do. Was she a member of the demimonde? "You have me at a disadvantage, miss. You appear to know me, yet I do not know you."

"Yes, I know you. You are accused of Nell's murder."

Lord! She could feel her reputation slipping away. "Miss Brookes had been stabbed when I found her."

"I never believed you had anything to do with it. The police are fools to think so."

"I want to find out who the real murderer is."

"Because it will clear you," the woman concluded in a cynical tone.

"I want to see justice done. Whoever did this to Nell should pay for it. Please help me find her killer. I just want to ask a few questions. Will you tell me your name?"

There was a long silence before the woman spoke again. "My name is Flora Denton."

"Thank you, Miss Denton. How long have you known Miss Brookes?"

"Since I arrived in London. For a few months we…worked at the same establishment. She was my dearest friend." She turned and regarded Dianthe through dark eyes. "I heard people talking about how closely you resemble her. Your hair and eyes are nearly the same, and the shape of your face and figure, but you haven't her sophistication."

"Where did you hear all this, Miss Denton? The murder was only three days ago."

She nodded. "The police have been by to search Nell's rooms and belongings. The gentlemen talk. Nell's favorites have come to pay their respects and to comfort one another."

For some inexplicable reason, Dianthe was pleased by the thought that Nell's lovers mourned her. "Were there many?"

Miss Denton gave a short laugh. "Yes. Too many. For one of us, very few."

"One of you?" Dianthe asked.

"The demimonde, Miss Lovejoy. The half-world of London, or the shadow world, as your kind would call it. The part proper ladies like you do not even speak of."

Dianthe walked along for moment, not knowing how to reply to such a statement.

"Have I shocked you, Miss Lovejoy?"

"No, Miss Denton. My family was impoverished and I have occasionally thought that, but for the grace of family who cared for us, my sister and I might have fallen into a similar fate." She recalled Squire Daniels in Little Upton, who had offered to buy her a small cottage in exchange for her "company." She would have had to be a great deal more desperate to accept that offer.

"We are courtesans, Miss Lovejoy, not prostitutes. Many of us have several lovers, some have only one at a time. But *we* say who, and when, and where, unlike our poorer sisters. Nor do we sell our wares on the street."

Dianthe nodded, understanding that explanation. "Did Miss Brookes have many, few, or one?"

"A few."

"How many?"

"It varied from time to time."

"Had she recently argued with any of them?"

"I see where you are going with this, and I would like to help you. But I am afraid I cannot."

"But why?"

"Miss Lovejoy," she said as she increased the length of her stride, "I do not even wish to be seen in your company. Indiscretion and women who talk out of turn are frowned upon in my business. Should it be known that I have shared any sort of information with a woman of the ton, I would find it very difficult to earn a living. My gentlemen would withdraw their patronage, and I would find myself on the streets in short order."

Dianthe caught up to her and entreated, "Just tell me the names of her protectors. I shall question them myself."

"Miss Lovejoy, are you not sensible to the difficulty of what you have taken on? Do you really think men of the ton will discuss their affairs with you? The very thought is absurdly naive. And Nell's other friends will not be as forthcoming as I have been."

Her spirits plummeted. "Then how will I ever discover what happened to Miss Brookes?"

Flora Denton stopped and turned to face her. She laughed and shook her head. "That will never happen, Miss Lovejoy. Give it up. You would have to be one of us."

Mouth agape, Dianthe watched the woman lose herself in the crowded market at Covent Garden. *One of them?*

Mr. Renquist was waiting on the street outside St. Martins Church by the time she made her way back. He looked anxious and heaved a sigh of relief when he saw her. "I wondered where you had got to, Miss Lovejoy. I do not know how to find you. Where are you staying?"

An impression of Lord Geoffrey's flashing smile passed through her head and she shuddered at what Mr. Renquist would say about her choice of lodgings. "It would be best if you do not know that, Mr. Renquist. Then it will not be a conflict for you."

"It is already a conflict," he grumbled. "I should be hauling you before a magistrate this very minute."

She winced, knowing Mr. Renquist was compromising his job every moment he spent with her.

"I recognized three or four of the men, Miss Lovejoy. The others should not be hard to find."

"Is it usual for such funerals to be so…small?"

"No one wants to be associated with a murder—at least until after it has been solved. Most of the men who attend upon the demimonde could not withstand the scrutiny."

Dianthe's frustration mounted. "Then how shall we ever solve this?"

"The truth has a way of coming out, miss. In its own sweet time."

"I do not have time, Mr. Renquist. I could hang before the truth is known."

Renquist gave her a sober nod. "Yes, I can see the problem, miss. And that is the very thing I am trying to prevent."

She sighed as Flora Denton's words rang in her head. *You would have to be one of us.*

Geoff paced the small rented room above the tavern in Whitefriars while Sir Harry scratched a few lines on a piece of paper. "Anyone else?"

"Edgerton's cub," Geoff told him. "I heard he was pursuing Nell but that she'd told him to come back when he inherited."

"That was cold."

"*Nell* could be cold. I imagine we would be, too, if our survival depended upon it. It wasn't a courtship, for God's sake, it was a business arrangement."

Sir Harry nodded. "That's it, then? I thought you said there'd been a dozen men in attendance. I've only got six names."

"I will investigate the others, Harry. Apart from the six I just gave you, there are myself, two women, and a man I suspect was sent by Bow Street."

"And the women?"

"Veiled. One, I think, was Flora Denton, Nell's friend."

"And the other?"

Geoff hesitated. Even though she'd been shrouded and veiled, he'd recognized the set of Miss Lovejoy's shoulders, the slender lines of her form, the grace with which she moved. He wasn't certain he wanted to bring her name into this.

Even while he'd been angry to find her at the funeral, he had to admire her ingenuity. He wasn't particularly concerned that Flora had given her any information. No, Flora Denton was too canny for that. She knew discretion was her only choice. Now, almost certainly, the little dilettante would be flummoxed. She'd give up and sit quietly until someone from her family arrived to handle the matter for her. She had neither the experience nor the grit for more.

"The other woman?" Harry prompted again. "Did you recognize her?"

"I'll take care of it, Harry. You follow up on the men."

"Men? That's a waste of my talents, Morgan. Trying to regain your reputation as a lady's man?"

Geoff raised an eyebrow, remembering the days when he'd been known as the "Sheikh." He'd had a way with women then, and a lighter heart and readier smile. And a much greater tolerance for social games and feminine wiles.

And, blast it all, he was about to pay for those days by having to keep a closer eye on the Lovejoy girl.

Late the following afternoon, Dianthe slipped quietly in the door of La Meilleure Robe and reached up to silence the little shop bell. She did not want Madame Marie's clients looking into the corridor to see who had come in. The ladies would be waiting for her in the large fitting room in the back, so she hurried along the dark corridor and rapped twice before entering.

"Dianthe!" Sarah exclaimed. "Thank heavens you've come. We feared something had happened to you."

"This arrangement really is not satisfactory," Lady Annica pronounced. "What if we'd needed to contact you, Dianthe? What if you hadn't been able to come? How would we have known where—oh! That reminds me. I have a letter from Afton for you. Mr. Thayer brought it by this morning. It was posted before your troubles, dear."

Dianthe tucked the letter into her reticule. Thank heavens the ladies were there—Sarah, Annica and Charity. She removed her gloves and sat on one of the stools used for marking hems. "If you knew where I was staying, you could hardly plead ignorance if the police had come, could you?"

The ladies exchanged a telling glance.

"They *did* come, did they not?" she guessed, a knot tightening in her stomach.

"Well, yes," Charity admitted. "And I confess that it was a relief not to lie. My husband would have known it immediately."

Dianthe glanced at Annica and Sarah, and they nodded in admission. So, it was official. The authorities were in pursuit of her. But first things first. "I am sorry I was late, but I didn't get much sleep last night. In fact, I only dozed off near dawn."

"If you are not sleeping—"

"It is not because of my bed or accommodations. I am quite comfortable, but I ache to be doing something, and that makes me restless."

Sarah sat forward. "Mr. Renquist told us that you went to Miss Brookes's funeral yesterday. Are you mad, Dianthe? What if you'd been seen? You could have been thrown in jail!"

Dianthe remembered the funeral attendees who had watched her every move. "I wore a veil and only spoke with a friend of Miss Brookes's, but she would not tell me anything. She is suspicious of me. Of anyone, in fact. She said that her income depends upon her discretion."

"Oh! I had not thought of that!" Charity said. "Men— husbands and fathers—would not want their loved ones to know what they have been doing. And with whom."

"All the same, a number of them were at the church. Mr. Renquist has their names and will be questioning them."

Annica sighed. "This is apt to be a lengthy process. I would feel better if we knew how you were situated, Dianthe. I cannot bear to think of what hardships you may be enduring just to remain out of sight."

Hardships? She was living in the veritable lap of luxury. She could not imagine what Lord Morgan had told the servants, but her every whim, her slightest wish, was catered to as if she were a visiting dignitary. "I am quite comfortable. Please do not give it a second thought."

"Are you protecting your reputation, Dianthe?"

"I…am doing what needs to be done. I know that you, too, have run grave risks to accomplish your goals, and I am not taking unreasonable risks." She'd known from the moment she'd decided not to taint her friends with her problem that she was risking her reputation—if, indeed, she had one left. What else could she do? Drag them down into ignominy with her? Never!

Annica frowned. "I do not like this the least little bit, Dianthe. You should come to one of us at once."

She squared her shoulders and lifted her chin, ready for battle. "My reputation is the least of my problems. It is already in shreds. Confess! What is the *on dit* concerning me?"

Another awkward pause told Dianthe almost all she needed to know. "How bad is it?"

"People hush when we enter a room, as it is known that we are friends," Sarah admitted. "My brother, Reginald, told me this morning that…that there is an order sworn to apprehend you. The only question people are asking is *why* you did it."

Dianthe sighed deeply. Well, she had suspected as much. Gossip hates a void, and she'd become the juiciest topic yet in the slow summer months when most of the ton had retired to the country.

"Auberville is trying to persuade the authorities otherwise," Annica said. "He provided them with a letter you had written me some time ago, so that they could compare your handwriting with the handwriting on the note found at the scene. It did not match, of course, but that did little to convince them. Auberville says there is some other piece of evidence they have against you, but he would not tell me what it was."

"I cannot imagine what it could be. That was the only time I'd ever seen Miss Brookes."

"That is what we tried to tell them," Annica said. "But there is speculation now that there was some sort of secret connection that has been kept from common knowledge. I cannot imagine what but, given the girl's occupation, I shudder to imagine what is being said."

Dianthe took a deep breath and braced herself. "The point now is that…well, I've become fodder for the gossip mills."

"Whatever is whispered behind fans can be overcome when the truth is out, my dear," Charity said.

"Doubtful," Dianthe murmured. "Once something like this is whispered, one cannot reclaim a spotless reputation. I only hope the truth will redeem the portion my friends and family have lost."

"Drats!" Annica cursed. "This is so unfair! All you did was stop to help someone you thought was ill."

"And I'd do it again," Dianthe admitted. "So there is no use in agonizing over this. I simply wanted to know if there was any advantage in coming forward."

"No!" the ladies exclaimed in one voice.

Sarah stood and began to pace circles around the small

room. "My husband says you should not have hidden. He says they—the police—have likely taken that as an indication of guilt. But it is too late to undo that now."

Then it was even *worse* than she'd suspected. "I doubt I will be going out much. The risk of recognition is too great."

"Disguise," Sarah said.

"Or go out only after dark," Annica advised.

Dianthe donned her bonnet and gave them an uncertain smile. If she went forward with her new plan, and if she could conquer her fears, she would be doing both.

Chapter Four

Dianthe curled up in the overstuffed chair in her room and unfolded Afton's letter. She wanted to read slowly and savor every word. The letter had been written weeks ago and would be full of ordinary news and everyday observations. Oh, how she longed for something ordinary.

She took a sip of her tea and began reading.

My dearest little sister,

I write to you with some good news and some of a curious nature. First the good news. I am bearing a little McHugh. I have known for quite some time but have delayed telling anyone until I was certain all was well. Rob is completely overjoyed. I have never seen him so doting. We expect the blessed event to occur just before the New Year.

Dianthe counted backward on her fingers. Heavens! Afton was five months along. How wonderful. Oh, but a doting McHugh would never allow Afton to travel over rough Scottish roads in a delicate condition. Nor should he.

Afton should stay safe at home. And that meant McHugh would come himself. That thought made her more than a little uneasy. McHugh was not a patient man, and he would rush into the Bow Street office demanding to see any evidence against her, and that any charges be dropped. He'd likely end up in Newgate alongside her.

Oh, but she wouldn't think of that now. Afton was having a baby! What joyous news. If Dianthe could just get clear of this mess, she would hie to Scotland to be with her. She blinked her tears away and returned her attention to the letter.

And now for the curious news. The postmaster in Little Upton forwarded a letter to me here. To say I was surprised, even shocked, is an understatement. Do you recall that Mama had a sister, Aunt Dora, who emigrated to Australia? Well, it appears that was a lie to cover a more scandalous event.

A visiting dignitary seduced Aunt Dora, and Grandfather turned her out when he discovered her transgression. She did not go as far as Australia, however. She went to London and took up with a wealthy merchant. He was married, but kept Aunt Dora comfortably. She had a daughter, Eleanor. Just think! We have a cousin. It was she who wrote to us.

Aunt Dora died a few years ago, and would never discuss her family, so Eleanor only recently found out about us. Her father preceded Aunt Dora in death, and his family turned their back on Eleanor, refusing to acknowledge her or contribute to her support.

Here lies the difficulty, Dianthe, and I pray you will be gentle and not judge her. Lacking both family and fortune, Eleanor was left to her own devices

when Aunt Dora died. Untrained for any useful occupation, she had little choice but to enter the demimonde. She now wishes to leave that life behind,
and begs that we will help.

Toward that end, dear sister, I have sent her your
calling card, along with the Thayers' address, and I
have urged her to call upon you. When you hear from
Miss Eleanor Brookes, please assist her in any way
possible, and send her to us at Glenross. We shall take
care of her and help her build her life anew.

I know I needn't caution you to discretion. This
sort of news would provide grist for the gossip mill
for years to come, and the damage it could do the
Lovejoy name is immeasurable. Think of your future
prospects, Dianthe, and of our brother's future.

I hope to hear from you soon, and urge you to
come spend the Christmas season with us at Glenross.
Your loving sister, Afton

Stunned, Dianthe could only stare at the letter in her lap
while her mind reeled. Eleanor. *Nell*. Nell Brookes had
been her cousin. She had held her cousin and watched her
life seep away. And Nell had known—had probably followed Dianthe to Vauxhall to meet her rather than come to
the Thayer house. *Thank heavens 'tis you,* she had said.
And, as difficult as it had been, thank heaven Dianthe had
been there so Nell would not die alone.

Tears stung her eyes and blurred the words on the page.
Dianthe silently renewed her promise to find and stop the
man who had murdered her cousin. Of course she would
not breathe a word of this to anyone. Whether her own future had been irretrievably lost or not, her brother's must
be protected at any cost.

* * *

Geoff left his horse in the care of a stable boy and let himself in the kitchen door of the manse on Curzon Street. He'd departed the gaming hells early this evening for the express purpose of dealing with Miss Lovejoy but he wanted to get back to the hells for the deepest play. The risk of a high stakes game was the only thing that gave him relief from the endless monotony of life. Only then did the dark loneliness inside him ease. Only then could he forget his failure to Constance. And, dear God, his sister, Charlotte. But that pain was still too raw to bear thinking about. Now he had to add Nell to his list. He was no good for women.

He encountered Mrs. Mason as she came below stairs bearing a tray with a half-eaten meal of lamb chops and roasted potatoes. "Oh, Lord Morgan! I did not expect you tonight. Will you be wanting dinner?"

He shook his head. "I'll be wanting Miss Lovejoy. Is she about?"

The woman flushed and Geoff realized how his words must have sounded.

"I mean I'll be wanting to *speak* with Miss Lovejoy."

"Of course, milord. But I am afraid she has just retired for the evening."

"I'll be in the library. Please ask her to accommodate me. I will take only a few moments of her time."

Without waiting for a response, Geoff made his way to the library. He'd just poured himself a brandy when Mrs. Mason appeared at the door.

"My lord, I…Miss Lovejoy begs that you return tomorrow at a…" the woman colored again and took a deep breath "…at a respectable hour."

It took him a full minute to comprehend the enormity of that insult. It was his house, by God! And she was living on his charity! How dare she refuse to see him? Had she no manners at all?

"Thank you, Mrs. Mason," he said, trying to keep his voice even and calm. He dismissed the woman with a wave of his hand and finished his brandy in a single gulp.

Another brandy followed the first as he considered how to respond to her haughtiness. In the end, he was confounded. There was only one way to handle Miss Lovejoy.

He took the stairs two at a time, seething with indignation. Two sharp raps on her door were all the warning he gave before opening it and stepping through. She was sitting in an overstuffed chair with her legs curled beneath her and the pages of a letter in her lap. She looked up in surprise.

"Miss Lovejoy, when I request an interview with you, I expect to be accommodated."

She blinked those wide blue eyes. "As you can see, Lord Morgan, I am scarcely in a condition to receive visitors."

There was nothing wrong with her condition as far as he could see. Her pale blond hair, most often done up in a formal style or tucked beneath a bonnet, was loose and fell over her shoulders, to tumble down her back. A wealth of midnight-blue fabric swathed her form, leaving a deep V open from her neck to a spot midway between her breasts, where a film of white lace peeked through. No, her "condition" was quite acceptable. At least to him.

"I do not care what condition you are in. Common courtesy would dictate that you receive me."

She unfolded her legs, revealing bare feet. The deep blue fabric shifted to drape over her form most alluringly as she stood. He recognized the garment as his dressing robe. The cuffs had been rolled back several times, and the hem made a little puddle at her feet. The sight gave him such a sudden visceral reaction that he instantly stiffened with desire. He was jealous of his damn robe! *He* wanted to wrap himself around her, fall heavily over the soft swells of her breasts, get tangled between her long shapely legs.

He swallowed hard, his throat suddenly dry.

She stood, the pages of her letter drifting to the carpet with a soft whisper, and performed a mocking curtsy. "My pardon, Lord Morgan. I had thought your offer of shelter was given without pain of favors. Now that I know better, I shall, of course, leave."

"The hell you will," he cursed. "Where do you think you could go? You will simply treat me with due courtesy and respect. In short, as you would treat anyone else in the same circumstances."

"You are not 'anyone else.' You are a reprobate who gambled to win my friend in marriage. Your quarrel nearly got my cousin killed. And because of you, Mr. Lucas is dead. You care for nothing but yourself. I only accepted your help because I do not care what happens to you, and, to be frank, all your money will not buy you respectability."

"There were reasons for that wager, Miss Lovejoy."

"You take other people's fortunes on the turn of a card," she accused.

"I force no one to risk so much as a farthing. 'Tis their choice, and if I do not take it, someone else will."

"You nearly got my cousin killed!"

"Your cousin, of his own accord, lunged between me and a dishonorable shot from my opponent's second when my back was turned." She looked so like an avenging angel that Geoff felt guilty, though he couldn't have said for what. He'd be damned if he was about to explain anything further to this piece of fluff who thought him guilty of all sorts of misdeeds.

She lifted her pert little nose in high moral indignation.

"I've no doubt at all that you can explain everything away, Lord Morgan, but I've no interest in hearing excuses. Now, why have you come to my room?"

She had him in such a state that it actually took him a moment to recall why he'd come. "Miss Brookes's funeral, Miss Lovejoy. I saw you there."

He detected a crack in her hard veneer. She turned and walked slowly toward the fireplace, speaking over her shoulder. "Why should I not have gone? After all, I was the one to find her."

"And the one the authorities are looking for. I thought you were smart enough to stay out of sight."

"I thought I had. I was swathed in black mourning and heavily veiled. How did you recognize me, Lord Morgan? I doubt my own sister would have."

He could hardly tell her he had recognized her figure and the way she moved. It would never do to let her know the effect she was having on him. She was already too sure of herself. He would have to settle on something more vague. "Perhaps you are not as clever as you thought."

She halted and her spine stiffened. "Then I suppose I shall have to be more careful."

"I'd advise it, Miss Lovejoy, though staying out of sight entirely would be preferable."

"I believe we've had this discussion before, Lord Morgan. Do I not recall you saying that you 'make it your policy to never interfere in the personal matters of others, nor to question their actions or motives'?"

"That was before you were being so widely sought."

"Nevertheless, giving me shelter does not grant you the right to dictate my actions. Disavow yourself of that notion. If you are unable to do so I shall have to leave, because I do not intend to sit docilely by while the police make a case against me. Since no one else has come forward to do it, I shall champion myself."

Was she suggesting that *he* should champion her? Surely not. She'd made it obvious that she could not even bear the sight of him. Perhaps he could reason with her. "Did you learn anything new today, Miss Lovejoy?"

"Well, no. I only spoke with one person, and she was not at liberty to…that is, she—"

"Wouldn't tell you anything," he finished for her. "And what does that tell you?"

"That people are afraid to talk."

"That people are unwilling to talk to *you*," he corrected. "You cannot expect those close to a murder to simply begin blurting every little detail they might recall. Investigation requires a little more finesse than that, Miss Lovejoy. You are far too naive to know how to go about this sort of thing."

She finally turned toward him and smiled. "I have a new plan. One that will open doors for me and answer whatever questions I have. And, by the by, what were *you* doing at Miss Brookes's funeral?"

Damn. "Where I go and what I do is none of your concern, Miss Lovejoy. Just stay out of my way."

"Nor is what I do or where I go yours, Lord Morgan. And I shall be quite pleased to stay out of your way. Now, are you going to toss me out of your house on my ear?"

"You know I won't," he growled. "And you're counting on that. But once your cousin is back—"

"All bets are off," she finished for him with a wicked little quirk of her lips.

Oh! That impossible man! He leaves me alone for days, then simply appears in the middle of the night, demanding to see me, and telling me what to do!

Dianthe tossed her brush aside and stared at her reflection in the dressing table mirror. What was it about her that brought out the worst in that man? What was it in him that brought out the worst in *her?* She made a little moue in the mirror.

If forced to the truth, she would have to admit that Geoffrey Morgan had been as kind to her as she had allowed, and she hadn't made even that easy for him. There was just something about him that set her on edge. Was it that he didn't fawn over her like other men? Or that most of the time he just seemed annoyed by her?

She stood and glanced at the massive canopy bed. Had Lord Morgan ever slept there? She tried to imagine him lying tangled in the pristine sheets of satin-weave linen, his intense hazel eyes closed in slumber. Her breathing deepened and her heartbeat skipped. His lordship had an intangible air of danger and darkness about him that made her other beaux seem almost effeminate. She'd certainly never pictured any of *them* in a bed.

But this was foolishness! She had no intention of allowing herself to waste time in such utter nonsense as dreaming of that scheming devil. She untied the belt of her robe and shrugged out of it. A whiff of masculine shaving soap floated up to her from the discarded heap on the floor, and her knees weakened. What was wrong with her?

Geoffrey Morgan was everything she disliked in a man. He was arrogant, unscrupulous, ill-mannered, ruthless, cold, demanding and autocratic. Everything about him set her teeth on edge.

Then why couldn't she stop thinking about him?

She closed her eyes and saw his face as he'd stood in her doorway. His eyes had burned into her and caused an answering heat to rise from somewhere near her belly. When he'd taken three steps into the bedroom, she'd wondered if he'd come to ravage her. And she was distressed to realize that thought did not trouble her much.

Or was it guilt that gnawed at her? Yes. That had to be it. Willingly or not, he'd given her shelter when she'd been desperate. He'd made certain his staff would see to all of her needs, and had given her relative independence. And she had repaid him with churlishness. Though he wouldn't know it, she really had better manners than she'd shown him.

Yes. Henceforth, she'd give him no cause for complaint. She'd show him the respect he'd asked for. She'd be as civil to him as she would to any polite stranger. She'd be the very model of decorum and ladylike calm. She wouldn't allow him to rankle her, no matter what he said or did.

Dawn was spreading a pink glow over rooftops and chimney pots when Geoff finally arrived at his house on Salisbury Street. The day servants had not arrived yet, and only his valet, Giles, and Hanson, the cook, lived in. Although the house was certainly large enough to warrant a live-in staff of five or so servants, he did not like the intrusion upon his privacy. Giles and Hanson, though, had come with him from his estate in Devon, and their absolute loyalty and discretion could be trusted.

He let himself in, tossed his jacket and vest on the foyer table and headed for the ballroom, rolling up his shirtsleeves as he went. He was too restless to sleep. First there'd been that absurd confrontation gone awry with Miss Lovejoy, and then he'd actually *lost* at vingt-et-un. It wasn't the loss of the money that bothered him—he'd lost more in an evening. It was the fact that he hadn't been able to concentrate. His mind had been too full of blond hair and blue eyes—and an edge of transparent lace peeking from the V of his dressing robe.

Clearly, he needed to get rid of Dianthe Lovejoy as quickly as possible. Was there any point in sending a letter to her cousin in Italy? No. Certainly someone else had done that already.

Instinctively in tune with Geoffrey's moods, Giles had left chandeliers alight in the ballroom, and the fireplaces lit at each end of the room. Light glittered off the mirrored walls and the crystal prisms of the chandelier, setting the room ablaze with reflected brilliance. Geoffrey walked the length of the room, trailing his index finger along the rack holding everything from lances to swords. He selected a claymore, savoring its weight and length. He needed something taxing tonight. Something to banish the memory of his robe draping a delicate frame.

He hefted the claymore and sliced vertically, then horizontally through the air. The whoosh of the blade satisfied something deep in his soul, and he smiled. He worked through a routine of standard moves, then offensive moves, then defensive ones. The echo of his boots on the marble floor and his heavy breathing from the exertion were the only sounds to rupture the silence. By the time he was done, a fine sheen of sweat dampened his skin and his white shirt, but he was not yet fatigued enough to sleep. He replaced the claymore in its slot and picked a deadly rapier—light in weight, sleek in build, treacherous at its point. Ah, yes. This blade *sang* as it slashed the air.

With an edge vertically to his forehead, he saluted his reflection in the mirrors. Working through a different routine, watching his form for mistakes or openings that an opponent could pierce, he found the lighter, more familiar blade almost became an extension of his arm. Only when the rising sun penetrated the French doors along one wall did Geoff replace the rapier in the rack. He hesitantly caressed the hilt of his cutlass, but turned away in exhaustion.

Now, perhaps, he'd sleep. Spent as he was, the guilt, the memories of Constance, Charlotte, Nell and the other women he'd failed, would not rise to haunt his dreams. Worse, he might dream of Dianthe Lovejoy. Her steadfast defiance amused him. Her beauty drew him. Her instinctive intelligence intrigued him. And his hunger for her was reaching a fever pitch. If he started seducing her in his dreams, would he be able to resist her in his waking moments?

Ah, but he'd have to claim Dianthe in his *dreams,* because he'd never claim her anywhere else. He'd make love to her there because, awake, he'd never risk loving her. He'd hold her close in his dreams, because he'd never allow her to rely upon him in life. He'd never take that risk of failing again. Never.

And when the isolation and solitude became too much to bear, he'd shut himself away with Flora Denton or one of the other lovelies of the demimonde again, for a few days or weeks, until that particular monster had been tamed enough to lock away for another term of penance.

He climbed the long curve of the staircase to his room, hardening his heart, reducing his hunger and need to a mere physical act. That's all it was. That's all he'd ever let it be.

The summons from Harry Richardson several hours later came as a surprise. Geoff hadn't expected to hear from him for several days. Information packets from Tangier were slow in coming—at least during the summer months.

When he opened the door of the rented room, Harry jumped to his feet. "Glad you could come so quickly, Morgan."

Geoff glanced at the small wooden table where charts, maps, pen and ink were laid out in waiting. "El-Daibul is on the move?" he guessed.

"We think so," Harry replied.

"Think? You don't know?" Geoff crossed to the table and looked down at the charts. Tangier, Gibraltar, Spain, Portugal. What was going on?

Harry shrugged. "We've lost him."

Geoff fastened the man with an asking stare. How could an experienced operative lose a man of el-Daibul's infamy and importance?

"He has disappeared," Harry explained, looking a bit pale from Geoff's study.

"When?"

Harry went to the small table beside the cot where the whiskey bottle was waiting. He poured himself a glass and quirked an eyebrow at Geoff.

Since he'd only risen an hour ago, that would be like drinking whiskey for breakfast. He hadn't sunk to that level yet. "Too early," Geoff said, though he had no doubt the male half of London was drinking by teatime.

After a swallow, Harry met Geoff's gaze again. "We don't know when, exactly. It just came to our attention that no one has seen el-Daibul for a month or more."

"Christ! A month! Where can he have gone?"

"Don't know. We haven't been able to pick up his trail. We've got operatives searching Algiers to see if he went back there. So far, no luck."

"Any word from the desert?" Geoff pointed to the Sahara on the map.

"No one has reported him moving overland."

"Has the political climate changed? Any clues there?"

"Nothing new. The Americans are still harrying the Corsairs, but the underground market is still good for white slavery."

"Always," Geoff murmured. "Have you tried tracking his men?"

"They are all in place. Nothing unusual there, and one of the reasons it took us so long to realize that el-Daibul himself had not been seen for quite some time. It looks as if he went to considerable trouble to lull us into complacency."

Geoff ran his fingers through his hair, smoothing a stray lock. Damn! What could the man be up to? Geoff could only hope this latest development was not a prelude to increased activity. Unless… "Harry, what's the news from the docks? Any increase in reports of missing women?"

"Not in London."

"Send men to Liverpool, Portsmouth and Dover. Contact Culver in France, Groton in Hamburg and Peters in Venice. Verify with them that the traffic is quiet. If there's an increase, no matter how small, and no matter where, I want to know immediately."

"What are you thinking?" Harry asked. His eyes narrowed suspiciously.

"I'm not certain. Just…verify. He's up to something, Harry, I can feel it."

Harry shook his head. "We'll need evidence to get help from the Foreign Office."

He sat and studied the maps. "Last time…when he was quiet, it was because the demand for Englishwomen was high enough to warrant certain…risks. Educated women of a higher social standing were in demand. Virgins."

Harry nodded. "I remember. 'Twas 1816. The year Auberville nearly lost his wife. The year Constance Bennington was killed."

Geoff said nothing. He still couldn't talk about the hor-

ror and pain of finding Constance's body in a pile of discarded rags. She'd come too close to learning the truth
about the disappearing women, and she'd fought her at-
tackers. Oh, God, if she just hadn't fought! He could have
gone after her. She might still be alive.

But Mustafa el-Daibul had wanted retribution in retaliation for their systematic closing down of the white slavery trade. And he hadn't cared what form it took.

"So." Harry exhaled. "You think this may be the same
thing? You think he's stepping up activity?"

Lord, Geoffrey almost hoped so. That might be better
than the possibility of retaliation. He, at least, did not have
a woman to worry about this time, but Auberville would
have to be warned. He'd have to set guards over his wife
and children.

Damn! Why did these things have to happen when he
could ill afford the division of his attention? He'd give
anything for a two-week respite—just long enough to get
Miss Lovejoy off his hands. Or to get rid of Miss Lovejoy
long enough to deal with el-Daibul.

"What is it, Morgan?" Harry asked. "Isn't this what
you've been hoping for? Haven't you been trying to force
el-Daibul's hand? Flush him from hiding?"

Geoff nodded. "There are complications. If I didn't
have…a personal obligation at the moment, I'd be halfway
to Gibraltar right now. I wish I knew where the hell the
blighter was."

"If you were to guess?"

"I'd say he's gone back to Algiers. Or Tunis. That's
where the buyers are. Most likely, Tunis. The Dey of Algiers blamed him for the Bombardment in 1816. I think
el-Daibul has been out of favor since then, which is why
he shifted operations to Tangier. He blames Auberville and

me for that particular debacle. El-Daibul's wife and children were killed in the Bombardment, and that has given him another reason to hate me."

"You make it sound personal, Morgan."

"It is personal." In point of fact, he suspected Constance had been killed as much for her place in his heart as for the fact that she'd fought her kidnappers. He could easily imagine el-Daibul ordering a "dead or alive" order to take Constance. Hide and seek. Cat and mouse. Attack and retreat. They'd played out all the stratagems. There wasn't much left that hadn't already been done. He and the white slaver had been engaged in a global duel to the death for the past five years, and nothing was sacrosanct, no rules inviolable.

Wisely, Harry remained silent. He went to the window and stood gazing out while Geoff made a few marks on the maps and a notation at the bottom.

What was it? What piece of the puzzle was just out of his grasp? A message? A taunt? There was a clue somewhere, something he should see and understand.

"Bloody goddamned hell!" He slammed his fist down on the table, rattling the ink bottle and miscellaneous pens.

"Easy, Morgan," Harry soothed. "I hate it when you get this way. You're too hard on yourself. Ease up a bit and let it come on its own."

Geoff pushed back from the table. "Send for word from the ports, Harry, and get news to me the minute you have any. Steer clear of the Foreign Office. They'd have our heads if they thought we were compromising the uneasy peace they've forged."

Harry nodded. "Where are you going?"

"To warn Auberville."

Chapter Five

Dianthe sat at a dressing table in Madame Marie's back fitting room and made a tight coil of her pale hair before pinning it at her crown. She watched *Madame* lower the black wig over her head and snug it into place.

"Ah, *chérie!* This is the mistake, no?"

Dianthe stared at her reflection. With every strand of blond hair covered, she had taken on a foreign look. Pale skin with a hint of pink on her cheeks, clear blue eyes and a beauty patch on one cheekbone made her virtually unrecognizable.

"Mistake?" she asked. "You think the beauty patch is too much?"

"*Mais non, chérie!* But the idea was to make you less noticeable. This—" she waved at Dianthe's reflection "—will turn 'eads."

"I do not care about that, *Madame.* More to the point is if I will be recognized." Indeed, Dianthe was nearly desperate to change her appearance. She hadn't been outside without her bonnet and veils since taking refuge at Lord Geoffrey's house. Anything to evade the killer who, according to Nell, would come for her next.

Madame Marie stepped back to study her critically. "Never!" she said.

Dianthe pulled one curl down and watched as it sprang back into place. She rather liked the way she looked, and she certainly felt safer.

Madame Marie arranged the style in an artful manner and stood back to observe her work. "I did not think you could be more beautiful, *chérie,* but I was wrong. You look so…*à la française.*"

Just the thing she wanted. Her French was very good, and she knew she could fake a believable accent. She'd worn a veil to Marie's shop but she wouldn't wear one when leaving. She wouldn't need it.

Best of all, this disguise would be perfect for her new plan. With the wig, an accent, a sophisticated attitude and a new name, she would be worlds apart from Dianthe Lovejoy of Little Upton, Wiltshire. Soon. Very soon.

"*Là!*" Madame Marie exclaimed. "I do not like that look, *chérie.* You are 'atching some plot, are you not?"

Dianthe blinked. "I am sure I don't know what you mean, *Madame.* I am just pleased that I will not have to go about veiled and shrouded. 'Twill be nice to see where I am walking. Would you have a few cosmetics to further disguise me?"

Madame Marie rummaged in a small kit. "You do not need it, *chérie,* but I 'ave a powder that will warm your pale complexion and lip rouge and kohl for the eyes and lashes."

A knock at the door drew Madame Marie's attention away. "That will be François," she said. "'E said there are matters to discuss with you."

Francis Renquist opened the door a crack and called in. "Are you decent, Miss Lovejoy?"

"But of course she is decent, François." Madame Marie smiled at her husband. She let him in and went around him, speaking over her shoulder. "She looks just like *ma mère,* Lizette Deauville. I 'ave an appointment, *chérie.* I shall see you tomorrow when the ladies come, eh?"

"Oui," she called, turning from the mirror to face Mr. Renquist. "Do you have news?" she asked.

Mr. Renquist looked dumbstruck. His eyes widened and he stared at her with his mouth agape. "I, ah. You…*are* Miss Lovejoy?"

She smiled. "Then you do not think I'd be recognized on the street?"

He shook his head, his eyes never leaving her. "But do not let that make you reckless, Miss Lovejoy."

"And once I shed the disguise and go back to being Dianthe Lovejoy?"

"No one would link the two of you together," he confirmed.

Thank heavens. Now she was free to proceed with her plan. But first, she asked, "Did you learn anything, Mr. Renquist?"

He shook his head as if to clear it. "No. The men I interviewed are well-respected family men. All have alibis for the night of the murder."

Dianthe wondered how any man who'd dallied with a courtesan and had been fond enough of one to attend her funeral could be a "family man." "And the others?" she asked. "Did you learn their names?"

"Yes, miss. Nigel Edgerton and Lord Geoffrey Morgan among them. I have not interviewed them yet."

"As it happens, Mr. Renquist, my cousin and aunt are well acquainted with Lord Morgan. If you will speak with Mr. Edgerton, I shall interview Morgan." The last thing she wanted was for Mr. Renquist to question Geoffrey Morgan. If he should slip and give her whereabouts away, Mr. Renquist would call him out.

"I am not certain that is a good idea, Miss Lovejoy. Lord Morgan has a reputation as the worst sort of rake."

"But he owes my cousin a favor. He will not harm me in any way. Set your mind at ease on that, sir. But I wonder if you might indulge me in a few questions. You see, there is no one else I can ask."

Mr. Renquist frowned. "What sort of questions?"

"About the demimonde, sir. And their…well, practices."

"Here now. You ought not to be concerning yourself with such things."

"I fear it is too late for that. Miss Brookes was of the demimonde, and therefore certain elements of it are of grave concern to me. They may have bearing on her murder. Perhaps her killer was a patron, or a jealous competitor."

Considering her words, Mr. Renquist went to the door and peeked out. He shut it again and turned the lock. "If Marie catches me talking about such things, I'll be hard-pressed to find supper or a bed tonight."

Dianthe nodded in understanding.

"Ask, then," he instructed with a nervous glance over his shoulder.

"I think it would be helpful to know how a woman of the demimonde goes on."

Mr. Renquist looked bewildered. "Goes on?"

"Conducts herself," Dianthe clarified, covering her embarrassment. "I assume that, if she has a protector, he would escort her places and see to her business and needs. But what if she does not have a particular protector, as Miss Brookes did not? Did Miss Brookes go to events alone? In groups with other ladies of the demimonde? Or would she always have an escort? The possibilities are bewildering, you see, and they could make all the difference in why Miss Brookes was where she was, and in what happened to her. I would ask you to investigate that for me, Mr. Renquist, but I know Madame Marie would have your…hide pinned to a wall should you spend time with that sort of woman."

A hint of fear passed through Mr. Renquist's eyes. "I quite agree, miss. Well, not that I am knowledgeable about such things, but the rules of polite society do not apply to the demimonde. Miss Brookes could have gone wherever she wanted, excepting in society."

"Alone?"

"If she chose."

"What sort of places would she have gone?"

"Public places, mostly. The theater. Vauxhall Gardens. Her escort the night of her murder was never found. Likely she went alone to meet friends."

To meet her, Dianthe thought. But the theater? That was an idea. She could purchase a ticket and observe the goings-on. "Where else would a courtesan go?" she asked.

"Where she could meet men. Where ladies do not. Such women would not be admitted to Almack's or balls and soirees."

Then what of hells and public houses? Hells. A woman could expect to meet a better sort there than at a public house. Men who had enough money to gamble would be men who could buy an expensive woman's favors. Nell Brookes had seemed the sort who would prefer men with money, and she'd been pretty enough to attract them. Her friends would have frequented the same places and have known the same men.

And they were the women whose trust Dianthe must

win. Only then would she get the answers to her questions.
You would have to be one of us....

Precisely what she had in mind.

Dianthe dropped her brush on the dressing table and
went to pour herself another cup of tea from the pot on her
bedside table. She couldn't believe she felt so lonely. Her
brother, Bennett, was abroad with a schoolmate's family
for the summer, Afton was in Scotland with her husband,
and Aunt Grace was on her wedding trip. Dianthe had
thought she'd be quite merry with the Thayers until au-
tumn. She wished, now, that she'd gone to stay with Afton
and the McHugh in the Highlands. Instead, she was now
homeless, bereft of family and at the mercy of a man she
had always believed was completely ruthless.

The mantel clock struck the hour of ten and Dianthe
rolled her eyes. Hortense and Harriett would be frisking
through the salons of the ton at this very minute, with nary
a thought of bed for many hours to come, and dozens of
young swains in pursuit, while her only company was the
monotonous tick of the clock. Tedium coupled with unease
made her nerves jangle.

She glanced down at the leather-bound volume on her
chair. She'd finished *The Taming Of The Shrew,* and hadn't
brought anything else upstairs with her. Perhaps she should
go down to the library and find something more interesting to read. Something on the upper shelves, perhaps. Yes,
something not fit for delicate female eyes. She'd like to
know that there was something more shocking than her
own life at the moment, and she longed for anything that
would distract her.

Without distractions, her mind always returned to Vauxhall Gardens and her cousin dying in her arms. Tears

welled in her eyes and she dashed them away with the back of her hand. Every day that she delayed taking action was a betrayal of her promise to Nell.

Dianthe hadn't heard anyone stirring for quite some time, and figured Mrs. Mason and Pemberton had undoubtedly retired for the night. They would have extinguished the lights in the library, so she picked up a lit candle to take with her. Anticipating the library ladder she would have to negotiate to reach the higher shelves, she kicked off her slippers. She'd be more sure-footed on the treads without them.

Despite the pervasive silence, there were a good many lights left burning—one in the foyer, one in the back hallway and another in the sitting room. She'd never known anyone to use the sitting room. Still, the running of the house was none of her business. Perhaps Lord Morgan's orders had been to be prepared for his arrival at any and all times.

The ornamental umbrella stand in the foyer was tipped over, and she paused to right it and replace the umbrellas. How had that happened? She glanced around but could find nothing else out of place.

With a shrug, she continued to the library. One lamp by the desk was still lit and the fireplace still glowed, the embers a bright orange-red. She closed the door to ensure her privacy should Pemberton come to make one last circuit of the house. She had no desire to explain her taste in reading materials while standing in a nightgown.

She placed her candle on the desk and returned the volume of Shakespeare to the shelf. With heightened anticipation, she climbed the library ladder to read the titles on the top shelf. Oh, for an illicit copy of something naughty—just the very thing to chase worry from her weary brain. Perhaps something by the Italians. Dante or

Ovid's *Ars Amatoria,* Shakespeare's *Venus and Adonis,* or some other "indecent" work.

But she found nothing to titillate or even raise an eyebrow. She descended the ladder and pushed it along the shelves to a new position. The sound of a footfall outside the library door stopped her. Was it Pemberton coming to lock up for the night?

She was on the verge of calling out when another possibility occurred to her. Had Lord Morgan come to devil her? She really was in no mood for such a possibility. She found their encounters increasingly taxing on her nerves.

A faint moan was followed by a muffled footfall. A prickle of misgiving raced up Dianthe's spine. This wouldn't be Morgan. The sounds of that night in Vauxhall Gardens came back to her, and she made an instinctive move toward the desk and the knee well beneath it. For the first time, she noticed that the middle drawer was open and the floor beneath it was littered with papers. She glanced over her shoulder and saw the doorknob turning. Dropping to her knees, she scooted beneath the desk, hugged herself and held her breath.

The door opened and a shaft of light from the foyer spread across the wall behind her. Whatever had been dragged was dropped, and the library door was closed with a quiet click.

Dianthe scarcely breathed. Her heartbeat hammered wildly against her rib cage and fear rose in the form of a solid lump in her throat. Oh! The candle! She'd left it burning!

A gurgling chortle slid through the silence. "I know you're in here," a man's voice whispered.

Geoff left his horse saddled in the empty stables and strode toward the house. He'd only be a minute. Just a quick word of warning to Pemberton and then he'd go on to the hells. Not that he had any particular fear where Miss Lovejoy was concerned, but with el-Daibul's whereabouts unknown, it was better to err on the side of caution than live with regrets.

Auberville hadn't been a happy man when Geoff gave him the news that el-Daibul was "at large." Nevertheless, he agreed that he would have to send Lady Annica and the children out of town at once. And not to the country estates. No, Auberville intended to send them all the way to his hunting lodge in Scotland until they could locate and neutralize el-Daibul. Geoff gathered that Lady Sarah and Charity MacGregor would be sent away, as well.

He let himself in the kitchen door and glanced around. A broken bowl filled with dough lay on the floor and flour scattered a white dusting across the worktable. A wooden chair was overturned and several tins of spices had spilled off the shelves. His pulse quickened and readiness raced through his bloodstream.

Weak thumping caught his attention. He followed the sound to the pantry door and opened it wide. Mrs. Mason lay bound by her apron strings and gagged with a dish towel. Geoff unfastened the bonds and removed her gag, signaling her to silence with a finger to his lips.

With tears streaking down her face, Mrs. Mason gasped for air before she whispered, "He hit Pemberton over the head, milord."

"Who?" he asked, though he had little hope Mrs. Mason would know. "And when?"

She shook her head to deny knowledge of the first question and went on to answer the second. "Ten minutes ago, sir. I heard him rummaging in the library and upstairs in your room. Oh, milord! Pemberton was so still!"

"Miss Lovejoy? Where is she?"

Mrs. Mason's eyes widened and she bit the knuckles of her right hand. "Oh, I'd forgot her, she's that quiet!"

"Go out the back and bring the night watch. *Run.*" He slipped his dagger from his boot and turned toward the hall-way to the front of the house.

Keeping his back to one wall as he edged forward, he listened intently for any noise, looked for any telltale sign of an intruder. Was it el-Daibul's henchman? A random robbery? And what the hell had he done with Pemberton?

Geoff's stomach seized with a biting cramp. Miss Love-joy? *Had* she been the target in Vauxhall Gardens, and had the killer tracked her here to finish the job?

A piercing scream suddenly rent the air and Geoff was galvanized to action. He sprinted toward the library with an answering shout and threw the door open. He was pro-pelled backward, flailing his arms to keep his balance. A knife blade slashed out, slicing through his jacket and vest as he and the assailant rolled over together. The other man, shrouded in a hood and cloak, stumbled to his feet and sprinted toward the front door. Geoff lunged after him and grasped an edge of the dark cloak, ripping a corner away.

Another scream sounded. His split second of hesitation to look back at Miss Lovejoy cost him the kill. If anything happened to her…. He turned again as the assailant disap-peared out the front door, then back to Miss Lovejoy, who fell to her knees by Pemberton's prone body. Geoff lurched forward and dropped to his own knees, on the other side of Pemberton, pushing the scrap of the intruder's cloak into his jacket pocket and his knife back into his boot.

Miss Lovejoy's hand shook as she examined a lump on Pemberton's graying head. "He…he's breathing." She sighed with relief.

Geoff gripped her shoulders. "Miss Lovejoy, are *you* all right? Did he hurt you? What happened?"

"N-no. He heard you coming and…"

Pemberton moaned and opened his eyes. "My lord," he said, struggling to sit up.

"Lie back, Pemberton. Mrs. Mason has gone for a constable."

Pemberton felt the lump on his head gingerly. "I am as right as rain, sir. A small headache is all. Do not trouble yourself."

Geoff nodded and scanned Miss Lovejoy's form. She was just barely holding herself together. Fear burned in her eyes, her hands trembled and a darkening patch of skin on her neck just below her ear told him that the man had tried to strangle her. A moment later, she'd have been dead.

His voice was tight as he asked, "Did he say anything?"

"He said he knew I was in here—the library. I don't know why he was dragging Mr. Pemberton with him. It all seemed so…insane."

"Wanted…wanted me to show him where…your personal papers were, sir," Pemberton said, ignoring Geoff's order to lie back. "He didn't hit me until I tried to get away."

"What did he look like? Did you recognize him?"

"Masked, my lord," Pemberton said.

Miss Lovejoy nodded. "And he whispered," she said.

Yes, voices were harder to recognize in a whisper. The man knew his business. And now it appeared that the invasion had been aimed at him, not Miss Lovejoy. Geoff studied her again. Her light cotton nightgown was ripped at the shoulder, and curling tendrils of pale blond hair had come loose to form a frame about her face. The bruise on her throat stood out like a reproach. He should have realized that Miss Lovejoy would be in danger, just as he should have seen the signs with Constance. He should have been there. He should have stopped it.

Something long dormant, something nameless and primal, stirred in him, and he reacted without thinking. He stood and lifted Miss Lovejoy to her feet. "Pemberton, will you lie quietly until Mrs. Mason returns?"

"Aye, my lord."

"I do not want you to become dizzy and fall. When Mrs. Mason brings the authorities, do not mention that Miss Lovejoy was here. It could…compromise her reputation."

"But—"

"Tell them that I had urgent business and that I will come 'round to the offices tomorrow to give them a full report."

"Where—"

"Somewhere safe," he answered.

Miss Lovejoy understood and, for once, did not argue. "I'll go pack my things."

"No time," Geoff told her. "We'll send for them in the morning."

"But I need to—"

"We need to go *now*, Miss Lovejoy," he said in an undertone. "The *authorities* are on the way."

She blinked. "My slippers?"

He looked down at her bare feet, peeking out from beneath the hem of her gown. "You will not need them," he said as he swept her up and carried her toward the back of the house.

In the stables, he lifted her to the saddle of his horse and swung up behind her. She was shivering in the night air and he quickly shrugged out of his jacket to drape it over her shoulders. He reached around her to take the reins, and kicked his mount to a gallop. The well-trained chestnut stallion did not balk at the added weight, and caught Geoff's urgency.

He watched over his shoulder to be certain they were not being followed, and negotiated the streets quickly—a surprise, given the distraction Miss Lovejoy's warmth and softness provided. Her scent, jasmine blended with warm feminine skin, awoke a fire in his blood and a swelling in his loins. How was he to keep his distance from the chit now that they were about to take residency together?

In the courtyard behind the house on Salisbury Street, Geoff slid off the stallion's rump and held his arms out for Miss Lovejoy. She leaned forward, placed her hands on his shoulders and hesitated.

"Where are we?" she asked.

"My house on Salisbury Street." He was certain she was about to give him an argument, listing all the reasons this was a bad idea, but she merely took a deep breath and allowed him to lift her from the saddle.

He carried her through a set of French doors leading into his office, or, as Giles and Hanson liked to call it, his library. He placed her on her feet and then closed and locked the door. Embers glowed in the fireplace, so Geoff touched a piece of kindling to the coals, lifted the globe of the lamp and touched the wick. Miss Lovejoy looked around as the dark corners of the room came into view.

"Not nearly as grand as the house on Curzon," he admitted, "but more to my taste."

She nodded with an uncertain smile.

"What is it, Miss Lovejoy? You've been quiet and given me no arguments. Are you in pain? Is your throat swollen?"

"I…I owe you my life, Lord Morgan. If you hadn't come when you did…" She stopped and cleared her throat.

"Hmm, well," he said, uncomfortable with her gratitude. He'd rather have her berating him. "We need to talk about that. What were you doing in the library at that time of night?"

"I went down to find a book to read. I was bored."

"Still bored?"

She laughed and some of the tension seemed to leave her shoulders. "I must say, Lord Morgan, that excitement seems to follow you."

"Me?" he chuckled. "I'd swear 'tis you, Miss Lovejoy. From the moment I saw you at Vauxhall, my life has been in an uproar."

Unexpected tears filled her eyes and she looked down at her bare feet. "I wish I knew how to stop all this, but…"

Damn! He'd meant to lighten the mood. She looked so lost and forlorn that he stepped forward and drew her against his chest, half expecting her to resist or curse at him for trying to take advantage. Instead she laid her cheek against his chest and gave a shaky sigh.

In a voice so faint he swore she hadn't meant him to hear, she whispered, "This is the first time I've felt truly safe since I stopped to help Nell."

Bloody hell! He couldn't, he *wouldn't,* let her rely on him! He couldn't live with *her* death on his conscience, too.

"If I haven't said it before," she said in a stronger voice, "thank you." She tilted her face up to him, came up on her toes and pressed those unutterably soft, delicate lips to his cheek.

He groaned, wanting to claim her mouth and kiss her until those lips were swollen with his passion, and wanting at the same time to thrust her away and leave the room before his baser nature asserted itself. He leaned toward her at the very moment she stepped away from him and looked around.

"Do you live here alone?"

He shook his head, regaining his composure. "My valet, Giles, and my cook, Hanson, live in. I believe there are some other servants, but I rarely see them. About that, Miss Lovejoy. I—"

"Dianthe," she said. "You saved my life. You have earned the right to call me by my given name, my lord."

That stunned him. Should he reciprocate? God, no! If she called him Geoff, he'd find some way to use that familiarity to seduce her. He picked up the lantern and opened the door to the corridor. "If you will follow me, Miss—"

"Dianthe," she corrected, softly but firmly.

"Follow me, please. I'll show you the house. You will, of course, choose a room that suits you." He prayed it would be in the opposite wing from his.

The first floor was quite lovely, Dianthe decided. Quietly elegant and comfortable. She was surprised by the ballroom on the ground floor, which he had converted into a practice studio for various skills, primarily fencing and boxing. Aside from his office, there was a sitting room, dining room, morning room, parlor and music room. Though he did not show her, he told her the kitchen and laundry room were below stairs, as well as staff quarters for Giles and Hanson, and he did not want to disturb them. On the second floor were several bedrooms, a privy, a bathroom that held a large tub and washstand, a private receiving room and a nursery. The third floor, which would ordinarily hold the ballroom, contained a schoolroom, governess quarters and another water closet.

"Did you win this one, too?" she asked softly.

He shook his head. "I bought it from a barrister who was moving his family to the countryside. It's close to my work, Waterloo Bridge and the Beaufort Wharfs."

She could tell from his wary look that he was waiting for her to make some comment about his choice to stay close to the gaming hells of Covent Garden. "It is lovely," she commented.

"Well, now you've seen it, which room do you want?"

A little bubble of fear rose in her throat. She could still feel that awful man's hands around her neck, squeezing, closing off her windpipe—could still see the flashes of light as she began to lose consciousness. "The one next to yours," she blurted.

His eyebrows lifted nearly to his hairline. "Miss Lovejoy, need I tell you how inappropriate that would be?"

"No," she admitted. "But I would feel better if anyone who wanted to hurt me had to pass you first."

A smile twitched at the corners of his mouth. "Ah! And as the man is murdering me, you can make your escape?"

"Precisely," she said. "And it is only for tonight, after all."

Lord Geoffrey grinned. "Not exactly, Miss Lovejoy. I have run out of London houses, and my estate is far into the countryside. Would you rather go there?"

"No!" If she went there, how could she keep her promise to Nell? "I must stay in London. My brother-in-law is on his way to fetch me now. It is too late to intercept the letter, so how would he find me in the countryside?"

"I know the McHugh. I could contact him and—"

"There must be somewhere else I can go?"

His jaw tightened. "I regret to say, Miss Lovejoy, that you will have to remain here if you remain in London. I cannot be certain what was behind this attack tonight, and I doubt you will want to return to Curzon Street. If you would prefer to go to the country, I shall make my estate available to you and staff it with guards. Your choice."

She longed to argue with him, but she could see he was implacable. Dianthe desperately wanted to flee to safety but, in the end, there was only one decision she could make. "I shall stay. If I must, then I'll stay here. I know how inappropriate this whole situation is, and I know that my reputation is already in ruins. Society may not believe we are blameless, but my family will."

"If we are careful, Miss Lovejoy, no one need ever know. Your secret is safe with me and my servants will never gossip."

His assurance surprised her. Indeed, his behavior the entire evening had surprised her. Perhaps he was not quite the scoundrel she thought him. Her aunt had not considered him "beyond the pale," nor had certain members of the Wednesday League spoken out against him. When he'd put his arms around her in the library, Dianthe had felt so safe and peaceful. Only that dreadful awkward moment after she'd kissed him had marred his composure. To Lord Geoffrey's credit, he had not berated her, but his unwillingness to use her given name was a certain sign he did not welcome her familiarity.

"Very well, Lord Geoffrey. I am sensible to how difficult it would be for you to protect me if you cannot be near me."

He winced and his lips thinned into a tight line. "I am *not* protecting you, Miss Lovejoy. Never mistake that, and never count on it. I am giving you safe harbor. Shelter— that is all. And just how safe it is depends entirely upon your behavior."

She stepped back, feeling his vehemence like a bitter wind. "I shall remember that, Lord Morgan. See that you do." She turned away from him and climbed the cold marble stairs to the room she intended to claim as hers. And to think she had nearly let her guard down—had nearly confused the arrogant lord with a human being!

Chapter Six

⁓⁓⁓

The harsh morning sun glared through the French doors of Geoff's office, washing over Hanson and Giles, who sat across the desk from him. They were staring in unabashed astonishment. That was not a good sign.

"A woman, milord?" Giles asked again, as if certain he had misheard.

Geoffrey nearly scalded his tongue on his second cup of coffee. Would that it were whiskey! He was still trying to figure out how he'd fallen into this trap. "She's the cousin of a friend of mine. I am required to lodge her until her cousin can return to town and reclaim her. She appears to be in somewhat of a pickle. Danger of some sort. I want you both to keep an eye on her."

"Are…are we to follow her, milord?" Hanson asked, a look of horror on his usually placid round face.

"Of course not. But during her residence, I do not want you admitting any strangers, no matter the excuse or explanation. I want all outside doors locked at all times. It would be best if you put the day staff on leave until further notice. Paid leave, of course." Geoff watched the two shocked faces across from him with a modicum of sympathy. They'd always been a household of males, and now he was asking them to accept and serve a very feminine female.

"But, my lord," Giles said in a pleading voice as he sat forward in his chair, a look of earnest confusion on his face, "we have no female staff. Who will attend her?"

"She will attend herself." Geoff suddenly wondered if Miss Lovejoy required an abigail. She seemed fairly self-sufficient, and Mrs. Mason had not mentioned her needing assistance in dressing or bathing. Surely Giles and Hanson wouldn't intrude on... "I expect you will respect her privacy in all ways."

Hanson nodded. "And which room is she staying in, my lord?"

Geoff cleared his throat and glanced down at the papers in front of him. "The one next to mine," he murmured, knowing what they would think. But, damn it all, what else could he do? It wasn't as if they had adjoining doors, after all.

Last night after she'd gone up to her room, he'd remembered that she hadn't any clothing with her, and he'd taken her one of his shirts to use as a nightgown. She'd snatched it out of his hand and slammed the door in his face. He'd gone back to the ballroom and boxed the sandbag dummy until his knuckles were red and he was exhausted, then he'd fenced his reflection until dawn. And still he hadn't been able to sleep.

Another gulp of coffee fortified him and he met his servants' eyes. "You will, of course, treat her with the respect due a guest in my home. Her valise will arrive this morning and you will leave it outside her door. Do not enter her room unless she has vacated it. Whatever she wants, give it to her. If it is not within your power to grant her wishes, communicate them to me, and I shall take care of them."

"Will you not, ah, have occasion to speak with her, milord?"

"Infrequently. I have my own business to tend, and she has hers. I do not wish you to interfere with her in any way. Simply keep her safe and well tended within the confines of this house."

Giles scratched his balding head. "Then you and this... Miss Lovejoy, are keeping separate lives? We will not wait dinner for you, nor expect you to rise at this hour every day, sir?"

Rise? Hell, he hadn't been to bed. "For the time being, arrange the household schedule to accommodate Miss Lovejoy."

"Yes, milord." Giles nodded. "We shall do as you ask."

Geoff waited until they'd left the office, then stood and ran his fingers through his hair and along the stubble on his jaw. What next? Bed? Or a bath and a shave? He cursed softly, recalling his promise to meet with the authorities this morning to give a report of last night's break-in on Curzon Street and then go through his papers to see what he was missing. He'd need to clean up before he left the house. He trudged up the stairs and shut himself in his room. One glance in the mirror made him wince. He looked like hell.

After shaving and changing into fresh clothes, he found himself unable to resist the siren's call and opened his door and went to the next.

When his houseguest didn't answer his soft knock, he opened her door a crack. Had she been angry enough to leave while he'd been busy in the ballroom?

No. She lay beneath the red coverlet, her blond hair loose and scattered across her pillow, one hand peeking from beneath his shirt cuff, the fingers curled toward her palm and resting beside her face. Violet smudges beneath her eyes gave testimony to her sleeplessness. Her lips were parted and a soft snore drifted to him and made him smile. So, little Miss Lovejoy was not perfect after all.

That knowledge did not comfort him. No, it only made him want her more, as he had from the moment months ago when he'd first seen her in her aunt's parlor. Two minutes later, she'd denounced him with words that still echoed in his mind. *Are you so bereft of friends that you could not find anyone but a stranger to stand up with you? You are a devil disguised as a man!*

Ah yes, she'd had him pegged even then. He closed the door softly and headed for the stables.

In disguise, Dianthe hurried toward Madame Marie's salon, thinking what an odd lot Lord Morgan's servants were. They'd left her breakfast on a tray outside her door this morning, along with her valise, which had been delivered from the house on Curzon Street. She'd only seen their shadows thus far. Nevertheless, it was pleasant to have her privacy.

Mrs. Mason had thoughtfully sent along her wig, as well as the dressing gown of his lordship's that she'd been using. She'd wrapped herself in that and hurried along the hall to the bathroom, where the invisible servants had left hot—now lukewarm—water for her to bathe. Clean and refreshed, she'd dressed, donned her dark wig and beauty patch, and set off for her meeting with the ladies.

She rounded the corner from Piccadilly and entered La Meilleure Robe, setting the shop bell to jingling. Before she could remove her bonnet and gloves, Madame Marie appeared from the back and dragged her into a dressing room. Only Charity MacGregor had arrived, and she stood near the door with an anxious look on her face.

"*Chérie!* Thank 'eavens you 'ave come," Madame Marie exclaimed.

A feeling of dread washed through Dianthe. What now?

Charity's astonished look gave way to concern. She took Dianthe's hand and led her toward a chair. "Sit down, Di. I have some strange news, and I fear it will affect you."

"Afton is not coming?" she guessed. "Or has Aunt Grace been delayed on her return?"

"Not that." Charity took the chair across from her, removed an envelope from her reticule and passed it to Dianthe. "Annica and Sarah have left town rather suddenly, and I am next. Once my husband got wind of what's been happening, he's made arrangements to ship me off, too."

Dianthe shook her head in confusion. "Is it me? Have they found out that you were helping me?"

"No! Heavens, not that. 'Tis a case we worked on four years ago. The local conspirators were caught, but the organizer of the plot escaped due to his residency in a different country. Now, it seems, he is up to his old villainy, and our husbands are insisting we be put out of harm's way. Annica and Sarah have been sent to Auberville's hunting lodge in the Highlands. Andrew is arranging for my departure even now."

"Oh! Of course you must go," Dianthe agreed. Fear, almost stronger than last night, constricted her breathing. She'd be alone. Truly alone, with no one to help her find her cousin's killer and no one to rescue her if she were arrested or attacked as Nell had been. She tried to hide her panic.

"Come with us, Dianthe. Fetch your bag and we can be gone before nightfall. Please, come with us and let us keep you safe."

Dianthe blinked back threatening tears. "No. For your sake as much as mine. How could I hope to finish what I've begun if I were in Scotland?"

"Drat! We were afraid you'd say that. There is a coaching voucher in the envelope, and we beg you will use it to follow us. If not today, then soon."

Dianthe took a deep breath and put on an air of bravado. "I am in a position where all the demons of hell would not be able to get to me. I vow I could not be safer anywhere else on earth. And I was not even in London four years ago. There is nothing to connect me to that case. I am certain I will be quite safe."

"Consider coming, Dianthe," Charity entreated, and gave her a quick hug before hurrying out the door.

Dianthe looked down at the envelope in her hand. Perhaps she could turn the voucher in for cash. Her own meager supply was running out.

Sitting at the vanity staring at her reflection, Dianthe could scarcely believe her transformation. Not only did she look different, she felt different. The cosmetic box Madame Marie had given her earlier completed her disguise to perfection. With heightened color to tone her pale complexion and kohl to darken her lashes, she had become Lizette Deauville, the miniature portrait of Madame Marie's mother. She hoped the modiste would forgive her use of the name.

She knew from hearing Madame Marie's descriptions that courtesans dressed more provocatively than women of the ton, and she looked at herself in the cheval mirror to see if something could be done to her pistachio-green gown to remake it into something fitting for a courtesan to wear. A ruching of lace trimmed the low scoop of her neckline, and light fabric sleeves fell from the puffed off-the-shoulder straps.

She slipped out of the dress and retrieved a pair of embroidery scissors from the dresser. With a few snips, the lace ruching was gone, and so were the sleeves. When she pulled her gown on again, she smiled at her reflection. What an amazing difference bare arms could make. And the scandalous sweep of skin between her chin and neckline revealed far more than it hid. The lace trim had been more important to her modesty than she would have guessed. She dared not take a deep breath lest she reveal all.

Stuffing a five-pound note into her black beaded reticule, she added her light kerseymere shawl in multiple jewel-tone colors and a painted silk fan before leaving her room and heading for the front door.

A shadow disappeared down a hallway on the main floor, and she smiled to herself. She felt as if she were living entirely in a shadow world, being served by fairies and followed by ghosts. She was still debating whether to accept this odd behavior or force some sort of acknowledgment when she rounded the corner and crossed The Strand. She wouldn't need a coach to go the few blocks to the theater, but she thought she'd make more of an entrance arriving in one, so she summoned a large black conveyance. The driver slowed, took one look at her and passed her by, shouting something insulting about "her kind." She stiffened her spine and walked the distance.

She had just become a courtesan, complete with the insults. She smiled coquettishly at a few men milling near the theater entrance as she purchased her admission. She took a deep breath and bought the seats for an entire box. She prayed it would be worth the expense. People would look at her if for no other reason than that she was the *only* thing to see in her box. And she hoped it would proclaim her as a new entry to the demimonde. Certainly no proper lady would engage in such fast behavior.

Once settled in her box, Dianthe let her shawl slip from her shoulders and expose the daring cut of her gown. She reminded herself that she was not Dianthe any longer, but Lizette Deauville, and this was the only way she could think of to gain entry to the circles she sought. She opened her fan and moved it slowly, lazily, alternately revealing and shielding her cleavage, and took comfort from the fact that no one would recognize her.

A liveried footman who had, evidently, accompanied his employer to the theater delivered a glass of wine to her. She glanced around at the other boxes to see if she could find her benefactor. A tall, distinguished looking man dressed in elegant gray and red saluted her with his own glass and nodded. He was several boxes to her right, and she suspected he would call on her at intermission.

This was a good beginning, but she wanted to make the acquaintance of the demimonde, not the gentry. Where were the courtesans? Where were Flora Denton and her ilk?

The curtain went up and, under the cover of diverted attention, Dianthe studied the boxes around her and the seats below. There were a few faces she recognized and some she knew well. Thank heavens the Thayers were not there, or she'd likely give herself away. In the box opposite her, she spotted a merry group of men and women. This was interesting. The women definitely did not look entirely respectable. Generous use of cosmetics proclaimed their status. These, then, would be the women whose trust she would need to win. Unfortunately, they seemed determined to snub her.

Within twenty minutes, she felt the weight of eyes upon her. With as much elegance and composure as she could muster, she folded her fan and laid it across her lap before taking another sip of her wine. Looking casually to her left, she found a group of three vaguely familiar men watching her and whispering among themselves. She smiled at them and nodded before turning away.

There was a shuffling behind her and she turned to find the man in gray there, bowing sharply at the waist. He had not waited for the intermission.

"If I may be so bold, miss, have we met? I feel as if I should know you."

She suspected this would be the case with many men she would meet while in disguise. Men who could afford courtesans and mistresses were men with money. Men of the ton. The same men she had seen and met at soirees, balls, routs and crushes. She would know them, but they would not know her. She tilted her head to one side and offered her gloved hand. "Mademoiselle Lizette Deauville, *M'sieur.* I do not think we 'ave met, as I 'ave only recently arrived in England."

He bent over her hand and gave her a charming smile. "Then I count myself the most fortunate of men to have met you before the others. Perhaps that will give me the advantage over them."

"You flatter me, *M'sieur.* I do not think I shall draw so very much interest, no?"

"Most certainly yes. Do you see those scoundrels over there?" he said, gesturing in the direction of the three men she had noted earlier.

She nodded. *"Mais oui."*

"The Hunter brothers. Charles, Andrew and James. To a man, they look as if they have plans for you."

Good heavens! Sarah's brothers! That was why they looked familiar. Regaining her composure, Dianthe returned her attention to the handsome man in gray. "And you, *M'sieur?* What is your name?"

"Reginald Hunter, seventh earl of Lockwood," he said.

She coughed. How had she not recognized one of the ton's leading bachelors?

Misreading her reaction, he hastened to explain. "Yes, they are my brothers. But I am the eldest. And, I must say in all modesty, the best of the lot."

Had she, indeed, been a courtesan, she couldn't have asked for a better protector than Lord Lockwood. Or any of his brothers. All unmarried, they had the reputation of relentless rakes, but their names had never been connected with cruelty or stinginess.

Glancing back at Lord Lockwood, she smiled and tilted her head to one side. "*Enchantée,* Lord Lockwood."

"*Mais non! Je suis enchanté, Mademoiselle.*"

His French was flawless and she smiled in approval. Goodness! He hadn't flirted so outrageously when he'd danced with her at one of Sarah's balls. Men, she realized, had a different standard of behavior with their sister's friends than with women of the demimonde.

"What are you doing after the play, *Mademoiselle?*" he asked.

"I am going 'ome," she said. "Tonight was for the purpose of...'ow you say, making my feet green?"

"You, Mademoiselle Lizette Deauville, may say it any way you wish. The English, however, get their feet *wet* when they are green behind the *ears.*"

"*Là!*" Dianthe laughed merrily. "I am the novitiate."

Now Reginald laughed. "Pray not, Miss Deauville! A novice to the language, perhaps, but were you an actual novitiate, my heart would be broken."

She smiled with relief. He had believed her mixed metaphors. Now he would be utterly convinced of her recent arrival in England. "As you say, my lord. I am the amateur."

"I doubt you are an amateur," he contradicted with a knowing smile.

Aware of what he was thinking, she felt a blush rise to her cheeks, and tried to think of a way to counteract it. Surely a courtesan would not blush at so mild a comment? She lifted her fan and began waving it as if she were suddenly warm. Though their conversation had been whispered, out of courtesy to the actors, she could tell that she and Lord Reginald were drawing rather more attention than the stage. She feared if she invited him to sit, the conclusion would be that she and the handsome lord had reached an agreement, if not for the future, at least for the night. She glanced up at him again and tried to think how to dismiss him.

"I thank you for the wine, my lord, and pray that we shall meet again soon?"

"Are you certain I cannot take you to a late supper, or show you some of the more…provocative entertainments of London? Dampen your toes, at least?"

"Per'aps another time, no?"

He sighed in mock disappointment. "Perhaps another time, yes. And, should you wish to hone your English skills, I stand ready to assist you."

She offered her hand again and, with a bow and a kiss to her palm, Lord Lockwood was gone. She noted the other Hunter brothers elbowing each other in the ribs and exchanging banknotes. They had been betting on the outcome of the encounter! How amusing. Just to muddy the waters, she gave all three a little wave.

By the time intermission came, Dianthe was awash in curious stares and veiled attention. Though it was what she'd wanted, she began to feel uncomfortable. Hostility fairly coiled around her. From the women of the ton? From the other courtesans, who would regard her as competition? Or from the killer? Surely he would not recognize her.

She had meant to mingle with the demimonde during the intermission, but suddenly she hadn't the faintest idea how. Did courtesans have a separate retiring room than the ton?

She stood and pulled a few dark curls over her shoulder to cover a fraction of the vast expanse of her décolletage. With a deep breath, she grasped her reticule, drew the curtain of her box aside and looked about for a group of courtesans or some indication of where they might have gone. Would it be rude of her to intrude upon their company? Perhaps she could start a conversation by asking about Lord Reginald.

As she turned toward the mezzanine staircase, she found a sea of masculine faces staring up at her. To a man, they bowed and began coming up the stairs to join her. Panic began to set in. How would she ever manage such a horde? She stepped back but a strong hand clamped around her arm.

Warm breath brushed her ear as someone leaned close. "Are you utterly insane?"

Geoff fought his rising anger as he waited for Miss Lovejoy to turn toward him. It was a slow process. He watched the flush sweep up the curve of her cheek, saw the chill bumps rise on her arms, and felt the little shiver pass through her. When her eyes lifted to his, he could see her shock.

"You have two seconds to smile and nod, or I shall expose you at once," he said between gritted teeth.

It took her five seconds to process her precarious position. Her glance shifted to the waiting men below and then back to him. A soft smile lifted the corners of her delectable mouth and she nodded once, as if giving consent to something. At least she had some sense of what he was trying to accomplish.

"Very nice, Miss Lovejoy. Now take my arm and come down the stairs with me. We shall go outside and I shall hire a coach. Do you understand?"

"My fan. My shawl."

"I shall buy you new ones."

Once on the street, Lord Lockwood, waiting for his carriage to be brought around, turned and gave them a long look. After a moment, he smiled and nodded. "Geoff, Miss Deauville. I thought you only meant to make your feet green tonight."

She glanced up at "Geoff" before replying with a French accent. "*Là!* It is only Lord Geoffrey, my lord. 'E is a mere dampening of my toes."

Lockwood laughed and Geoff wondered if she was truly mad to taunt him thus. He'd always liked Lockwood—until this moment. He tightened his grip on Miss Lovejoy's arm and led her toward a hired coach with a nod in Lockwood's direction.

When the vehicle pulled away from the curb, she turned to him and took a deep breath. "What was that about, Lord Geoffrey?"

"That was about saving you from complete ruin."

"None of them even knew it was me."

"*Miss Deauville?* Where the hell did you come up with that?"

"How did *you* recognize me, Lord Geoffrey?"

He couldn't tell her he'd have recognized her smile from much farther away than across a crowded theater. Or that the real beauty mark just above her left breast would have given her away at close range, or that her laugh had become as familiar to him as his own. Instead he answered with another question. "Do you have any idea what those men thought you were?"

"A courtesan," she said.

My God! She *had* done it deliberately. Her reply gave rise to at least a dozen more questions, but the most burning one at the moment he voiced. "Can you even begin to know what men like Lockwood would expect from you?"

"I believe so, but—"

"Little fool! You couldn't possibly have the slightest notion of the depth of intimacy that would be demanded of you to even skirt the edges of the demimonde." Before he could think better of it, he pulled her into his arms to teach her that particular lesson. "Best you learn it now, before it is too late to turn back."

Her little gasp of surprise did nothing to call him to his senses. He pressed her against his chest until there was not an inch of her, from the soft swell of her breasts to the pounding of her heart, that wasn't burned into his memory. Her arms came up to push him away, but he was beyond recall. He loosened his hold enough to lift her chin, then took her mouth in a bruising kiss. She had to know. She had to be prepared for the insatiable appetite of men like Lockwood. Of men like him.

Her heat, her scent, her wildly beating heart filled his senses and urged him to deeper intimacies. He lost any sense of time. Somewhere between anger and the need to teach her a lesson, the kiss had turned into more. Her pounding on his chest had given way to her arms curling around his neck and her fingers twining through his hair. Her lips parted at his insistence and she welcomed his tongue with a faint moan.

He shouldn't. He was the worst sort of reprobate. Ah, but he couldn't stop. The pull was too strong, his hunger too great. His mouth still on hers, he moved his hand from her chin, down the curve of her throat to the slope of her breast, swallowing her little squeal of surprise. Her décolletage was so low that it took little effort to lift one perfect ivory orb free of its confines. He kissed his way downward, then captured the tight bud of her nipple between his teeth, giving it a gentle nip before taking it between his lips and rolling it with his tongue. My God! She tasted like summer strawberries—warm, sweet, ripened to perfection. He ached with a need so fierce it took him by surprise. It had been months since he'd had a woman, and his hunger rose to taunt him. A minute more and he'd throw all his lofty principles about teaching her a lesson aside.

She gasped. But it wasn't with the shock he expected. It was with passion. Her head fell back with a hungry moan and she slipped her fingers through his hair to cup his head and hold him against her. He'd have given his life to draw out that moment of madness, but the coach stopped with a lurch, recalling him to his senses at last.

As abruptly as he had begun the kiss—and with considerably more difficulty—he ended it. Leaving her to repair herself as best she could, he stepped down and paid the driver, then turned and lifted the would-be courtesan out.

Without a backward look or the least regret, he headed for the door as the coach pulled away, noting Miss Lovejoy's angry footfalls behind him. When he opened the door, she stormed past him, vilifying him on her way. As well she should. For his part, he did not regret a second of it.

Chapter Seven

Caught between passion and anger, Dianthe burned with humiliation. How could he have used her so? How utterly unconscionable. *"Libertine!"* she exclaimed. *"Devil!"*

"At the very least," Morgan agreed as he slammed the door with an echoing bang.

"Oh, the unmitigated gall to use me in such a manner! Who do you think I am?"

"That is precisely what I was trying to demonstrate. Had you been a demirep in truth, I'd have had you on your back with your legs in the air by the time we arrived here. One more trip around Covent Garden and I'd have been done with you."

From the corner of her eye, Dianthe caught a shadow scurrying down the servants' hall. She was past caring what the servants she'd never seen thought. She threw her reticule at Morgan's head.

He swatted it away and gave her a cynical smile. "Still want to masquerade as a courtesan now that you know a small measure of the consequences, Miss Lovejoy?"

"How dare you question me? You swore you would not

interfere with me in any way. You said you made it your business never to interfere. You said if I came here we would be leading separate lives."

"And so we are, Miss Lovejoy. I just thought you might like a little taste of what you were courting."

The memory of his tongue pushing past her lips in a most intimate manner, of his mouth on her breast, drawing forth a wild sweet yearning, nearly made her dizzy. How could she have forgotten herself so completely? Her uncertainty must have shown, because he stepped closer to her and lowered his voice.

"Not that you weren't quite delectable, my dear. I'd have paid dearly to have you whilst you were still fresh and before some other man had ruined you."

She gasped at the undisguised sexuality of that comment. "It was never my intention to…that was not what I planned—"

"And speaking of that, what in God's name *was* your plan?"

"To…to test the waters. To see if I could pass as a courtesan."

"The answer is a resounding *yes!*" He spread his arms wide. "But why the bloody hell would you want to?"

"That is not your business, Lord Geoffrey." She planted her feet firmly and placed her fists on her hips.

"I quite agree. I should have left you standing on the stairway of the Theatre Royal with a multitude of men ready to tear at you like a pack of dogs. It was just a mistaken notion that you would not want that. A mistake I shan't make again."

"I should hope not!" she said, lifting her chin in defiance.

"Indulge me, Miss Lovejoy. Why, precisely, would you want to pass as a courtesan?"

Dianthe clamped her jaw shut. Oh, how she did not want to tell him. He would just ridicule her. But if she didn't, he would continue to dog her footsteps and get in her way. And the truth was kinder than what he was thinking. Two days ago, she hadn't cared in the least what he might think of her, but today, for some reason unknown to her, she did.

"I am waiting, Miss Lovejoy. Astonish me with your brilliance."

"Very well. My plan is to enter the demimonde and befriend Nell Brookes's friends. They will tell me nothing unless they trust me, and to trust me, they must think I am one of them."

Lord Geoffrey seemed to consider this. "Not a bad plan, Miss Lovejoy, for one more experienced than you. But last I heard, virgins were not common in that circle. You *are* still a virgin, are you not?"

Dianthe could feel the heat of a blush from her toes clear up to her forehead. She sputtered for a moment, completely at a loss for words. Then she exclaimed, "Once again, Lord Morgan, you prove your lack of breeding!"

"Yes, I can see that you are." He nodded, completely ignoring her attempt to divert him. "How did you plan to avoid the interest of men? Or, more to the point, how did you plan to turn away all comers and still look the part?"

"I…I thought perhaps I could be coy. Let them think I was taking my time before making a choice."

He shook his head and grinned. "You really are naive, are you not? Were you a demimondaine, your income, your very *existence,* would depend upon your willingness to entertain men."

"Any man? But they would think I was a…a—"

"Courtesan?" he finished. "Was that not the point?"

"But would I not lose value with the number of men I entertained?"

He laughed. "To the contrary, Miss Lovejoy. In your profession, experience is a more valuable commodity than innocence. The more you learn about pleasing a man, the greater your value. Men who consort with Cyprians are not looking for a wife to bear his heir. They are looking for a woman who will do things a wife will not, and without the incumbent obligations. One night. Two. An exclusive arrangement for a period of time. It matters not. What matters is that she should have skills that would be unspeakable with your kind, and that she give pleasure without demurring. *Inexperience* is a novelty, soon gone, but experience is compelling…seductive."

Unspeakable skill? Pleasure without demurring? Dianthe swallowed her astonishment. "Could I not just put them off?"

"It would be remarked upon that you were not in the game. And it would take considerably more skill than you possess to play that game. The men waiting for you at the foot of the stairs tonight—what would you have done with them? How would you have come away unscathed?"

She shook her head. She had been in a panic when she had seen so many of them waiting for her. She had been the object of many men's attention before, but this was beyond anything she'd ever encountered. And she had seen the look in their eyes. They would not have been as easy to put off as Lord Lockwood. "Why?" she asked, voicing her confusion. "Why did so many of them want me?"

"Because as a demimondaine, you have a power over them that their sisters, mothers and wives could never wield. You have what they desperately want. What every man wants."

She held her breath as she asked, "What?"

"Freedom to be themselves. Release. Peace, if only for a moment. Pleasure beyond description. Gratification without guilt. Acceptance without judgment. Comfort in a cold world."

She shuddered and closed her eyes for a moment to regain her composure. "If this is all true, then is this not the woman you should marry?"

He laughed and shook his head. "Good God, Miss Lovejoy, how naive. A respectable man would never marry a courtesan. Nor would he traffic with a courtesan's family. *I* would never marry a courtesan."

Never marry a courtesan? "But if she can give all those things—"

"She cannot give the assurance that the child she bears is yours. She cannot attend a state dinner or a ball without numbering the men whose bed she has shared. And the fact that she suits you between the sheets does not mean she is suitable in all other areas. Intelligence, education, common goals, trust and loyalty are what a man needs in a wife. The other—the courtesan—he can purchase."

Of course. And that was why the two worlds existed side by side. One for pleasure. One for the future. And then the full impact of his words slammed into her. *Nor would they traffic with a courtesan's family. Her family.* He was too good for the Lovejoys? She tilted her chin upward and gave him her coldest glare.

"Thank you for the education, Lord Geoffrey. But I am set on my path. And I intend to hold you to your vow not to interfere with me. And as for you…well, I hope you get just what you deserve."

His expression thunderous, he threw his hands up in surrender and turned abruptly, heading for the front door. If this was victory, it was hollow.

* * *

In the cold light of day, Geoff was still furious with the stubborn little minx. She didn't have an ounce of common sense. Well, he would not take responsibility for her, and she would not back away from a dangerous course, so she could not complain that he had taken certain measures. What other choice had she left him?

He paced the length of the ballroom, keeping one eye on the door and the other on a disapproving Joseph Prescott. He wished to hell he could predict her reaction to his next plan. Either way, she would not make this difficult. He would see to that.

To his chagrin, he could not banish the memory of what had happened in the coach last night—of what he'd done to Miss Lovejoy. He'd completely lost his senses and it must never happen again. He needed distance between them, and perhaps the best way was to use a courtesan. Surely once he was sated, Miss Lovejoy would not hold such a fascination for him.

Prescott lowered his bushy dark brows in disapproval. "This is most improper. Furthermore, I have no experience in this sort of endeavor."

"You were relentless where I was concerned, sir. I expect you will do no less for her."

"Daily, my lord? Could we not schedule it weekly?"

Geoff stopped his pacing and studied the tall wiry man. Nothing of his form or grace betrayed his middle years. Built more like a dancer than a fighter, he was as fit as he'd been when he'd taught Geoff. "Is it money, Prescott? I'll pay more."

"It is the entire…unsuitability of the scheme. Not to mention the futility. Women are not gifted by nature with either the spirit or physical endowments."

Geoff smiled, thinking of Miss Lovejoy's spirit. There was nothing lacking there. As for the physical endowments, she was blessed with more than her fair share, but perhaps not in the sense that Prescott had meant.

"She needs to learn as quickly as possible, Prescott. Her life may depend upon it."

At the sound of her footsteps on the stairs, he crossed to the center of the room, praying she'd at least be civil. In his experience, Miss Lovejoy could be quite a shrew. If so, Prescott was likely to say there was not enough money in England to take on the task.

She had tied her hair back in a ribbon this morning and was wearing a frock of a light fabric embroidered with flowers in a cluster pattern. Stripped of her disguise, she looked younger than she had last night, and years more innocent. He wondered if that would help his argument with Prescott.

"You summoned me?" she said, the accusation that he'd been arrogant in her tone once again. "And can you not do something about your staff? They slip notes under my door and leave trays with no more than a timid knock. Have you told them I eat servants for breakfast?"

Ignoring her complaint, he gestured Prescott to come forward. "I'd like you to meet Mr. Joseph Prescott, Miss Deauville. He is undoubtedly the best fencing master in England."

She turned to regard Prescott, who was running his finger along the edge of the cutlass blade. He looked up and his gaze swept Miss Lovejoy from head to toe. To Geoff's dismay, he noted a flicker of admiration in the man's gray eyes. She bobbed a quick curtsy and turned back to him, clearly waiting for an explanation.

"I have hired him to instruct you," he said.

She blinked. Had he actually managed to surprise her?

"He is not particularly pleased with the task, so I must ask you to cooperate as much as it is in your nature to do so," he continued.

"Might I ask why, Lord Morgan?"

"I have told you that I will not be your protector, true? I will not rescue you, nor will I interfere with your business. And, since you insist upon putting yourself at risk, you had best learn how to defend yourself."

She laughed and her china-blue eyes sparkled merrily. "Do you fear someone will challenge me to a duel?"

"Not as much as I fear you will place yourself in some foolish position that will require you to defend yourself. You'd best know how, Miss Deauville, since I will not be there next time."

"You are serious? You think I will engage in a sword fight?"

"The principles will be excellent training and are the same for most defensive arts. What you must learn, and quickly, is concentration, composure when faced with danger, feint and thrust, advance and retreat, forming a strategy quickly and following through. Instinctive reactions."

"You think me capable of such things?" She glanced again at Mr. Prescott, an uncertain look on her face.

"Do not doubt his abilities, Miss Deauville," Geoffrey told her. "He taught me, and he will teach you. Additionally, I shall hire a boxing master to instruct you in the pugilistic arts."

"Boxing?" She laughed outright. "Should someone of your stature attempt to box me, do you really think I could prevail?"

"You needn't *win,* Miss Deauville. Often just living another day is prevailing. You are capable of learning enough to put your opponent off his guard. Or of putting him at a disadvantage with an elbow or knee."

Prescott circled Miss Lovejoy, his gaze sweeping her in appraisal, as if analyzing her strengths and weaknesses. "Miss Deauville will require suitable clothing unless you wish her to practice in her pantalettes—something fitting closer to her body, and without frills. I will require her to have a keen sense of the blade and be free enough to wield it."

Geoff tightened his jaw at the thought of her in a chemise and pantalettes. Could that be a prick of jealousy that had his hackles up? Prescott was entering into this with rather more enthusiasm than a few minutes ago. Judging by the look on the fencing master's face, Geoff should have her fitted for a pair of trousers and a shirt.

Miss Lovejoy stepped forward. "Pardon me, my lord, if I seem confused. Do I have no say in this at all?"

"None, unless you are courting my interference. As you will not listen to good sense, you will need to prepare to defend yourself, since I do not intend to be in the vicinity."

"Ah." She smiled. "A salve to your conscience."

"I have no conscience," he reminded her.

"Quite right. Very well, then," she replied cheerily, "if it will keep you at a distance, I shall be glad to comply with your wishes."

"Capital. I shall bring you a pair of my trousers and a shirt. You may take them to your modiste for a fitting this afternoon. I collect that recutting would be faster than starting from scratch. Have her send the bill to me."

"How generous of you, my lord. And when she asks why Lord Geoffrey Morgan is paying my bills, what would you like me to say?"

Damn. He hadn't thought of that. He could simply give her the money, or…. He glanced at a clock on the mantel

at the far end of the room. "Fetch your wrap, Miss Deauville. I shall take you to a modiste I know."

By the time Dianthe had donned her dark wig and hurried downstairs to the foyer, Mr. Prescott had departed and
Lord Geoffrey was waiting. Pacing, actually. She could not
imagine what he was thinking. Hiring her a fencing master so he would not have to defend her? She hadn't realized she was so loathsome to him.

He rushed her out the front door, handed her into his private coach and climbed in after her. Instead of sitting beside her as he'd done last night, he sat across from her and
watched her with cool intensity.

She cleared her throat. "I was not aware that men were
familiar with modistes, Lord Geoffrey."

"I've known a few," he said.

"Through your women folk?"

"I have no women folk."

"Then—"

He leaned forward, resting his forearms on his thighs.
"If you must know, Miss Lovejoy, I know them from my
mistresses. You will learn, once you enter the demimonde,
that Cyprians prefer to have their patrons pay for their bau-
bles and frippery. I confess I've made more than one trip
to a modiste for a new gown or a special luxury."

Dianthe glanced out the window, unable to meet his
gaze for fear he would see her discomfort. She had suspected he'd had mistresses—perhaps many—but she
hadn't been prepared for the sudden annoyance his admission caused her. A flash of memory of last night in this very
coach kindled an unaccustomed pain when she thought of
him doing such things with other women.

"Have I discomfited you?" he asked.

"I suspect you have done it on purpose. Several days ago I vowed to give you no trouble, Lord Geoffrey. Alas, I fear you have tested me rather more than I anticipated, and I have veered from that course. But now I know your game, and you shall not provoke me so easily."

He sat back again and folded his arms over his chest. Though he said nothing, she knew she'd surprised him. He made no further comment until they arrived at an expensive looking shop. There was no sign above the door, just a needle and thread painted in gold on the window to the street.

The moment they entered, a lovely woman with auburn curls hurried from the back room. When she saw who it was, she clasped her hands together and grinned widely.

"*Là!* Lord Morgan, 'ow nice to see you. I cannot remember 'ow long it 'as been. A year? Two?"

"Two," he admitted. He glanced down at Dianthe and turned back to the modiste. "This is Miss Lizette Deauville. I'd like you to fit her for trousers and a shirt. She is going to take fencing lessons. We shall need them by tomorrow morning. Lizette, this is Madame Genevieve LaFehr. She is the premiere modiste to the demimonde."

Madame LaFehr gave a throaty laugh as she led them toward a dressing room. "It is a specialty, Miss Deauville. As you know, there are sometimes unique requests, eh? Per'aps a game or two to play? A fantasy to indulge? Lord Morgan, though, 'as not requested anything so exotic in the past. I collect 'e 'as found a new passion and a new game, eh?"

Dianthe turned to Lord Geoffrey in time to note a slight twitch at the corner of his eye. If she could keep her own embarrassment at bay, this could be amusing. "Yes, Madame LaFehr. Something close fitting and without frills."

"But feminine, yes? Lord Morgan would not want you to 'ide your…assets." Madame LaFehr turned to him and asked, "Do you wish to stay as usual, my lord, or will you wait in the parlor?"

"Surprise me, *Madame*. I'll wait in the parlor." He left them and went down another hallway.

Madame LaFehr led Dianthe into a square room with a small dais and a separate dressing closet. "Strip down, pe-tite Lizette," she instructed, "and I shall take the measures."

Dianthe went into the little closet and did as she was told. When she was finished, she stepped onto the dais in her pantalettes and chemise. Madame LaFehr began knot-ting strings for the measurements as she kept up a steady stream of chatter.

"So you are Morgan's new obsession, eh? I knew 'e was due. Per'aps overdue. I am a little surprised, no? You are so fresh, *chère*, not 'is usual sort at all."

"No?" she asked. "What is his usual sort?"

"More experienced, of course. You look to be new at this trade. You are so fortunate to 'ave found Morgan so soon. 'E is a most generous man, no? Oh, and the things 'e can do! *Là!* Are the others jealous, *chère?*"

"Others? What others?"

"The women who aspired to be next, *chère*. 'Is former paramours? They all call 'im the Sheikh."

The Sheikh? What could he have done to earn that title? Dianthe wondered as the modiste brought bolts of cloth from another room. Heavens! Had he kept a harem?

"Now, *chère,* what is the game?"

"Game?"

"For which 'e orders the clothes. Fencing, eh? Will there be real swords, or just the…figurative sword?"

Dianthe realized what the woman meant and couldn't

stop her blush. "Real, *Madame.* I am actually to take fencing lessons."

Madame LaFehr raised an eyebrow. "Yes? From the *on dit,* I would not 'ave thought Morgan would like it… rough." She pulled several skins from the pile she had amassed. "This one for the trousers, eh? We would not want you to suffer the cuts."

Dianthe felt the texture. It was a very fine suede that felt like chamois. She tried to imagine what it would feel like next to her skin. There were skins in black, tan and a deep rich brown. She stroked the brown wistfully, knowing it was far too expensive for her.

"The brown." Madame LaFehr nodded. "Usually not a good choice with the black 'air, but your coloring requires it. And now, for the shirt," she said, pulling several rolls of fabric from the pile.

"Oh, *Madame*, I really cannot afford—"

"*Mais non, chère!* Morgan will pay. 'E always pays when 'e brings 'is women."

So this was a pattern with Lord Morgan? The odd annoyance was back. Dianthe glanced at the fabrics again, wondering which ones were the most expensive. She touched a rich ivory fabric that felt like cool liquid, and when she lifted it between her fingers, it slipped over her hand like a second skin. Such a fabric would be very expensive, indeed, and since Morgan was paying… "This one, *Madame*," she said.

"*Voilà!* Perfection!"

"Will you obtain approvals from Lord Morgan now?" she asked, relishing the prospect of his chagrin when he found she was squandering his money.

"Ah, Lizette. 'E will not care. I 'ave seen 'im insist upon finer fabrics and patterns, never poorer. And there is no time, eh? 'E said these must be delivered no later than to-morrow morning. I will 'ave four girls sewing all night."

Dianthe shrugged. She hoped she could be present when he opened the bill.

"Shall we begin with the Four Governors?" Mr. Prescott asked the next afternoon as his gaze swept Dianthe's form. She felt nearly naked. The leather breeches hugged her hips and legs while the shirt draped her form, laying like water on her skin, the ruffle on the sleeves falling over her hands. She'd never been so revealed in front of a man before. Mr. Prescott, though, seemed not to notice. He lifted a rapier from the rack and cut a pattern through the air, then handed it to her, hilt first.

She took the sword and gripped the hilt as he demonstrated. "The Four Governors?"

"Perception, distance, timing and technique. The essential elements of swordsmanship, Miss Deauville. You must master them all to prevail."

"Perception, distance, timing and technique," she repeated. That did not sound beyond her.

"Stand beside me," Mr. Prescott instructed. "Imitate my moves while I walk you through a basic exercise. Watch your form in the mirrors and concentrate."

His tone, deadly earnest, led her to believe that this might be a serious endeavor. Mr. Prescott moved with the grace of a dancer, showing her a series of moves including lunges, parries and passes.

"There is much more, Miss Deauville," he said after an hour or two. "And we shall get to that. For now, practice what I've taught you. I shall be back tomorrow, in the morning, I think, whilst you are still fresh."

Dianthe rolled her neck to relieve the tension that had

built up with her concentration. "Do you really think any of this will help me, Mr. Prescott? After all, I haven't the advantage of strength, size or stamina."

"I thought not, Miss Deauville, but now I think I was wrong. You have a natural grace that will compensate for much. You can master all the important elements, except, perhaps, distance. Your sword arm is not as long as most men's, but you can offset that with speed. You are quite agile and there are defensive moves that will leave your enemy confounded."

"Then you think I should continue with the lessons?"

"Most certainly. You will be effective in the riposte and the traverse. Your opponent will not expect that from you." He frowned and then laughed. "He will not expect any resistance from you. Listen well, Miss Deauville, because this may be the best advice I give you—*do not allow your enemy to know your skill.* Surprise will be your greatest asset, and if you follow surprise with finesse, you'll have a fair chance at victory."

She laid a finger against her lips to indicate that she would keep her silence.

He smiled and nodded. "I think I shall teach you the Mysterious Circle first. It is the quickest method to develop your skills. And then we shall learn *al la macchia,* the rough-and-tumble fighting you would encounter if trying to defend yourself against attack."

Al la macchia? Dianthe nodded in understanding. She was not likely to be formally challenged to a duel, but an attack could come from anywhere. She shivered as she remembered that horrible voice in the library on Curzon Street. Yes, she would learn, and as quickly as possible.

Mr. Prescott bowed from the waist again and departed, leaving her in the ballroom. In the mirrors she saw a quick skittering movement behind her and knew it would be either Giles or Hanson. She'd yet to meet them, and she'd begun to think of them as cockroaches, always disappearing when she turned a corner or lit a lamp. She'd begun to make a game of trying to surprise them.

Well, there was nothing to do until supper. She straightened her spine, lifted her chin and saluted herself in the mirror as Mr. Prescott had taught her to do. She might as well perfect her moves. God knew it was better than thinking of Geoffrey Morgan's mouth. Or the wild yearning he had created in her.

Chapter Eight

The morning light in Lord Geoffrey's office spilled onto Dianthe's lap as she settled into a comfortable chair. A soft summer breeze filtered through the open French doors. She threaded a needle and lifted the pink satin gown awaiting her attention. A little snipping and cutting, and it would be fit for an evening gown. She had thought of going to Madame LaFehr's and having a new gown made, but she suspected the modiste would be much too expensive for her means. All she had left was five pounds and she imagined a gown by Madame LaFehr would cost twice that.

Judging by the reaction she'd garnered at the theater, she only needed to lower her necklines and leave her arms bare. There was more to seductive dressing than that, she knew, but nothing she could accomplish with her limited resources. And she could ill afford to sit around any longer. She had to take action tonight—before the killer found her.

She sighed and glanced up at the portrait above the fireplace. An enigmatic beauty with long dark hair falling to the middle of her back stood beneath a tree, a straw bonnet in one hand. Her gown was a maidenly pink trimmed in white, and a wistful smile curved her full lips. By the manner of the subject's dress, the portrait had been painted no more than ten years previous, perhaps seven, judging by the style of her bonnet. Dianthe knew it couldn't be the fabled Constance Bennington. She'd seen a miniature of that woman in Lady Annica's sitting room.

She could not tear her eyes from that portrait. There was something very familiar in the vulnerable face and the grace of those hands. A cautious curiosity shone from the woman's dark eyes and made Dianthe smile. She fancied she would have liked this woman.

"Miss Lovejoy? Did you need something?"

She turned at the sound of Lord Morgan's voice. He carried a hat and gloves, and she suspected he was on his way to an appointment. She shrugged and held up her pink gown. "I just came to find some good light to repair my gown, my lord."

"Ah, well…" He looked awkward. "I shall have Giles bring additional lamps to your room."

"Am I not allowed in here?" she asked.

He hesitated, then shrugged. "You have access to anywhere in the house but my apartments. You were quite right. The morning light is best in here. Pray continue." He took several steps toward the open French doors to the back terrace.

"Lord Geoffrey?" She waited for him to halt before she continued. "Who is the girl in the portrait?"

"My sister, Charlotte," he said without turning.

That was it! That was why she'd looked familiar. She had the same dark eyes, the same hint of sweetness beneath the surface. The same graceful, expressive hands. The same vulnerability? But Lord Geoffrey was not vulnerable, was he? And hadn't he said he had no women folk?

She turned back to him with the question on her lips, only to find that he had slipped out the open doors. At almost the same instant, she caught a scurrying in the hallway just outside the door. She raised an eyebrow as misplaced frustration snapped a thread of restraint. She would deal with Giles and Hanson. But Mr. Prescott would be here soon for her lesson. She needed to change. Giles and Hanson would wait.

Exhausted from her lesson, Dianthe rubbed her right shoulder and rolled her head to ease the tension in her neck. She never would have guessed that fencing could be so strenuous. Of course, the three hours of practice after her lesson hadn't helped. Her calves and thighs hurt, her arms and shoulders ached and even her buttocks were sore.

When she left the ballroom, she found her luncheon waiting outside the door—another sneak attack by Giles or Hanson. She picked up the tray and headed for the kitchen with a deep sigh.

When she heard soft voices in the pantry, she silently placed it on the worktable and took a chair. She'd sit there as long as it took them to come out. In the end, she did not have long to wait. They obviously hadn't heard her coming.

Both appeared to be in their middle years. The taller one was lean, with a balding head and gray hair, while his companion was shorter, plump and had dark hair shot through with silver. And both stopped dead in their tracks to stare at her in horror. They obviously were not accustomed to being encountered in their kitchen.

"Good afternoon," she said as pleasantly as she could manage. She followed with a smile, wondering if even that would put them at ease. "I wasn't aware that you'd brought my lunch and I lost track of time while I practiced. Could I trouble you to warm my soup, please?"

"I, ah…" The shorter man hurried forward and lifted the bowl of fish chowder off her tray so fast that it almost spilled over the polished surface of the table. "S-sorry, miss."

"I do not believe we have met," she said. She stood and bobbed the slightest of curtsies in polite respect. "My name is Dianthe Lovejoy, late of Bloomsbury Square."

The taller man, who, by his more circumspect manner, seemed to be in charge, bowed deeply, as if determined to outdo her in politeness. "I am Giles, Lord Morgan's valet, Miss Lovejoy. And this—" he waved at the plump man "—is Hanson, the cook."

"How very nice to meet you both." She settled herself at the table again.

"Would you not be more comfortable in your room, miss?" Giles asked.

"I do not wish to put you to the trouble of bringing the tray up." She watched their faces with veiled amusement. They really had no idea what to do with her. She couldn't resist teasing them. "Please spare me a few moments. I've been lonely since coming here, and since we are all here now, we should become acquainted. I must admit that I was beginning to think it was fairies that brought my meals and changed the linens."

A deep flush stained Giles's face and she instantly regretted teasing the man. "Has Lord Morgan told you that I am a fire-breathing dragon?"

"No, miss," Hanson answered over his shoulder as he ladled fresh soup from the pot on the stove. "He said we were to keep an eye on you but leave you alone."

Yes, that sounded like Lord Geoffrey—always walking a fine line between helping and hindering. He might call it "not interfering," but she called it infuriating. She buried her irritation and smiled reassuringly again. "I would not take conversation amiss, Mr. Hanson. Indeed, I would find it quite reassuring."

Giles stepped forward and bowed again, slightly. "Very well, Miss Lovejoy. What did you wish to talk about?"

She shrugged and picked up a spoon as Hanson put the bowl of hot soup in front of her. "Well, we could start with my presence here. What has Lord Morgan told you about that?"

"That he owes your cousin a debt of honor, miss, and that he has agreed to keep you safe until your relative returns to town."

"And that you're in a bit of a pickle," Hanson contributed. "I think he is a little afraid for—"

"That's enough, Hanson," Giles said with a stern look. "No sense in frightening the young woman, is there?"

Hanson nodded before turning back to Dianthe. "Cup of tea, miss?"

"Yes, thank you." She debated the wisdom of taking the two men into her confidence. If Morgan had wanted them to know the details of her "pickle" he'd have told them. Instead, she decided to tell them why Morgan felt he needed to…well, not protect her, but shelter her.

"You've heard of the incident?" she asked after she'd related the story.

"Of course, miss, though not quite the same as you describe it," Giles explained.

Irritation reawakened in her. Of course Morgan would tell his version—that Mr. Lucas's shot had been deliberate. Mr. Lucas would never have done anything dishonorable. But she hadn't come to argue. She only wanted to set these men at ease around her. She took several spoonfuls of soup while she quieted her nerves.

Giles brought her a cup of tea. "I can see, then, why his lordship is intent on paying his debt. He always pays his debts."

"Mmm," she said. Some little devil urged her to add, "And collects them, as well."

"Yes, miss. Of course."

"Does he ever show compassion?" she asked.

"As much as he was shown by those his father owed."

Dianthe paused with the spoon halfway to her mouth. Had she heard correctly? "His father gambled?" she asked.

"He…" Giles flushed guiltily, as if he'd said too much. "It was a long time ago, miss," he finished.

She nodded, though she resolved to find out more about this little twist on Morgan's character. And while she was on the subject, she asked, "The portrait in the office? Lord Geoffrey told me it was of his sister, Charlotte. She is beautiful, is she not?"

"She was a delight, miss. So sweet and accommodating. Never a cross word from her."

"Ah." Dianthe smiled. "She's married and gone now?"

Hanson sighed heavily. "Dead, miss. An accident barely a year after she married. She fell down a flight of stairs."

Dianthe blanched. Dead. Then Lord Geoffrey had been telling the truth. He was more alone in the world than she. "How awful for the family," she said.

"Yes, miss. Fit to be tied, Lord Morgan was! We thought he'd—"

Giles cleared his throat and Hanson fell silent. She began to feel guilty for her veiled interrogation. She shook off the gloom and smiled again, attempting once more to put them at ease.

"Sudden deaths are so difficult," she said with a sigh, thinking of her mother, her father and, most recently, her aunt Henrietta. "I've had my share, as well, but life is relentless. It goes on, will we, nill we. And time sees us through the worst." She finished eating and stood. "Well, thank you for the soup. It was delicious. In future, please do not trouble about me. When I am hungry, I shall come find something to eat."

As she walked out the kitchen door she caught a snip of whispered conversation. "…seems nice enough…"

She grinned. It would, no doubt, rankle Lord Geoffrey to think she had made friends with his servants.

A footman handed Dianthe down from the hired coach but the uniformed doorman at the entry to Thackery's stopped her before she could enter. She took a deep breath and assumed the personality of Lizette Deauville, audacious flirt and courtesan. She kept a firm grip on her fear and prepared for her bluff.

"*Oui?*" she asked, and glanced haughtily down at the man's hand on her bare arm.

"Where is your escort, miss?"

"I am to meet 'im 'ere," she said with a little lift of her chin. In truth, she had chosen Thackery's because she had heard her aunt say it was the best of the hells. She took another step toward the inner sanctum as if she had every right to be there.

"Who is your…escort?" the man asked, with a tone that said he clearly had her identified as a demimondaine.

There was only one name she could think of that would give her entry—as much as she disliked to use it. "Lord Geoffrey Morgan," she said.

"Lord Morgan is not here, miss."

Thank heavens! "'E shall be along presently."

The youthful doorman studied her intently, indecision written on his face.

Her knees weakened. If he wouldn't admit her, her plan would fail. "Do you keep me waiting on the steps, *M'sieur?*" She lifted her chin in a last attempt to bluff her way in.

"Well, I…"

"'Ave I not the correct dressing?" she asked, noting that he was having a difficult time keeping his gaze above her neckline.

"Well, I suppose you could wait inside."

"Merci." She smiled. "I believe *mes amis* are waiting."

He held the door for her and she entered as if she'd been there a hundred times before. Heart hammering erratically, she knew the hardest part lay ahead.

Trying not to be obvious, she hurried past a cloakroom and found herself in what could only be the main salon. Brilliant crystal chandeliers lit the center of the room, leaving intimate dark corners around the edges. Two corridors opened off each end of the salon, and she concluded they must lead to private gaming areas. She lifted a wineglass from a footman's tray and smiled at him. With a glass of wine in her hand she'd look as if she belonged.

"Upstairs, miss," he told her.

"Pardonnez-moi?"

"Your party is upstairs in the mezzanine salon."

Her party? Ah, he meant her "kind." She nodded and strolled casually toward the curved staircase leading to the mezzanine, still dazzled by the decor.

She'd never seen such opulence. Deep, plush wine-colored carpeting cushioned her footsteps, rich embossed wall coverings absorbed harsh sounds, and gleaming, deeply carved mahogany paneling, moldings and wainscoting trimmed the room. A string quartet played quietly in one corner, while men bent over tables, intent on cards or dice. Very few women were present, and most of them were hanging on the arms of wealthy looking men. Dianthe wondered if the gathering in the mezzanine salon would match this one.

Here and there she recognized a familiar face—one of the Hunter brothers, a magistrate, a few peers, Dr. Worley, and some anxious looking individuals she assumed were losers at one game or another. Across the room at a faro table, Laura Talbot's brother—the very man who had wagered with Lord Morgan for his sister and lost—placed another bet. Dianthe turned her back to him and began a slow ascent to the mezzanine, using the vantage of height to memorize the floor plan. She wanted to look completely comfortable and at ease with her surroundings.

At the top of the stairs, a wide marble promenade edged the walls, affording views of the happenings below. Rooms opened off the promenade, providing further venues for risking one's fortune. What appeared to be the largest of the rooms was at the head of the staircase. Glass doors stood open in invitation, and the sounds of muted laughter and conversation floated outward.

Gripping her reticule tight to still her trembling, Dianthe strolled into the salon with as much confidence as she could muster and glanced around. Yes, there were women here—pretty women who were daringly dressed. The space was dimly lit compared to the rooms below, but the mood was lighter, as if gambling was only a part of the festivities. As she watched, a man linked arms with a ripe redhead and walked toward the door, whispering something in her ear that made her laugh. Dianthe had the distinct impression they were not in search of another gambling table. Heat flooded her cheeks and she shivered uneasily.

One wall was paneled with mirrors that reflected the sparkle of crystal prisms from candlelit chandeliers. The opposite wall contained a cushioned banquette for seating, and murals in muted colors. Dianthe could not make out the subject, but there were trees and streams. A landscape, she assumed.

Even to her inexperienced eye, and to her great discomfort, the atmosphere in the salon seemed heavily sexual. Men appeared to be assessing the women around them, and the women were vying for attention. Dianthe moved to the edge of the room, wanting only to find an opportunity to speak with the women. She saw Flora Denton in conversation with a handsome elderly man, laughing at some jest and plying her fan in a flirtatious manner.

Dianthe sighed with regret. She could have used a fan to cover a portion of her bared chest. Her scissors had snipped a little lower than she'd intended, and now no more than a quarter of an inch saved her modesty.

Flora excused herself from the elderly gentleman and moved toward a sideboard to leave her wineglass. Seeing her opportunity, Dianthe hurried toward her.

Flora glanced up at her approach. She gave Dianthe an impersonal smile and moved to the side, allowing access to the sideboard. Nothing in her manner suggested that she recognized her from Nell's funeral.

"Miss Denton, is it not?" Dianthe asked.

Flora smiled politely. "Have we met?"

"Mais non," Dianthe answered. "I know you by reputation only."

"Oh?" Flora commented noncommittally. "And you are?"

"Mademoiselle Lizette Deauville. I am newly come to town."

"Newly arrived," Flora corrected. She glanced around. "Are you here alone?"

"*Oui.* For the moment."

Flora seemed surprised by this answer. "How did you gain entrance?"

She laughed. "I told the falsehood."

After an uncertain moment, Flora laughed with her. "You are bound to make a splash, Miss Deauville. I am certain you will have invitations aplenty by the time you leave tonight."

Dianthe indicated a dim corner with a sweep of her hand, inviting conversation. When they were certain they would not be overheard, Flora arched an eyebrow in a query.

"This—it is all new to me, Miss Denton. I 'oped you to tell something of the London customs to me. That I need the escort for admission to the gambling 'ell, I did not know."

Flora nodded. "There are a few public assemblies to which you may go alone. Thackery's, as well as many of the other better gambling clubs, are private, and admission is by subscription or invitation only."

"But 'ow does one gain entrée to this society?" she asked.

"One takes a patron. Or acquires a sponsor," Flora informed her. She gave Dianthe a searching look, as if suddenly suspicious. "For instance, the sponsorship or protection of an Abbess."

Dianthe had heard that term before. It referred to a female operator of a brothel. "*Là!* I do not wish to do the business this way, Miss Denton."

"If not, you must find a protector at once. Come, I will introduce you around." She took one of Dianthe's hands and started to draw her toward the gaming tables.

"*Mais non!* Can we not converse a little longer?" she begged. The last thing she wanted was a protector! Nor did she want a repeat of the disaster at the theater. She had already noted that she and Flora were drawing a few interested glances from some of the men.

Flora dropped her hand. "You know my name, Miss Deauville. Why is that?"

Dianthe would need an ally if she was to carry the masquerade off. She sighed and abandoned her French accent. "Nell Brookes."

Narrowing her eyes, Flora studied her face. "Did Nell introduce us? I do not recall that, Miss Deauville."

She shook her head. "Nell's funeral."

"Good heavens! I would never have known you! What are you doing here?"

"I am here at your suggestion, Flora. You said I would have to be one of you for Nell's friends to talk to me."

"I never thought…that is not what I meant, Miss Lovejoy. I meant that you do not have a prayer of learning anything from us."

Dianthe frowned. "I do not understand. Why do you not care who killed your friend? I should think you would want to find the villain even more than I."

"I *do* want the villain found," Flora said. Tears filled her eyes and she swiped at them angrily. "But there is nothing we can do. The authorities will not pursue the killer. Apart from searching Nell's rooms, they have done nothing. We have not been questioned, nor have we seen the authorities again."

"But that is why *we* must investigate, Miss Denton." Dianthe lowered her voice and glanced around. "Nell was not dead when I found her. With her last breath, she entreated me to find and stop her killer. She said he had killed before and would again. It could be you next time. Or me. Or any of the other women here tonight."

Flora paled. "Dear Lord," she murmured. "That must mean that she had learned something. But if the runners and police cannot find anything out, how shall we?"

"By not giving up. By caring about Nell and the next victim more than they do. That is why I am here. I want justice for Nell. And…" her voice caught with the memory "…I promised her I would stop him. But I need your help. Please say you will give it."

"Miss—"

"*Lizette,*" she whispered with a furtive glance around.

Miss Denton sighed and her shoulders sagged. "The greatest favor I can do you, Lizette, is to deny you."

"But you will not," she guessed. "Because you want justice for Nell, too."

"Yes. Yes, I do." She squeezed Dianthe's hand. "What do you want me to do?"

"I need introductions to the other…"

"Demireps? Yes, I can manage that, but do not expect them to tell you much. They will not like you, as you are their competition."

"If…if you could vouch for me, that would help my credibility."

"I shall say I met you while abroad last summer, and invited you to come visit me."

"Thank you." Dianthe felt the tension leave her shoulders. She'd taken a risk admitting to Miss Denton who she really was, but she still couldn't admit that Nell was her cousin.

"What would you like me to tell the men, who are already beginning to ask questions about you?"

Dianthe glanced across the room to see a small group

drinking brandy and watching her and Flora. Their study was openly carnal, and a prickle of fear unsettled her. "I do not know. What will satisfy them?"

Miss Denton shook off her gloom and laughed. "Why, that you are surveying the scene before making a choice. I shall say you are quite fastidious in your selections. They will beg introductions and you will have to talk to them and let them believe they have a chance, and that should send them into a frenzy of anticipation."

"I told the doorman that I was meeting Geoffrey Morgan here," Dianthe admitted. "It was the only way he would let me in."

"Lord! Why did it have to be Morgan? He is such a hard man. So unforgiving."

"He was the only one I knew to frequent this establishment. I gambled that he wouldn't be here."

"Lucky bet! But I wouldn't tempt fate again." She stood and pulled Dianthe to her feet. "Come, the evening is still young."

Chapter Nine

Geoff moved his whiskey glass aside to spread the reports on the small table in the room over the tavern. He scanned the pages, then went back to read them more carefully. Bad news came in abundance these days.

Harry Richardson went to the window, open to the humid summer night, cursed the noise in the street, pulled the panes closed and latched them, then paced in circles, obviously impatient.

Finally, Geoff pushed his chair back and stood. "It's as we thought, Harry. More disappearances."

"I'll take the reports to the Foreign Office," Harry said.

"We'd better keep them to ourselves for the moment. Until Barrington's successor has been named, we cannot be certain who to trust. I'll brief Auberville, Travis, McHugh and Lockwood in private."

"They're still involved in this?" Harry asked.

Geoff sighed and stretched the kinks from his back. "Involved *again*—since I told them el-Daibul was on the move. We've all had a brush with the devil, and we've always known he would come after us someday. To a man, we'd like to see him dead. God knows nothing short of that will stop him.

"In fact, I think el-Daibul may have something to do with Nell's death. She was killed either because she was getting close to the truth, or because she and I had been... intimate. I'd lay odds he sent one of his henchmen to do the dirty work. Furthermore, I believe he is behind the break-in on Curzon Street. That is my only known address. My papers had been gone through. He's sent his men to look for something. He wants to learn how close we are to uncovering his operation, how much we know and what evidence we've gathered."

"I suppose that makes sense," Richardson said. "But how does the break-in connect to Nell?"

Geoff gestured at the reports on the table. "Activity is increased in all the major ports—New York to Copenhagen. And this time the prime target is courtesans and kept women. The demimonde. El-Daibul must be thinking no one will miss these women, or bother to investigate. That's what tripped him up last time. Nell either learned something, stood in his way or was targeted because of our relationship."

"That's a leap, Geoff. There's got to be more. Accidents happen, robberies happen, people are murdered. There are any of a dozen wives who might have wanted Nell Brookes dead. Even Miss Lovejoy could have lost a beau to Nell. You said they looked enough alike to be sisters. One of her suitors may have thought he could spend a little money on Nell and purge the Lovejoy chit from his blood. And that may not have sat well with Miss Lovejoy. Apart from that, Nell could have had a host of enemies on her own. She wouldn't be the first demirep who tried to make a little extra money extorting a former lover, or who had taken a dangerous man to her bed."

Geoff grimaced. "You've never asked me what I was doing in Vauxhall Gardens that night."

Harry squinted in a frown as he asked, "So, what were you doing in Vauxhall Gardens that night?"

"I was following a lead from one of our operatives that a suspected agent of el-Daibul's was on the hunt. The whispers had it that he 'had a job to do.' I didn't know if that meant another kidnapping, or something else."

"And the only thing that happened in Vauxhall Gardens that night was a murder," Harry finished.

"I'd just gotten there. I must have missed him by seconds." Another failure to protect a charge? A heaviness settled over him and he removed a scrap of fabric from his pocket and held it out for Richardson to see. "I caught the edge of his cloak when he broke into the house on Curzon Street, and this is what I came away with." He turned the scrap over in his hand. Black worsted on one side and scarlet silk on the other.

Richardson raised one eyebrow in a query. "A bit flashy, wouldn't you say?"

"But useful," Geoff told him. He ran his finger over a stiffened section of the red lining. "It would disguise blood. If you wanted to murder someone in a public place and make an escape, a red cloak could be an advantage. I waited at the gate when Dr. Worley said the murderer would be covered in blood. Nothing. Unless it was disguised by something like this." He turned the fabric in his hand once again before replacing it in his pocket.

Richardson ran his long fingers through his hair. "Should we expect a break-in on Salisbury Street next?"

"I've left that house under the previous owner's name as a protection. No one but you and a small handful of trusted people know I have that residence. I think we'll be safe enough."

"We? Are Hanson and Giles still with you?"

"Always," Geoff said, hoping to end the subject before Richardson became too inquisitive. He had no desire to explain Miss Lovejoy's presence on Salisbury Street.

He kept seeing her in his mind as she'd been that morning in the library—sitting there mending a gown. He found it deeply disturbing that something so mundane could have awakened such a strong yearning in him. He'd never thought he was the sort to find domestic scenes so charming, nor to pine for someone to sit with, share the news of the day, laugh with or watch a toddler weaving his way across the room to him. But all that and more had come to him in a rush when he'd seen Dianthe Lovejoy mending her gown. Absurd. Utterly ridiculous. He would get rid of her the moment—the very second—he could.

Ah, but the weight and softness of her breast in his hand drew his mind back again…wanting, needing, something he could never have.

He swept his hat from the table, tossed down the remains of his whiskey and headed for the door. He needed to forget as he always forgot, at a gaming table or in another woman's arms. "I'll see you later, Richardson. I hear the hazard tables calling my name."

"Your party has arrived ahead of you, my lord," the footman said as Geoff handed him his hat.

"My party?" he asked, wondering if he'd forgotten an engagement.

"Upstairs, my lord."

He nodded, purchased some counters and continued into the main salon. The footman had confused him with someone else. He wasn't expected here tonight, nor had he made any arrangements to meet anyone. He was sure of it.

Most of the tables were full. It was a busy night at Thackery's. He nodded to several acquaintances and filled a brandy glass from a sideboard. As he strolled past the tables, there were no whispers about any high stakes games, nor were any of the usual pigeons looking particularly flush. It appeared, in fact, as if it would be a dull evening ahead.

He was contemplating going on to another club when an acquaintance stopped him.

"Congratulations on your latest mistress, Lord Geoffrey. She's a stunner, right enough."

"My…mistress?" he asked, the hair rising on the back of his neck.

"I was coming in right behind her and heard her tell the footman that you'd be along soon. I must say, I hadn't seen her before. She has every red-blooded man here under her spell. Did you import her? Or find her when she was just come to town?"

He forced a neutral smile and tried to keep from gritting his teeth. "Just," he said. With a polite nod, he headed for the stairs. He knew who the fraud was as surely as he knew his own name. He finished his brandy in a gulp and put the glass on a footman's tray. The liquor burned its way downward and seeped through his veins as he climbed the stairs. What a pity he did not have time for a few more before he confronted his "mistress."

When he passed through the glass doors of the mezzanine salon, he focused on a tight group around a faro table at the far end of the room. She had her back to him, and she was wearing the dark wig and the pink confection she'd been mending this morning. Good God! He'd thought she was sweetly domestic, when all the while she'd been fashioning a temptress's gown! And why the hell did he feel betrayed by that?

Flora Denton, who had been laughing at something, paled when she saw him coming. She touched Miss Lovejoy's arm and whispered in her ear. Miss Lovejoy's shoulders squared and she turned slowly to face him. Three or four young bucks who'd been courting her attention also turned to him. Only his former brother-in-law, Lewis Munro, held his ground.

Smiling grimly, Geoff stopped close enough to see her rapid pulse in the hollow of her throat. He recognized the fear in her eyes and knew she was wondering if he would expose her. He'd sworn he would after the incident at the Theatre Royal. He should. He wanted to. That would remove her from his life once and for all. And, had it been any other man than Lewis Munro leering at the cut of Miss Lovejoy's gown, he might do just that. It would rid him of the unsettling, conflicting emotions she awoke in him. Ah, but then how could he make her pay for reawakening those torturous ghosts?

"Good evening, my dear Lizette," he purred. "Sorry I'm late."

She blinked. "I—"

Munro groaned. "Say you haven't made arrangements with Miss Deauville already, Morgan. That wouldn't be fair. The rest of us haven't had a chance at her yet."

Geoff turned a cold eye on him. "Life is often unfair, Munro. Miss Deauville and I have reached an understanding. Have we not, my dear?"

His question pulled Miss Lovejoy from her trance. "*M-mais oui. C'est vrai.* We are…understood."

He took her arm with every appearance of civility. "Come, my dear. Shall we find some privacy? I believe it is time for a little *tête à tête*."

She looked as if she would protest, but his firm grip on her arm persuaded her differently. To the sound of theatrical moans on the part of her erstwhile swains, and a covetous glance from Munro, Geoff led her to a private corner and sat beside her on the banquette. He kept hold of her hand, suspecting she might bolt if he released her.

"Well, Miss Deauville, what do you have to say for yourself?"

"I did not know you would be here tonight."

"That would be the reason you told your lie. What I want to know is why you are here at all."

"To do what I planned to do. I am winning the confidence of the demimonde so that they will trust me enough to tell me their secrets. Specifically, who would wish to harm my...Nell Brookes." Dianthe tugged at her hand, trying to free it from his grasp.

"Tut-tut, my dear. People are watching. You wouldn't want it to appear that we've had a spat, would you? One of those eager young gentlemen over there would be all too happy to take you off my hands. Especially Munro. He'd relish the opportunity to break you in."

She stopped struggling and gave him a sober look. Thank heavens she was considering the consequences of her masquerade, Geoff thought. With a little luck, he might yet get her untangled from this charade. He lowered his voice. "Look around you, Lizette. What sort of place do you think this is? Why do you suppose these women are here? And what do you think would happen to your reputation and future prospects if these men knew who you really are?"

She glanced around and her eyes widened as she took in the murals behind them. What at first glance had appeared to be mere country landscapes now revealed satyrs chasing nude women among the trees and rocks. Some had caught their prey and were pictured in various poses of copulation. More were ravishing unwilling women, while their fellows carried still others off to unknown destinations. The subject was explicit and decidedly unpleasant and vulgar to any gently reared woman.

A maidenly blush suffused her cheeks and her gaze swept to the center of the room, where one of the courtesans sported a gown cut so low that the deep rose areolas of her breasts peeked above the fabric. The young buck talking to her ran his finger along her neckline and she giggled and licked her lips. In response, he fondled her openly while she trailed her fan from his chest to his crotch.

Miss Lovejoy bit her lower lip and turned back to Geoff. There was nowhere left for her to look but in his eyes. "Be certain you want to be a part of this, Lizette," he whispered, "because, if you do, a dozen men here would be happy to accommodate you. Including me. I usually avoid virgins like the plague, but I'd be willing to make an exception in your case."

She gave him a tremulous smile "I thought you avoided getting involved, my lord."

"Involved? I was willing to give you shelter. Correct me if I am wrong, but I do not think I agreed to allow you to use me and my name to further your scheme. You are the one who stepped over that line."

She frowned and thought about that for a moment. "I just assumed you would not care."

How could she drive him insane with so little effort? How had she found his weak spots so easily? His temper snapped and he unleashed it in a flood of sarcasm. "Why did you think I would not care? Did you consider me so lacking in pride or social consequence that I would leap at the chance to associate myself with the new whore in town? Or that my reputation is so sullied that it could not be damaged further by anything *you* could do?"

Her cheeks reddened and he knew she was about to lie. "That thought never occurred to me. I simply thought… well, I did not think of the consequences to you. The doorman stopped me, and to gain entry I had to tell him I was meeting someone. Your name was the first that came to mind. I did not think you would be here tonight. If I have offended you, I apologize."

He narrowed his eyes, not believing a single word. "In the future I will require previous notice if you want to use my name. I do not like being surprised with a mistress."

"Yes, my lord."

Was she being serious or facetious? With Miss Lovejoy, it was difficult to tell the difference. The upshot was that now his plan to take a mistress of his own choosing in order to dull the fine edge of desire Miss Lovejoy had honed in him was no longer possible. What was he to do with that pent-up energy now?

She sighed and shrugged, quite unaware of the turn his musings had taken. "How would you like me to undo this? We could say we had a falling out. Or that I did not…suit. Or that—"

"Not suit?" he asked softly. He leaned down and met her lips with his. She gasped at this public display and started to pull away, but he held her steady and warned her, "Coyness is not a part of the demimondaine's makeup, my dear. Hold still. We have yet to determine whether you 'suit' or not."

Her eyes darkened, whether in fear, anger or desire, he couldn't tell. But she held her ground when he deepened the kiss, and her eyelashes fluttered, then settled in perfect crescents against her flushed cheeks. He could feel the tension drain from her shoulders and he'd have sworn she had forgotten where they were.

Memories, sweet and innocent, flooded him, dragging him back to his first kisses with Constance Bennington. Languid, honeyed, deeply arousing, they'd been filled with hope and promise for the future. She'd been the first woman he'd loved. He should feel guilty for shaming Miss Lovejoy so, but his own hunger, aye, his need to punish himself, drove all other thoughts from his mind. Until she laid one delicate hand against his cheek.

He broke contact, noting her bemused expression. "No, I think we suit quite well, *Lizette.* You won't be rid of me so easily."

"But—"

He shook his head to silence her protest. "I am afraid the fat is in the fire," he told her in a low voice. "You have locked us both into your little lie, like it or not. If you do not continue posing as my mistress, you will be pressed to make another choice. Which of these men would you choose, Lizette?"

Trapped, she glanced around the room.

"Come now, my little would-be courtesan. Are there none that you can picture yourself naked beneath? At the disposal of? Doing unspeakable things for? I think you should aim high, my dear. Virgins are a rarity." He nodded toward a balding gentleman with bushy gray eyebrows. "Lord Peebles would be able to pay the price. Of course, after the initial novelty wears thin, you would become a liability until you'd learned some tricks. How quickly do you learn, Lizette? I'd stay away from my brother-in-law, though. I've heard Munro has a mean streak."

The hunted look in her eyes should have made him relent, but he wanted to punish her. Like it or not, she had landed herself in the middle of his investigation. He couldn't tell her what he was up to and, God knows, he couldn't stop her from her course. Munro's interest in her added to the mix, and that was more deeply disturbing than Geoff would have thought. Indeed, it chilled his blood. Before he'd let Munro—who'd killed his sister and gotten away with it—have Miss Lovejoy, he'd take her himself. Yes, his only choice now was to keep as close an eye on her as possible.

And use whatever information she uncovered.

Taking a deep breath, he stood and held his hand out to her. "Well, Lizette, I think you've done enough damage for one night. Shall we go home?"

"But I haven't—"

"Of course you haven't gotten answers. Did you think you would simply arrive on the scene and the others would begin spilling information? It will take more than one evening to get past their reserve."

She pressed her lips together and he smiled. She was trying to control her temper. It was a start.

"Did you leave your wrap downstairs?"

"I do not have a wrap. Or a fan. I seem to have left them at the theater."

Ah, yes. He'd forgotten all about that. He looked her up and down. "My mistresses do not dress so shabbily. You reflect poorly on me, Lizette. We shall have to remedy that."

Unable to sleep, Dianthe stared at the flickering candle beside her bed. Her thoughts were in a jumble and her emotions held her on the verge of tears. What was wrong with her?

Geoffrey Morgan, of course. On the other side of the wall, a garbled epithet carried to her, and the clink of a bottle against a glass. The soft slide of his window opening was followed by the creak of his bed. She pictured him throwing his covers back to the warm summer night and lying prone on the down mattress. Her heartbeat skipped.

Why had fate played such a cruel jest on her—to place her in the hands and at the mercy of a known rake and reprobate? A man she'd once vowed to dislike for the rest of her life?

She fluffed her pillow and turned over. The cool linen soothed her heated cheek and reminded her of Geoffrey Morgan's palm cupping her face as he kissed her at Thackery's. A kiss so sweet, so consuming, that the room had narrowed to only them. A touch so scorching that she'd have surrendered whatever he asked. There was magic in those kisses, and she did not know how to deal with the emotions they evoked.

Who was this man who exerted such power over her? What manner of man was he? As near as she could tell, he was abrupt and stern and vaguely threatening. She disliked being so dependent upon his goodwill, yet she prayed his debt to her cousin would prevent him from turning her out. She needed him more desperately than she wanted him to know. And could he be truly wicked if he had never used his position to abuse her?

Fear had stalked her every footstep since that night in Vauxhall Gardens. Each man she met as Lizette Deauville could be Nell's killer—a man who would kill *her* if he found out who she was. Every sound in the dark could be a return of the intruder who'd choked her in the library on Curzon Street. And every moment she breathed, she remembered vividly holding her cousin as her life slipped away. Since that very moment, the only time she'd felt safe was with Geoffrey Morgan. But how could that be when everything she knew of the man urged her to run?

She had caught glimpses, mere hints, of depths, vulnerabilities, loss and hidden pain beneath his dark demeanor. She'd learned that he'd endured tragedy, though he never spoke of it. He'd loved Constance Bennington, and lost her, and the look in his eyes when he'd gazed up at his sister's portrait yesterday had been anything but remote and cold.

Heavens! Dianthe sat bolt upright in bed. Had she completely misjudged the man? Had his brusqueness been a sham? A device to protect himself from further pain? If so, then it was no wonder he resented her intrusion in his life. The best she could do, then, was to give him no more trouble. Yes. She'd be the model of civility and, lacking provocation, he would cease troubling her.

Geoff stood in the shadows outside the ballroom early the next afternoon and watched Miss Lovejoy at her fencing lesson. She was learning quickly. She had excellent form and a natural athleticism that would advance her quickly. But it was her figure, straining against the snug buckskin breeches and the loose shirt that draped her shoulders and arms that drew most of his attention. He had a fine imagination, and was pleased that every curve he'd longed to see was visible now. Even the firm little buds of her nipples pressing against the fluid cloth of her shirt were evident. The unwilling response of his body gave testament to the fact that he found her completely irresistible. Merely a physical response, he told himself.

She delivered a riposte to Prescott's parry and then attempted a quick retreat. The button on the end of Prescott's foil pressed firmly to Miss Lovejoy's left breast, just above her heart. Panting, she grinned at the teacher and spread her arms wide in surrender. God, what Geoff would give to have her face *him* in so charming a surrender.

"Your match, Mr. Prescott," she said.

"You are doing remarkably well, Miss Deauville. Another week and you will acquit yourself in any setting." He lowered his sword to point it at her feet. "Better, of course, if you had boots and did not slide when riposting."

Geoff looked down at her stockings. Of course she wouldn't have suitable boots. He'd remedy that today. A pair of handmade Hessians. Yes, those trim calves would look good in Hessians.

Prescott saluted her with his sword and Geoff did not like the look in his eyes. He'd be willing to wager that swordplay was not the only thing on the teacher's mind. Geoff came forward, covering his annoyance.

"Ah, here you are, Miss Deauville. Go change, if you please. We are going shopping."

She turned to him, her eyes alight. "Shopping? Am I to get a new shawl and fan as you promised?"

"At the very least," he told her.

Prescott replaced his foil in the rack and shrugged into his jacket. "Tomorrow, Miss Deauville. Practice your lunges, eh?"

She nodded and hurried from the ballroom. Geoff had never seen anyone so anxious to go shopping. She must be more bored here than he'd thought. He'd have to come up with some other ideas to keep her busy. The busier she was, the less likely she'd be to get in his way. Or in trouble.

He walked Prescott to the door and couldn't resist a warning. "I would take it badly, Prescott, if I should learn that there is anything improper going on between you and Miss Deauville."

Prescott looked offended. "Miss Deauville is a fine, high-spirited young woman with a natural ability for the blade. I believe she has the talent to outshine most of my students. My interest lies in that, Lord Morgan."

Geoff wasn't convinced but he let it pass. Almost before he could shut the door, Miss Lovejoy appeared at the top of the stairs in her plain blue gown and dark wig.

"Shall I need a spencer, Lord Morgan? Is it crisp outside?" she asked.

The gown was the same one he'd seen her in for three days. She couldn't have had much in the small valise she'd taken away from the Thayers' house. He knew she'd remade two of her dresses into evening gowns. It was unlikely that she would have much more with her.

"No, Miss Lovejoy. It is a fine afternoon. Come along. Madame LaFehr will be waiting. I made an appointment with her this morning."

Madame LaFehr opened the door to her salon and waved them in. "I 'ave been wondering where you were, my lord. As you instructed, I canceled my appointments to accommodate you."

"For which you will be compensated, *Madame*."

"*Mais oui.* I know your generosity, my lord. But some of my best patrons are not pleased that they were put off." She gave a typically Gallic shrug and turned to face Miss Lovejoy. "Miss Deauville, I cannot wait to dress you! Your coloring is unusual for a brunette, with the fair skin and the blue eyes, eh? We shall create a look that will be all the rage."

Miss Lovejoy's eyes widened. "A shawl and a fan, Miss LaFehr. That is all I've come for."

Geoff smiled. "I insist on a few new fripperies, Miss Deauville. Your appearance will reflect on me now, and I won't look penurious."

Miss LaFehr led them toward the same dressing room

she'd used for fitting the trousers, and Miss Lovejoy leaned close to him to whisper, "But I haven't the means for this, Lord Morgan. Truly, I haven't the means for the shawl and fan, but you said you'd replace those."

"I can bear the cost of a few gowns, Miss Deauville."

"But it wouldn't be proper. Accepting such things from you would be scandalous."

He gave her a wry smile. "A little late to be thinking of that, Miss Deauville. Everything you've done for the past week or more has been scandalous. And just think! You did not even need my help to get yourself into this predicament. You managed it all on your own."

"But I do not like taking gifts from you."

"From men in general, Miss Deauville, or just me? Then think of them as coming from your aunt, or your cousin, or even Mr. Talbot. After all, it is their money that will pay for your fripperies."

She looked up at him again and a slow smile curved her lips. "Very well. I shall love to spend your money."

And she did. After confirming the measurements she had taken for Dianthe's fencing outfit, Madame LaFehr brought out dozens of fashion catalogs from French, German and London designers. Geoff found that he actually enjoyed selecting styles that would complement Miss Lovejoy's slender figure and then pairing them with the rich array of fabrics and colors Madame LaFehr arranged before them.

After an hour, tea was brought to the dressing room and Madame LaFehr excused herself to check on her seamstresses. "I shall be back presently," she said as she shut the door. "Amuse yourselves, *mes amis*."

Geoff sat back and watched Miss Lovejoy pour the tea. She was touchingly lovely and a pang of yearning shot through him. He needed to distance himself from the girl before he became too attached. Reconciling himself to losing Constance had taken him years. If he went so far as to let himself love Miss Lovejoy, losing her would be the end of him. She had the fresh innocence of youth and a willingness to fully engage in life. Lord, she made him feel young again instead of the world-weary cynic he'd become. Ah, but he'd always been cursed with wanting what he could never have.

She handed him his cup of tea and sat back. "Are we done now, but for my shawl and fan?" she asked.

He shook his head. "We've only selected four evening gowns, and you have nothing for daytime but the dress you're wearing. I think you should have four of those. And, perhaps, some underpinnings."

A deep flush infused her cheeks and she looked down into her teacup. "You are spending entirely too much money on me, my lord. I've never had so many things at once."

"Not even for your presentation to society?"

"We saved for that for months and years in advance. Then, when I came to London, I was fitted with accessories. Gloves, handkerchiefs, stockings, dancing slippers and a few new gowns. After Papa died, we were in a terrible bind. Every pence we made from market and craft went to taxes, paying our brother's tuition at Eton and preserving his inheritance."

"You were poor?" He would never have guessed she'd been anything but the pampered, willful little debutante he'd thought her.

"As church mice." She nodded. "My aunt Henrietta had to come to town to earn a living, and later Afton came to be Aunt Grace's companion."

"Was it difficult?" he asked, trying to picture Miss Lovejoy washing dishes, doing laundry or cooking.

"In many ways it was the happiest time of my life. In London, I feel so useless. At least in Little Upton, I was doing something constructive and of value."

"Is that why you seek a murderer?" he asked, beginning to understand her determination.

"Yes." She sighed. "And help others when I can." She sipped her tea thoughtfully.

He waited. He'd read enough faces over gaming tables to know that she was on the verge of broaching a dangerous subject.

"Laura Talbot was my friend," she finally said. "I tried to help her. She came to me when her brother lost her to you in a card game. She told me her brother said you'd cheated him. I took her to Aunt Grace, and we vowed to do everything in our power to save her from that fate." She glanced up at him and winced. "Not that you are so awful that…well, she did not even know you, my lord, and your reputation is not exactly…reassuring. It seemed so unfair. How could she be no more than a pawn on her brother's chessboard?"

"Her brother is the worst sort of gambler," Geoff said softly, hoping she would understand. "Everything he possesses is subject to his addiction. If I had not won Miss Talbot, someone else would have. Perhaps someone worse, perhaps someone better. I, at least, would have provided for her and would not have abused her trust." And he would not have loved her. Their marriage would have been one of convenience, requiring nothing he could not give—love, commitment.

"But you would have…" she bowed her head over her teacup again "…exercised your marital rights."

Geoff fought his smile. "Yes. And I would have expected what any husband has a right to expect. Fidelity, loyalty, children. In exchange, she would have had my name and protection, every comfort at her fingertips, and an indulgent husband who would not have taken too much of her time or made unreasonable demands."

"But you did not love her. And you lost her in a game of chance with my aunt. Isn't that as reprehensible as what her brother did?"

Only he and Adam Hawthorne knew the truth of that wager, and he wouldn't betray it now. "I didn't lose her, Miss Lovejoy. Your aunt won only the right for Miss Talbot to make her own choice of marrying me or remaining at her brother's mercy. In the end, and at her request, I released her from her brother's debt. The choice was hers. And how has it served her? I hear she ran off with a fortune hunter who abandoned her when he learned of her brother's losses and that there'd be no dowry."

"Laura's judgment, it seems, is no better than her brother's." Miss Lovejoy looked up at him and, for the first time during the conversation, her clear blue eyes held no trace of suspicion or contempt. "She told me after her interview with you that you did not try to coerce her, nor behave improperly, and that you gave her that choice. For whatever it is worth, my lord, I have come to believe she made the wrong choice. For her, but not for you."

He was disconcerted to realize just how much it was worth. He put his cup aside and leaned toward her. "Why was it the right choice for me?"

"Because you deserve more. You deserve to be loved."

Loved? He hadn't expected that. That Dianthe could wish more for him... He leaned toward her, reaching out to cup her cheek.

Madame LaFehr hurried into the room like a small whirlwind. "*Eh bien!* Now we shall finish with the day dresses. I 'ave told my girls that they will earn extra to 'ave these things ready as you requested, my lord. And they will be ready for fittings within a few days." She clapped her hands and a seamstress bustled in with more catalogs. "Come, sweet'earts, make your choices!"

Chapter Ten

Lord Morgan deposited her on the doorstep of his house on Salisbury Street with a promise to fetch her after supper, but Dianthe was restless. She'd been caged for days on end with nothing to do but practice her fencing. She longed to stretch her legs. Instead of going inside, she turned right and headed for St. James Park.

Within twenty minutes, and with nothing more than her wig, a bonnet and a parasol to disguise her, Dianthe strolled past Hortense and Harriett Thayer's bench twice. She trusted the twins not to betray her, but she couldn't be certain of the maid. Dianthe took careful note of their abigail's position with other servants near the pond before approaching them.

"Psst. No greeting for your dearest friend?"

Hortense, the shyer of the two, glanced down at the path, presumably to indicate that they had not been introduced. Harriett, though, looked up and studied her face, narrowing her eyes.

"Do we know you, miss?"

"'Tis me. Dianthe. In disguise," she said.

Hortense looked up and met her eyes for the first time. "Heavens, Dianthe! We've been so worried! No one knows how to reach you or where you've gone."

"Oh! But this is too delightfully wicked!" Harriett whispered, pulling Dianthe down onto the bench between them. "Here we are, in the very center of polite London, speaking with a...well, an accused murderess."

Dianthe's stomach clenched in a sudden cramp. "Then it is official? I've been indicted?"

Harriett heaved a long-suffering sigh. "Everyone hushes when we come 'round," she complained. "They know how close we've been and they think they are protecting us from...well, who knows what. But we are unable to gather any news."

"Yes," Hortense agreed, "and Papa said last night at dinner that he was a little relieved you ran off. Especially after the authorities came to question us. He said bankers must be careful of their reputations and the company they keep, lest investors withdraw their funds."

Harriett shot her sister an angry look. "All the same, Dianthe, I think we should smuggle you home and hide you in our room. Our abigail would never tell, and then at least we would know you are safe. And where *are* you staying? No one has seen you in days!"

Sighing, Dianthe glanced around at the passing riders and pedestrians on the path. Any of them could be Bow Street runners sent to follow the twins and see if they met with Dianthe. "This is not a lark, Harri. I could hang. And all because I stopped to render aid."

"Oh, that's not all," Hortense volunteered. "The magistrate told Papa that when they searched Miss Brookes's rooms, they found your calling card, as if you had sent it to her by way of appointment."

Dianthe frowned. Yes. Afton had written about sending Nell her card. Now the authorities were using it as evidence of her guilt. If the truth came out—that Nell was her cousin—they'd consider it as additional motive to keep Nell quiet and prevent her from ruining Bennett's bright future and Dianthe's own marriage prospects.

Hortense leaned nearer and lowered her voice. "Papa said that, should we run into you, we must give you the cut sublime. But do not worry. We'd never do that, would we, Harri?"

"He believes I am guilty?" Dianthe asked.

"I do not think so. 'Tis just that, well, he thinks that, no matter the outcome, your reputation is irretrievably damaged. To become involved in a murder, no matter how inadvertently, places you beyond the pale, if you know what I mean."

Yes, she knew. "I should not compromise you further. What if I were recognized? Your papa would shut you in your rooms and not let you out until spring."

"There is not the slightest chance anyone will recognize you, Di," Hortense disagreed. "The dark hair and beauty patch completely threw us off. And *we* know you better than anyone outside your family."

She stood and smoothed her skirts. "I just wanted you to know that I was safe so you wouldn't worry. And I knew I could count on you to tell me the *on dit*."

"But when will we see you again?" Harriett asked.

"And where are you staying?" Hortense interjected. "Can you be certain they will not evict you if they learn what you are accused of?"

"They…they know. They—" Well, to be honest, she didn't know if Lord Morgan cared or not. She'd never asked. "I will not be evicted," she finished weakly.

"Can you meet us here tomorrow?" Harriett asked.

She shook her head and backed away as she saw their maid separating herself from her friends and coming toward the bench. "I shall look for you when I can, but I am not certain when I might come again."

"Keep well, Dianthe," Harriett whispered after her.

Head down, she hurried away, fretting over this news. Her family had come perilously close to losing credibility with the ton before, but they had always managed to avert disaster. But not this time. There was no hushing up her scandal, or sweeping it under the rug. No, this time all of London was privy to the details.

She most regretted what it would do to her family. Society would tar them with the same brush they used for her. Bennett would receive no more invitations from prominent families to spend holidays or vacations. Afton and her husband would remain relatively unscathed by virtue of his title, but Dianthe could no longer expect a good marriage.

Though the lighting was dim and subdued, Dianthe felt the weight of eyes upon her as she stood at the rouge-et-noir table in the main salon of the Blue Moon that night. Here, courtesans mixed freely with members of the ton and aristocracy. The lines between the classes were blurred and money was the only measuring rod.

She turned slightly and caught Geoffrey Morgan's gaze. He was standing alone near a door to a private room, leaning against the jamb in a pose of relaxed boredom, and jingling his counters in one expressive hand. He raised his glass to her and drank. Was he inviting her to join him? Or had he simply tired of the tables? She smiled. He was so disturbingly handsome that she could not resist.

"Ah, so it is mutual?" the woman beside her at the table asked in an undertone.

She returned her attention to her wager. She'd lost, and the croupier was sweeping the house winnings away. The little hoard of cash Lord Geoffrey had given her to gamble was dwindling quickly. Rather than place another bet, she linked arms with her new acquaintance, who introduced herself, and strolled toward a punch bowl. Miss Emma Tucker was a lovely dark-haired courtesan dressed dramatically in a red satin gown.

"It *is* mutual, is it not?" she asked again.

"Mutual? 'Ow do you mean, Miss Tucker?"

The woman shrugged. "It is plain to see that the others are right and Lord Geoffrey is smitten with you, but…well, as you know, women in our position cannot afford to be sentimental. If we allowed our hearts to rule our heads, we would die impoverished castoffs. I conceive your dilemma, however. Lord Geoffrey is so charming that you would have to be made of stone to resist."

Smitten? Lord Geoffrey was smitten with her? Absurd. Miss Tucker must need spectacles. As for resisting…well, she supposed she hadn't. Physically, at least. She couldn't forget that night in his coach when she'd—no, she couldn't think of that now. She must remember that she and Lord Geoffrey were from different worlds, and any connection between them would be utterly unsuitable. Ironically, he was now more respectable than she.

Miss Tucker gave a throaty chuckle. "Your pretty blush gives you away, Miss Deauville. Heavens! If Geoffrey can make a courtesan blush, he's lost none of his talent."

"T-talent?" she asked, though she suspected she'd regret it.

"Why yes. Have you not been universally congratulated on landing him?"

"No one 'as said a word, Miss Tucker. I am new to this town and still making my feet green. Enlighten me?"

"Ah, well. I suppose most of them are jealous, though they have no cause for complaint. Lord Geoffrey never repeats. That is widely known." Miss Tucker sighed deeply and gave a wistful smile. "He is quite the very best lover I've ever had and, my dear, I've had a few." She paused to laugh at her little joke before continuing. "He did not make me his mistress, although he came to me exclusively for a time. That's his pattern, you see. Long periods of abstinence followed by periods of intense indulgence. Almost as if he were trying to purge his need. All things considered, he is a single man in want of…companionship," Miss Tucker explained. "And he is most generous with the *congé.*"

Congé? If she recalled the finer points of her French, it meant a dismissal or farewell. "'Ow generous, Miss Tucker?"

"Diamonds, Miss Deauville. Necklaces and rings valuable enough to support them for years."

"*Là!* 'Ow long must they…serve 'im to receive such a *congé?*"

Miss Tucker accepted a cup of rum punch from a footman and raised it in a toast. "As a consort, no more than a week or two. As a mistress, never longer than two months. I do not exaggerate, Miss Deauville, when I tell you that every woman in this room would stand in a queue to be his next."

"Pourquoi?"

The courtesan paused and gave her a curious smile. "Why, Miss Deauville! You must be very exacting of your sponsors if you do not recognize Lord Geoffrey's uniqueness. Often, little consideration is given to our comfort, much less our needs. To have a lover who is inventive, athletic, talented and tireless is a rare thing. As you are no doubt aware, he has some esoteric tastes, but those are more a joy than…"

Dianthe looked down to compose her face as Miss Tucker continued. Good heavens! Esoteric? What in the world could that mean?

"Miss Deauville? Are you unwell? Have I said something to—"

"Mais non," she murmured. Poised again, she looked up and gave Miss Tucker her brightest smile. "You are correct, of course. 'E is most accommodating. I was simply curious, Miss Tucker."

"Why, I do believe you are jealous," Miss Tucker laughed. "How charming. No wonder Lord Geoffrey finds you entertaining."

Dianthe kept her smile fixed in place, pretending she hadn't noticed the insult. She did not want to alienate Miss Tucker, since she was the only courtesan she'd met who was willing to talk about the business of the demimonde. "Are there any 'oo would wish me ill for my…good fortune?"

"Some. But to no avail. As I've said, he never repeats."

"C'est vrai? A month?" But why was she astonished? Lord Geoffrey Morgan was unwilling to form attachments. His history forbade it. She glanced over at a table where vingt-et-un was being played. A brunette woman had been staring at her all evening. Dianthe made a guess. "The woman at vingt-et-un? Was she one of them?"

"Miss Elvina Gibson? Long ago," Miss Tucker said.

"Oui, and 'e never repeats." She sighed with resignation. "Are there many I should know about?"

Miss Tucker shrugged. "Fewer and fewer, Miss Deauville."

"*Oui?* Is 'e taking fewer mistresses?"

"Some have met with unfortunate accidents."

The hair on the back of her neck prickled. "*C'est vrai?*"

"Most recently, Miss Brookes."

Her cousin had been Lord Geoffrey's mistress? Dianthe turned to look back at him, still standing in the doorway watching her. Why hadn't he mentioned that little detail? "W-when?"

"Late last year. December, I think."

"And Flora Denton?"

"Not as a mistress. Flora is charming in her own way, but she lacks a certain je ne sais quoi. Lord Geoffrey looks for brightness. He prefers a cheerful disposition and a pragmatic turn of mind. He never involves himself with women who may want too much from him."

"But 'e gives diamonds," Dianthe mused. "'Ow much more could they expect?"

"Love. A lasting or long-term liaison. Nell wanted marriage, a house in the country, children. But she was too wise to ask. One such as Lord Geoffrey could never wed a woman like Nell—a woman of questionable reputation."

A woman like Nell. A woman like *her*. It was bad enough that she'd been accused of murder, but should her relationship to Nell be known… Oh, what did it matter? Ruined by association or accusation, the results were the same. "*Oui,*" she said. "And you, Miss Tucker? Why did your association with Lord Geoffrey end?"

"It lasted two weeks. Quite intense." She sighed dreamily. "Then, as quickly as it began, it was over. He'd fought back whatever demons haunt him, and could finally sleep through the night again. He'd sated his needs enough to bring them under control."

"*Oui! Oui, je comprends.*" Dianthe gritted her teeth. She

couldn't understand why Miss Tucker's constant harping on Lord Geoffrey's skill annoyed her so. Nor why the room had grown so warm. As fascinating as this subject was, it had wandered astray from her purpose. "I've 'eard of Nell Brookes. She was murdered, no? But why? What 'ad she done? What manner of person could do such a thing?"

Miss Tucker shrugged. "An angry wife? A rival?" Her eyes shifted to Miss Gibson, still at the vingt-et-un table. "Even a former lover. Lord Geoffrey, perhaps. I hear they did not part on friendly terms, although her *congé* was exceedingly generous."

"Why…why would Lord Geoffrey kill 'er?"

"I haven't the faintest notion, Miss Deauville. I only know they'd had words a few days before her death. Nell laughed about it, but…"

But she'd turned up dead just the same, Dianthe thought. And Geoffrey Morgan had not been far behind her. How long had it taken him to join the group around her body? Minutes? Seconds? Had he been hiding in the shrubbery all along? And was he sheltering Dianthe now so that he would know what she was finding out? And if she found out that he'd had something to do with Nell's death, would he kill her, too? Though she doubted he was the sort to kill a woman, she would have to tread carefully.

Miss Tucker took her arm and led her toward a group of men who had just stood up from a card table. She was grateful that she didn't recognize any of them. Two bowed politely and quickly hurried away, clearly more intent on gambling than socializing. She had already met one of the remaining men, and studied him as he bent over her hand.

"Miss Deauville, so pleased to meet you again. Dare I hope you are here alone?"

"*Mais non*, Mr. Munro. I am with Lord Geoffrey. I believe 'e is losing 'is money somewhere." She resisted the impulse to look over her shoulder to see if he was still watching.

"Losing? Geoff? I doubt that, Miss Deauville. He's the luckiest man I've ever known. He could fall into a barrel of manure and come up clutching a gold sovereign."

The other man laughed, and Dianthe turned her attention to him. He was lean, swarthy, clean-shaven and well-dressed. There was a faint scar over his left eyebrow. His eyes were as dark as obsidian, and she suspected he might be foreign. He, too, bowed over her offered hand while Miss Tucker made the introduction.

"Miss Deauville, may I present Senor Juan Ramirez. He has been visiting our fair isle from Barcelona."

Ah, that explained his dark good looks. *"Enchantée,"* she murmured with a little curtsy.

"I am pleased to meet you at last, Miss Deauville," he said in perfect English that bore just the faintest trace of a Castilian lisp.

At last? Had Mr. Munro mentioned her? "'Ave you been in England long, Senor Ramirez?" she asked.

"Perhaps two weeks. Alas, my visit is drawing to a close."

Dianthe opened her mouth to tell him not to miss the British Museum, but she remembered that she, too, was supposed to be new in town. "Such a short trip, *M'sieur.* 'Ave you come on business or pleasure?"

"A little of both, *Mademoiselle,*" he said with a charming smile.

"I 'ope you conclude everything to your satisfaction."

"That is why I have come myself, Mademoiselle Deauville. One should tend to the small details oneself if results are important, is it not so?"

"*Oui,*" she agreed readily. "The personal touch, yes?"

He chuckled, then shrugged apologetically. "I regret that it has become so late. I fatigue easily in England. I must return to my hotel. Perhaps we will meet again, Mademoiselle Deauville? Miss Tucker?"

"Have you and Mr. Munro come together?" Miss Tucker asked.

"I am afraid we have," Mr. Munro answered for his companion, a look of regret on his face. "I should return Senor Ramirez to his hotel. Will you be here later?"

Dianthe turned to find Lord Geoffrey still watching her. A hard expression had settled across his features and she recalled his warning about Mr. Munro. "I am growing weary myself, sir. I doubt I shall see you again tonight."

Munro bowed and departed with Senor Ramirez. Miss Tucker gave Dianthe a curious look. "Goodness! Senor Ramirez is quite the gentleman. I do not know the man well, but by the company he keeps I expect he will be very amusing. And he will have exquisite manners."

"The company 'e keeps?" she asked.

"Why, yes. As you know, Mr. Munro is a gentleman of the first order. So refined, and his manners are impeccable. He has had so much to overcome."

"*Oui?* What 'as 'e overcome? A low birth?"

"Heavens no! He is the second son of an earl. He is a true aristocrat in every sense of the word. He has had to overcome the tragic loss of his wife. He quite doted upon her. And I believe she was enceinte at the time."

Charlotte? Enceinte? That was something Giles and Hanson hadn't told her. Poor Mr. Munro, to suffer a double loss… She had noted the dullness of his eyes and had wondered the cause. Now she knew. The man was in deep mourning. "*Très tragique,*" she agreed with a little sigh.

"He has found solace in the demimonde, but he vows he will not marry again. He says he hasn't enough heart left for it. Quite disappointing."

Dianthe nodded absently, wondering what Lord Geoffrey could have done to make such an enemy as Lewis Munro.

Geoff decided to cut his losses before they grew. He wondered what could be behind his recent rash of bad luck at gambling. It really was unprecedented. Instead of losing more, he decided he'd see how Miss Lovejoy was passing the time.

He'd brought her to the Blue Moon—the seediest of the Covent Garden hells—hoping the atmosphere would disturb her enough to make her retreat from her ill-advised crusade to find Nell's murderer. But watching her from across the room, he witnessed the utter failure of his plan. Despite the presence of men like his former brother-in-law, she was none the worse for wear. It was well into the wee hours, and she'd lost none of her sparkle.

In a roomful of jades, Miss Lovejoy shone like a diamond. Men and women gravitated to her, drawn by her easy grace and humor. He began to see why she had earned the reputation as one of the ton's favored daughters. Ah, but no longer.

Now she had fallen so far from grace that she had become an inhabitant of *his* world—gamblers, cheats, rakes, courtesans and adventurers. And who better to tutor her than he?

She turned slightly and glanced at him as if she was aware of his study. A blush crept up her cheeks. If he had not known that she had nothing but contempt for him, he might have mistaken that blush for fondness. She was adapting well to the role of his mistress, although she still lacked a certain worldliness. Lessons in the demimonde might be just the thing. They would keep her busy and out of his way. He would look into that in the morning. Not that she actually needed tutoring in inciting his lust. His blood had begun to boil just watching her.

Miss Lovejoy separated herself from Emma Tucker and came toward him. "Lord Geoffrey," she said, taking his arm. "Are you ready to leave?"

Yes, he was, but he was not certain he should be alone with her at the moment. His hunger for her was disturbing, to say the least, and had she been a true courtesan, he'd have her in an upstairs room by now, naked, writhing and calling his name. She might drive him to distraction with her stubborn nature and her spirited defiance, but Lord, that body would be worth whatever obstacles came with it.

Alas, Miss Lovejoy was not a courtesan. And he was obligated to return her to his friend in the same condition she'd come to him. He looked down at her and sighed in resignation. "Yes, Miss…Deauville, I suppose we shall have to go home sometime."

The steady clip-clop of the horse's hooves and his own wayward fantasies of Miss Lovejoy in a negligee had lulled Geoff into unwariness when her soft voice brought him back. "I am finding Mr. Munro's company quite charming."

He straightened in his seat across from her. After the incident in the coach on the way home from the theater, he'd decided sitting opposite was safer than sitting beside her. "I warned you to stay away from him."

"I haven't encouraged him. He and Senor Ramirez simply stopped to have conversation with Miss Tucker. Do you know Senor Ramirez?"

"We have not been introduced. But if he is keeping company with Munro, he's bound to be a rakehell."

"Said the rakehell," she pointed out. "But I must say that my experience differs from yours. Mr. Munro, like Senor Ramirez, is civility itself."

"Munro has manners enough to get along in society, but that is a very thin veneer and covers something else entirely."

"What?"

He hesitated. If what he suspected was true, she'd be in danger. If it was false, he'd have slandered the man undeservedly. But he could tell her what he was certain of. "Munro does not possess the slightest compassion for anyone but himself. He cannot feel empathy or sympathy for others. It is not in his nature."

"That is harsh, Lord Geoffrey. As I understand it, he is in deep mourning. You cannot expect him to react as others who have not suffered."

"Pah! I know the man, Miss Lovejoy. Stay away from him or you will regret it."

"Are you jealous of him, sir, for the consequence and position in society that you forfeit because of your scandalous behavior?"

He gritted his teeth. She had a talent for sending him into a rage with the least provocation, but he wouldn't rise to her bait. He smiled into the darkness. He knew the perfect way to get even with her tomorrow.

Deciding a change of subject would be his best ploy, he asked, "Did you learn anything useful for your investigation this evening, Miss Lovejoy?"

"I'm afraid not. But I believe I've won the confidence of Miss Tucker. I think I could begin to ask more direct questions the next time I see her."

"Your progress is slow," he observed.

"Painfully so. I wish there were some way to hasten it."

"There may be." He folded his arms across his chest in an attempt to distance himself from her. "I shall take care of it tomorrow."

A short silence ensued and then Miss Lovejoy stirred in her seat. "Esoteric," she murmured.

"I beg your pardon?"

"What does 'esoteric' mean?" she repeated.

He mulled over the word. "I suppose it would depend upon the context."

"If one were said to have esoteric tastes?"

He couldn't see her face clearly in the darkness of the coach. "Considering the company you've been keeping, Miss Lovejoy, that could mean just about anything."

"Would it be like aesthetic?"

He fought his grin. "In one sense, yes."

"Which sense?" she pressed.

"Artistic."

Her little sigh carried to him and was so winsome that he longed to touch her lips with his and absorb the heat of it. "No, I do not believe that is what was meant. One of the ladies mentioned that…her gentleman has esoteric tastes."

His eyebrows shot up as he tried to think how to answer her question. "If someone were to tell me their mistress had esoteric tastes, and he had a smile on his face, I would take it to mean that she was…somewhat original, and that her particular preferences were…ah, exotic or specialized. Should he look annoyed or unhappy, I would assume they involved…" How could he explain little perversions, such as deriving pleasure from the giving or receiving of pain? Or erotic foreplay in the form of…? No. She was losing her innocence far too quickly without his help. He wouldn't hasten it. "I say, what the devil have you been discussing with the demireps?"

"Nothing much. They just say things and then laugh or sigh, and assume I know what they are talking about, but I don't. I hoped you would be able to educate me."

Bloody hell. If she only knew how *much* he wanted to educate her!

"But, on the whole, would you want a lover with esoteric tastes?" she persisted.

"I would certainly be intrigued enough to want to discover the exact nature of the esoteric pursuits."

Another sigh filled the chasm between them. "Just what I was thinking," she murmured.

Chapter Eleven

The more Dianthe thought about it, the more she began to understand just how wrong she'd been about Geoffrey Morgan. Oh, not about his scandalous behavior, nor any of the pertinent facts. But wealth was more a tool for him than a goal. So why did he gamble? Why was he escorting her to gaming hells? Indeed, why did Geoffrey Morgan do any of the things he did?

For example, he was escorting her to her fittings for gowns he had purchased for her. With no possible benefit to himself. He may want to pay his debt to her cousin, but he'd gone well beyond his obligation.

She twirled one dark curl of her wig around her finger as she studied him, sitting across from her in the coach. He was reading the *Times* and had only spoken to her in monosyllables since arriving home last night. She knew she had gone too far in goading him about his reputation, but he'd been so awfully prejudiced about Mr. Munro. Could he not see the man was suffering?

He folded the paper and tossed it on the seat beside him. When he noted her study, he gave her a cool smile and folded his arms across his chest. "How are your fencing lessons coming?"

"I am enjoying them immensely," she admitted. "But I still do not think I could actually hurt someone."

"That is the whole point, Miss Lovejoy. If you cannot disarm or kill your opponent, why bother?"

She could not dispute his logic so she merely shrugged. "I do enjoy my matches with Mr. Prescott. He says I am exceeding his expectations."

"That wouldn't take much. He was not expecting anything from you."

That stung. Would it have hurt him to let her have her little victory? Why was he being so disagreeable? She gritted her teeth and turned her attention to the window until they arrived at the dressmaker's shop.

Madame LaFehr met them at the door and hurried them to the large dressing room. A rainbow of organdy, muslin and silk gowns were hanging for inspection and fittings. They were stunning, and Dianthe suppressed a sigh of pleasure at the thought that they would all be hers. Well, for as long as she continued her masquerade, anyway.

"Come, little Lizette," Madame LaFehr urged. "I 'ave one in the changing room ready for you."

Dianthe glanced at Lord Geoffrey. Was he not going to whatever room *Madame* reserved for waiting men? As if to answer her unspoken question, he gave her a devilish smile and sat in one of the comfortable chairs facing the mirrors and fitting platform. Would she have to endure his ill temper throughout this ordeal?

Sighing in resignation, she entered the changing room with Madame LaFehr and closed the door with a slam. *Madame* pretended not to notice her loss of temper as she helped Dianthe undress and lift the gown over her head to let it settle around her.

"Come, *chère,* and see 'ow it looks. Lord Geoffrey will want to see it, too." She tugged on Dianthe's hand and pulled her into the fitting room. "Up," she prompted, urging her onto the dais.

Dianthe faced the mirrors and glanced at the reflection of Lord Geoffrey in the chair behind her. He straightened and sat slightly forward, a look of appraisal on his face.

Then she glanced at herself in the mirror. How had *Madame* managed a creation that was both seductive and innocent? The underdress, of an iridescent blue, clung to her form, while the overdress of sheer white embroidered organza lent her the modesty the sheath denied, and provided a small train in back. Low cut and trimmed in a narrow border of lace, the overdress hooked beneath her breasts, then separated down the front to reveal the clinging underdress.

She glanced in the mirror again to catch Lord Geoffrey's reaction. He was utterly still. Then his right hand came up and he twirled his forefinger.

Obediently, she turned in a circle, stopping when she faced him.

"This one has my approval, Genevieve," he said, and his familiarity told Dianthe that he had done this many times before. "I do not think it will require additional alterations."

"But—" Dianthe began. Had he not noticed that the top half of her nipples, while not quite obvious, were still visible beneath the sheer organza?

"Ah, I knew you would like it, Lord Geoffrey," *Madame* interrupted. "It shows 'er figure to good advantage, no? And should you wish something more alluring, *voilà!*" She unhooked the band beneath Dianthe's breasts and the overdress fell away.

Dianthe gasped. The organza had left her with some semblance of modesty, but the sheath left her none. Lord Geoffrey sat back in his chair and smiled as his gaze came up to meet hers. Her breasts puckered and hardened in response. Her cheeks burned and she brought her hands up to cover herself. Lord Geoffrey raised one eyebrow in a question.

"*Là!* She is so appealing, no?" *Madame* asked. "I can see 'er charm, my lord, even though she 'as not the complexity of your usual mistresses." She turned to Dianthe and gave her a mockingly stern look. "Do not deprive your benefactor of 'is pleasure, little Lizette. Come now, shall we try on the next?"

Dianthe was more than pleased to escape to the changing room. But as she tried on one gown after another, it was much the same—daring décolletages coupled with elegant, clinging fabrics. To her surprise, there were accessories to match all the gowns, from fans, shawls, pelisses and bonnets to satin slippers and reticules.

When she tried on the final gown, a sophisticated gold-and-blue-striped taffeta that rustled as she moved, Lord Geoffrey rose from his chair at last. He came toward her, removed a flat box from the inside of his jacket and handed it to her. Curious, she lifted the lid and found a stunning necklace nestled on black velvet. The gold chain was woven in a narrow lacy pattern and a clear blue sapphire pendant surrounded by small diamonds was suspended from it. She'd thought she'd never seen anything as beautiful in her life.

"It is yours, Lizette," he said when she looked up at him.

She blinked. "Th-the congé? So soon?"

Lord Geoffrey coughed. "Congé? Where did you learn about that?"

"From…the others. A parting gift, I believe? Are you sending me away?"

There was a long hesitation and Dianthe's anxiety rose. Her pulse quickened when she remembered the feel of that horrid man from Curzon Street tightening his hands around her throat. Where would she go?

Geoffrey removed the necklace from the box and moved behind her to fasten it. Then he cupped her shoulders and leaned close to her ear. "I should," he whispered. "God knows I should. But no. It is merely a gift."

"It is far too expensive, my lord. If I should accept such a gift, people would think I am—"

"A courtesan? My mistress? Exactly, and I cannot have them thinking I am miserly."

That never would have occurred to her. She sighed with relief. When his finger traced the woven gold where it lay against her throat, a tingle coursed through her. Then he stepped back and returned to his chair.

Unable to move, she stared as he pulled his watch from his vest pocket and checked it. "We have a little time, Genevieve. Continue, if you please."

"But this is the last of the dresses," Dianthe said.

"Ah, Lizette! Now the fun begins, no?" *Madame* gave her a little push toward the changing room.

Once she was down to her shift again, *Madame* opened boxes with an array of delicate items carefully wrapped in tissue. There were negligees, nightgowns, sheer stockings and soft ribbon garters. Corsets, stays, shifts, camisoles, drawers and dressing gowns. All were made of the most exquisitely soft fabrics Dianthe had ever seen—silk, lawn, finely woven muslin and satin. And they were all crafted so intricately that she swore they'd been made for royalty. Or made to…entertain in.

"Come, Lizette. 'Urry. Lord Geoffrey is not the patient man, yes? 'E is waiting."

Her jaw dropped. "You mean he expects me to dress in these and…and show him?"

Madame laughed. "But of course, *chère*. It is 'is money, is it not? 'E 'as a right to know what 'is money 'as purchased. Come. The dressing gown first. No! The white silk nightgown, and the dressing gown over it. Yes?"

"No!" She tried, unsuccessfully, to slap *Madame*'s hands away as she lifted her shift over her head. How humiliating! Dianthe had not worn stays this morning, in her haste to join Mr. Prescott, who had been waiting in the ballroom for her fencing lesson.

"*Là!*" *Madame* exclaimed when Dianthe was completely naked. "You are perfection! It is no wonder, then, that Lord Geoffrey 'as chosen you." She dropped the sheer white silk nightgown over Dianthe's head, helped her into the dressing gown and tied the blue sash around her waist.

"I cannot go out there like this," Dianthe whispered.

"But why not, *chère?*"

"It…it is indecent!"

Madame frowned. "Indecent? *Alors!* Are you the virgin or the woman of the world? Lord Geoffrey may find this modesty a novelty, eh? But 'e will soon tire of it, Lizette. I 'ave seen it before. 'E is a man of sophisticated tastes and 'igh expectations. This coyness of yours will grow old quickly. If you wish to keep 'is interest and succeed in the demimonde, you will 'ave to overcome this foolishness."

"I…I—"

"You flush, petite Lizette," the woman observed. A knowing smile came over her face. "Ah, 'e is your first protector, yes? You are new to the demimonde."

For lack of a better explanation, Dianthe nodded.

"Not to worry, my sweet," she said. "Lord Geoffrey is very kind. And very skilled. You could not ask for a better tutor to introduce you to this life. But do not strain 'is patience."

Heavens! Was there even one woman in the demimonde who had *not* slept with Lord Geoffrey? While Dianthe was still contemplating that question, Madame LaFehr opened the changing room door and pushed her out. She nearly tripped over the dais and stood facing her "protector."

He blinked, let his gaze drop to her bare feet, then sweep slowly upward until he reached her face. His expression did not change, but his breathing had deepened.

"Exquisite, is she not?" *Madame* asked.

"Exquisite," he repeated in a flat voice, his attention shifting lower.

Dianthe glanced down and moaned. The white silk was so sheer that it revealed as much as it hid. When she looked up again she caught a quick grin on Lord Geoffrey's face. The villain was enjoying this! He was extracting pleasure from her embarrassment. She spun around and hurried into the changing room, tossed the gossamer silk aside and pulled on the clothing she'd come in.

"Did he tell you how to cut the gowns, *Madame?* Or how much of me he wished exposed?"

"*Mais non,* Lizette! You were 'ere. You and 'e chose the gowns and fabrics together. The cut is identical to the gowns I make for the elite of the demimonde. And Lord Geoffrey's tastes are well known to me. I 'ave dressed 'is mistresses before."

So Lord Geoffrey hadn't expressly told *Madame* to cut the necklines so deep, or to use sheer fabrics? That fact calmed Dianthe considerably. Still, he had taken full advantage of the situation to make a spectacle of her.

Madame LaFehr crossed her arms and shook her head.

"This is not the way to please Lord Geoffrey. If you are not very careful, *chère,* you will find yourself put aside. 'Is attentions are brief as it is. If you could be as pleasing as possible, per'aps 'e will keep you longer than the rest."

Fear and anger mixed as Dianthe seethed inside. What was wrong with her? She was fully aware that her safety was only at Lord Geoffrey's sufferance. One minute she was terrified of losing it, and the next she was doing everything she could to insure that she would. But it wasn't all her fault. He'd been making a jest of her from the moment they'd arrived, allowing—no, *requiring*—her to pose in risqué gowns and underpinnings. He was a scoundrel and he deserved to…to be punished. Yes. She'd find a way to turn this back on him.

Despite that they were risqué, Dianthe's new gowns were the most luxurious and elegant she'd ever had. The small-clothes and nightwear were beyond beautiful. She folded them reverently and placed them in her bureau drawer.

Only a few of the gowns had been ready to come home with her, and the rest had remained with Madame LaFehr for further alterations. But the pendant lay on her dressing table where she could see it whenever she looked in that direction. She regretted that she would have to leave it behind when the killer was found and she could go home.

A timid knock on her door startled her. Surely Giles or Hanson hadn't come of their own accord?

She opened the door and had to stifle a giggle when she found Giles, red-faced and shuffling his feet. He held a silver salver with an envelope on it.

"Miss Lovejoy, there is a woman in the parlor who says she would like to see Miss Deauville. Would you like me to send her packing?"

Send her packing? Dianthe could rarely decipher what Lord Geoffrey's servants meant. She took the envelope and broke the seal. A single sheet of paper contained a few scrawled lines.

Miss Lovejoy, Please accommodate Miss Osgood, whom I have hired to instruct you. I shall return by nine o'clock to escort you to Thackery's. Cordially, Morgan.

How curious. She looked up at Giles and smiled. "Please tell Miss Osgood I shall be down presently."

"As you say, miss."

Dianthe returned to the dresser, pinned her hair up and donned her dark wig.

By the time she entered the small parlor off the foyer, Miss Osgood was removing her hat and gloves. She turned as Dianthe closed the door.

"Ah, Miss Deauville! Lovely. Yes, you are quite lovely. I can see why Lord Geoffrey would want me to undertake this particular task."

"Might I ask what task?" Dianthe inquired as she took the woman's measure. Miss Osgood was of a diminutive stature, very pretty for her years, and impeccably dressed. What did Lord Geoffrey have planned this time?

"Did he not tell you? Why, I am to instruct you in all things Cyprian."

"Cyprian?" she repeated. "Whatever do you mean, Miss Osgood?"

The woman laughed and the sound was a musical trill. "Why, the arts of your profession, Miss Deauville. I gather Lord Geoffrey dotes upon you, but he expressed his concern that you are just a little gauche in company."

"Gauche?" Dianthe fairly reeled from the insult. "He said I was *gauche?*"

"He said the word in all fondness, Miss Deauville. He simply thinks your skills could be improved upon."

"My…skills?"

Miss Osgood leaned forward as if sharing a confidence. "He told me you were new to the calling and had not perfected the art of seduction. He indicated that you would be a willing student. Is this not so?"

Dianthe opened her mouth to refute Lord Geoffrey's claim, but a sudden thought made her pause. If she could put her pride aside, as well as her modesty, this might be the perfect means to exact a fitting vengeance on the arrogant Lord Morgan. "By all means, Miss Osgood. When will this instruction take place, and how long will it last?"

"We can begin today, and I am to come every afternoon until Lord Geoffrey is satisfied."

Satisfied? Oh, make no mistake! She'd *satisfy* the lecherous rake! Satisfy him that he'd taunted the wrong female! She'd see to it that he got value for his money, and everything he so richly deserved. "Shall I send for tea, Miss Osgood?"

"Yes. I think we shall need it. We have quite a daunting task ahead of us."

Daunting? Good heavens! Dianthe tugged the bell pull and went to the door to request tea from Giles, then returned to Miss Osgood. With a sweep of her hand, she indicated a chair. "Shall I assume this can be done sitting down?"

Miss Osgood laughed again. "Most of it," she said. "The rest will be done reclining."

Wearing the blue sheath with the organza overdress and a shawl of white fringed cashmere, Dianthe took Lord

Geoffrey's offered hand to step down from the coach in front of Thackery's. They hadn't spoken on the way and all Dianthe could do was study his face and speculate as to his motives for educating her in the demimonde. At the very best, to prepare her to be convincing in her role. At worst, to provoke her into quitting. She suspected the latter.

To give her credit, Miss Osgood's first lesson had been nothing short of a revelation. The lecture had been about a woman's power over men, and Dianthe was reminded of Lord Geoffrey's discourse on why a man was attracted to a courtesan in the first place. Miss Osgood had also instructed her on how to tell if a man was interested in her, and how to use that interest to her advantage. Then she'd told Dianthe that men like confidence in a woman. She suggested that Dianthe practice her bearing, carriage and confidence in her mirror. Miss Osgood said that men found silence intriguing and mysterious.

And, judging by Lord Geoffrey's quizzical study in the coach this evening, Miss Osgood had been right. He would know that the woman had called on Dianthe, and he was waiting for her to rail against him or take him to task in some way. Her silence on the matter was obviously driving him to distraction.

There was one thing, however, that she hadn't been able to do. She simply could not expose herself in the gown as Miss Osgood had urged her to do. Instead, she'd tucked a narrow strip of lace into the neckline to shroud the pink crowns of her breasts. She'd never be brazen enough to reveal herself in such a manner.

In the foyer of Thackery's, Lord Geoffrey took her shawl and handed it to a footman. He smiled when he saw that she'd worn the sapphire pendant.

"I am going in search of a game, Miss Deauville," he

said, slipping a five-pound note into the top of her décolletage. "Try not to get in trouble, eh?"

He wore an expectant smile, waiting for her to slap his hand or make a protest. Recently schooled by Miss Osgood, however, she smiled back enigmatically as she plucked the note from her gown. "I shall try to make this last, my lord."

"Find me if you need more." He winked and headed for one of the rooms notorious for deep play.

Free to pursue her own goals, Dianthe strolled slowly up the curved stairway to the mezzanine, pausing halfway up to observe the crowd.

"Ah, Miss Deauville," came a voice from the landing.

She glanced up to find Lord Reginald Hunter descending toward her. "*Bonsoir,* Lord Lockwood," she answered.

He grinned. "I am flattered that you remembered me."

Here was a perfect opportunity to practice some of her new skills. "My lord, you are…'ow you say, not to be forgotten?"

"Memorable? Unforgettable?"

"*Oui.* Memorable."

He laughed and she wondered why she'd never noticed what a rogue he was. "Are you here with Morgan?"

"*Oui.* 'E is looking for a game."

"I see one right here. Is the man blind?"

She waved her white lace fan frantically. She'd had no idea that Lord Reginald could flirt so outrageously! "*Là!* I cost 'im money, my lord. The other game makes 'im money."

"I see that." He touched the sapphire pendant where it rested just above her breasts. He never would have dared such a move with Dianthe Lovejoy. "And I can see that he will be needing money. God knows *I'd* do whatever it took to keep you happy."

He frowned, and she looked up to find a flicker of something wary in his deep violet eyes. She lifted his finger away from the pendant with her fan and started to move around him.

"Are you certain we have not met, Miss Deauville? Those eyes. I know I've seen those eyes before."

"But of course we 'ave met, Lord Lockwood. At the theater." She continued up the stairs without a backward glance. She held her breath, praying Lockwood would not remember where he'd seen her eyes.

The instant she entered the mezzanine salon, Flora Denton excused herself from her group and came to Dianthe's side. "Thanks heavens you've come. I believe I have learned something rather startling."

Dianthe followed her to the banquette, almost afraid to hope. Once they were settled, Flora glanced around to make certain they would not be overheard. Dianthe patted her hand, trying to reassure her. "What did you learn, Miss Denton?"

"Elvina Gibson whispered that Nell was afraid of someone."

Elvina Gibson? Ah, yes—the dark woman who had glared at her last night at the Blue Moon. "Did she say whom? Or why?"

"She said that Nell had overheard a conversation and that something 'shocking' was afoot. Before Elvina could ask more, Nell hurried off. That was just days before she was murdered."

Puzzled, Dianthe frowned. "She must have spoken with someone in the meanwhile. Think, Miss Denton. Are you certain she said nothing to you?"

Tears sprang to the woman's eyes. "Do you think I have not asked myself that question a thousand times? It was not like Nell to keep scandal to herself. 'Tis true she was rather cryptic earlier that day, but she did not behave as if she was afraid of anyone."

"How was she cryptic?"

"I recall her saying that…that she had learned something that would set her up for life, but that it came with a difficult decision. It was so like Nell to dramatize her life. I assumed it had to do with an offer from one of her gentlemen. And still, I cannot be certain it was anything more than that."

Dianthe examined the statement, trying to think of possible explanations. Had Nell referred to an offer of the much-desired cottage and life annuity? Or could she have known something worthy of blackmail, and her victim killed her instead of paying hush money? A business venture could also explain such a statement. But it was more likely that she had been referring to Afton's offer of help. *Oh, Nell! Why couldn't you have found me sooner?*

"Heavens!" Flora whispered. "Here comes Munro and Senor Ramirez."

Dianthe looked up to see Lewis Munro and Juan Ramirez coming toward them. What was it about Senor Ramirez that piqued her curiosity? She could tell that Flora felt the same as she and Miss Tucker.

"Now how is this? The two prettiest ladies at Thackery's, and they have their heads together instead of with ours? Unthinkable," Munro pronounced.

Flora smiled and fluttered her fan, but Dianthe watched Senor Ramirez's face. His expression was curious, but faintly distant. As if he were observing only, and had no real interest in them. But then he turned his full attention to her and the intensity of his gaze told her otherwise.

She stood and took Mr. Munro's offered arm, turning

him toward the vingt-et-un table. "You know 'ow the fairer sex enjoys sharing confidences, Mr. Munro. Miss Denton and I are becoming dear friends, are we not, Miss Denton?"

In the absence of an answer, Dianthe glanced over her shoulder. Flora was flushed but silent, and Dianthe was surprised to see that even courtesans could form a crush. She was about to say something to draw the others into her conversation with Mr. Munro when Flora took a deep breath, tilted her head to one side and gave Senor Ramirez a dazzling smile.

A quick flash of something carnal passed across Senor Ramirez's face. Dianthe suddenly realized, in a way she hadn't before, what it meant to be a courtesan, and to have one's living, one's very existence, dependent upon pleasing men. To surrender one's very self to a virtual stranger in an intimate act was beyond her imagination. When she tried to think of herself with Mr. Munro or Mr. Ramirez, a shudder of revulsion passed though her—and a new sympathy for the women of the demimonde.

Mr. Munro patted her hand on his arm. "Are you cold, Miss Deauville? Shall I fetch your wrap or shawl?"

"No, *M'sieur*. It is gone. Per'aps there was a draft."

"Are you with Morgan again tonight?"

"*Oui*. Lord Morgan is my…my—"

"You have become his mistress?"

"*Oui*," she said, a little embarrassed that she had stumbled over the word *lover*. She had learned enough to know that a true courtesan would have declared such a thing with pride.

"Ah, you are Morgan's woman?" Senor Ramirez asked, a look of interest in his dark eyes.

"You know him?" she inquired.

"By reputation," he answered, and glanced at Munro. The other man cleared his throat. "I hope you will not think I have overstepped if I give you a gentle warning in that regard."

Dianthe gazed up into his pale blue eyes. "In regard to Lord Geoffrey? *Mais non!* Please do not 'esitate."

"Be very careful around him. Of course you know his reputation as a dangerous man to the women he is near, but have any of your friends warned you that, for all his cool control, he has a violent temper?"

"Oui?" She'd seen flashes of his temper, but it had always been tightly controlled. What might happen if it were unleashed? "No, Monsieur. Surely such a thing would be common knowledge."

Munro gave her a canny grin. "I did not mean that he is clumsy between the sheets. And, my dear, as you know, it could be foolhardy to expose a man's faults, especially as he is most generous with the congé."

"Alors! This is the conspiracy of silence?"

"One could say so." Munro sighed and squeezed her hand. "Discretion is the hallmark of the demimonde, which would explain why his women do not make public appearances for a time after one of his losses of temper."

Horrified, Dianthe paused and turned to face Munro, seeking clarification. "'E does violence? *Physical* violence?"

"I regret to say that has been the case in many instances. And now, with Nell…well, need I say more?"

A prickle of fear shot up Dianthe's spine. Had Lord Geoffrey been the "he" that Nell spoke of? She glanced at Flora for confirmation, but Miss Denton would not meet her gaze. This was very peculiar.

That a reputable man like Lewis Munro could believe such a thing about Geoffrey Morgan was sobering. After all, he had been married to Lord Geoffrey's sister. Surely he would know such personal things about his brother-in-law.

Chapter Twelve

Geoff studied Miss Lovejoy from his position facing her, wondering what had changed since their arrival at Thackery's earlier. The coach ride home promised to be as silent as the ride to the gaming hell, though there was considerably more tension now. Was her little escapade as a courtesan beginning to pall? He hoped so.

For his part, he was losing again. Every time he took Dianthe with him, his losses exceeded his gains. His mind was more on her whereabouts and well-being than on the game at hand. Oh, he hadn't lost enough money to endanger either the funding to trap el-Daibul or his own standard of living, but the matter was disconcerting.

Miss Lovejoy sighed and shifted in her seat. Her shawl slipped off her shoulders, affording a glimpse of the exposed skin above her neckline. Even in the dim light of the coach, the sight caused a constriction in his throat and a firming in his loins. Her gown and that shade of blue complemented her to perfection. He realized with a little pang of regret that, had she been a courtesan in fact, she'd have been far above his touch. He'd have had the money to pay for her, but never the social standing or consequence to win her.

She turned to him and caught his study. "Did you have a question, my lord?"

"I was wondering if you are making progress with your queries."

She glanced down at the reticule in her lap. "They have begun to bear fruit."

"Well?"

She looked up again, her expression curious. "I thought you were not interested in my investigation."

"Indulge me, if you please."

"Very well. I have learned that Miss Brookes told Elvina Gibson that she was afraid of someone. That she had overheard a conversation and that something shocking was afoot. But Miss Gibson did not know who Nell overheard, or why she was frightened."

Geoff sat forward. Now this was interesting. Why hadn't Elvina said anything to him about this? He'd have to quiz her on the subject. "Did she say anything else?"

"No. Very shortly afterward, Nell was killed."

He sat back, digesting the information.

"But Miss Denton said earlier that day, Nell told her she'd just learned something that could set her up for life," Dianthe added, "but that it came with a difficult decision. Miss Denton thought perhaps she'd had an offer from a gentleman. Later—afterward—she wondered if Nell might have been planning to blackmail someone."

Afraid of someone? Blackmail? Miss Lovejoy was right. She *had* been able to learn things as a woman and a member of the demimonde that he and Harry Richardson hadn't. "Anything else?" he asked.

She shook her head. "But I think I will seek Miss Gib-

son out and question her more closely. There may be something she did not realize the significance of."

The thought of Dianthe putting herself at risk for this
endeavor raised the hair on the back of his neck. Though
she'd made it clear that he hadn't the right to curtail her
in any way, his instincts urged him toward that. But,
damn it, he couldn't risk taking responsibility for her. For
her sake.

He crossed his arms over his chest, trying to shut her
out. "I was just reflecting upon how easily you've found a
niche in the demimonde."

"You sound surprised."

"I am. For one so high-minded and morally superior as
you, it must grate upon your nerves to associate with those
so clearly your inferiors."

A deep flush colored her cheeks. "Have you always
seen me in such a harsh light, Lord Geoffrey?"

"You've certainly been unforgiving with me, Miss
Lovejoy."

"That is different."

"How so?"

"You had social standing and threw it away for base pursuits. But the poor souls I have come to know are merely
surviving in the best way they can. And you, and men like
you, are only too glad to take advantage of them."

He grinned. "For your information, in regard to your
new sisterhood, I've always given more than I've taken—
in every possible way."

She gasped at his audacity and turned to hide what was
certainly a vivid blush.

He couldn't stop there. "And if I, and men like me, did
not take what these women offer, how would they support
themselves? Would you not say it is our obligation to see

that their efforts do not go for naught? What do you think their lives would be like if men like me did not purchase their wares?"

"Do not try to make something noble in…in—"

He laughed. "So," he persisted, "is your continuing disapproval of me based upon my gambling and taking mistresses? Would you like me better if I seduced young maidens, instead? The delicate flowers of the ton? I know men who do just that, yet stroll through drawing rooms as though they've not betrayed a single father's trust."

"I think I would like you better if you could control your…your base impulses."

He stopped himself before he could tell her exactly how much control he had exercised to keep from ravishing *her*. Instead, a different caution was in order. "Speaking of base impulses, do I need to caution you again in regard to Lewis Munro?"

"Do not bother. I cannot think what you have against him, but I have always found him to be a *true* gentleman."

"Have you?" Geoffrey was unable to keep the chill from his voice. "He is likely biding his time while he waits for you to be unprotected and easy prey."

"Oh! You are insufferable! The poor man is mourning the loss of his wife and the baby she carried."

An icy chill settled in his gut. Charlotte had been expecting? Bloody hell! Another death on his conscience! "Where did you hear that?"

"Miss Denton told me. Mr. Munro is quite bereft. I have nothing but sympathy for the poor man."

"That sympathy is just what will leave you vulnerable when he makes his move. He has cultivated it deliberately. The unconscionable bastard is an abuser of women, and I have reason to believe he killed my sister."

Her eyes widened. "That is preposterous! Slanderous! He warned me about you."

"Did he?" Geoffrey sat forward, resting his forearms on his thighs. "How interesting. What, precisely, did he tell you?"

"That you are prone to violent tempers. That your mistresses do not make appearances for many days after one of your outbursts. He...he suggested that you abuse women and that I should be very careful around you."

"Good God, Miss Lovejoy! You would be the first to know such a thing. No woman has ever tempted me more to violence than you, and yet you are still untouched. Munro has laid his crimes at *my* door—accused me of committing *his* sins."

A frown knit tiny lines between her brows as she absorbed this news. "But why would he tell such a lie, Lord Geoffrey?"

Did she find it easier to believe Munro than him? That stung. He gave her a disgusted look and she blinked.

Another blush pinked her cheeks. "You think he wanted me to distrust you and seek *his* protection?"

"What has he to lose? And if you are gullible enough to believe him, he'd consider it a personal victory. He destroyed my sister, and he'll destroy you, as well."

Her next question surprised him. "Why have you let him live, if you believe that? If someone killed my sister, I'd do whatever was necessary to obtain justice."

"Believe me, I've done everything possible to prove a case against him, but there were no witnesses. He said he found her at the foot of the stairs, the hem of her gown torn and caught on the toe of her shoe."

"It could be true," Dianthe said uncertainly. "It could have been an accident."

He shook his head. "Charlotte was ever graceful, and never untidy. She would not have left her room wearing a torn gown, nor would she have tripped on the stairs."

"But—"

"Bloody goddamned hell! You doubt every word out of my mouth, yet believe a bounder like Munro? Is there no end to your contempt for me?"

"Lord Geoffrey, I—"

"I tried to protect her and Constance and the others, but it was not enough! It's *never* enough."

"Protect…" The single word was whispered, as if something suddenly made sense to her.

She lifted her hand as if she would reach out to him, but the coach pulled up in front of the house on Salisbury Street. He jumped out and handed her down. When she was safely on the pavement, he left her to follow as he entered the house, then he walked through and out the back to the stables. He didn't dare stay in the same house with her in his present mood.

When he hadn't been at the tavern in Whitefriars, Geoff knew he'd find Harry at his favorite brothel. While the Abbess rousted his colleague from whoever's bed he was in, Geoff waited in a private parlor. He poured himself a healthy draft of bad brandy from a decanter on a cart and went to sit in front of the small fireplace.

Perhaps he should avail himself of a prostitute while he was here. He had better find some way to purge Dianthe Lovejoy from his blood. She was all he could see. She was constantly in his thoughts.

Worse, he was making her into a *demi-vierge*—a half virgin, technically untouched, but not inexperienced. He was making her into every man's dream—the virgin-whore. A prostitute would never satisfy when all he wanted was a prudish, judgmental, stubborn, headstrong, untried little minx just becoming aware of her own sexuality. What scant honor he still possessed forbade him taking her. What remained of his soul demanded it.

Geoff had done things—horrible things, unspeakable things—in his quest for revenge. Making el-Daibul pay for the countless murders he'd committed, the women he'd kidnapped, sold and killed, had become all he knew of life these last five years. And it had served him by making him unfit for the one thing he now wanted more than life.

"Blast and be damned," he muttered into the silence.

"Exactly what I was saying," Sir Harry exclaimed as he came into the parlor, still tucking his shirt into his breeches. "'What the bloody hell can Morgan want?' I'd have made you come to me, but Bess would have none of it. She'd charge me double, she said." He laughed and poured himself a brandy before joining Geoff at the fire. "Now what is this about?"

"Hire an investigator to look into Nell's past. I want to know who she really is, where she came from and what she was doing in Vauxhall Gardens that night."

"Hell, she was your mistress last year, Morgan. Don't you know her past?"

"Never came up," he growled.

Harry laughed. "I'll bet I know what did."

Geoff could only raise an eyebrow to express his distaste for the turn the conversation had taken.

"Fine," Harry said. "I'll hire one of Bow Street's best. But why the sudden curiosity?"

"Not so sudden," he muttered. There were so damn many factors at work here—Nell's death, and the manner of her death. The resemblance between Miss Lovejoy and

Nell Brookes had always bothered him, then Miss Love-joy's calling card showing up in Nell's lodging house. He was too cynical to believe in coincidences. Nell's death had to have something to do with either Miss Lovejoy or his investigation into the abductions. Not both.

He looked up at Harry again. "I think Nell's murder has something to do with el-Daibul. I heard that she thought she had found a way to set herself up for life. Sounds more like blackmail than a wealthy lover. Could she have stumbled across information about the kidnappings and demanded hush money?"

Harry's smile faded and he grew somber. "You're right. Where would she find a wealthy lover? Someone would have known."

"As it happens, I've also learned that she told Elvina Gibson she was afraid of someone. Blackmail is a filthy business. Nell wouldn't be the first to be killed instead of being paid. I'll question Elvina more closely on that tomorrow."

Harry emitted a stream of epithets, and then shook his head. "You didn't get my message? Elvina is dead. She was found earlier tonight behind the Blue Moon. Knifed."

Geoff's mind reeled. "It has to be el-Daibul's doing. He must have a henchman nearby."

"Hmm. If you didn't get my message about Elvina, then you don't know the rest."

"El-Daibul? We've found him?"

"Not precisely." Harry gulped his brandy and took a deep breath. "We don't know where, but it looks as if he's come to us at last. He could be in England."

"Could be? You don't know?"

"Our navy intercepted a ship in the channel, just off-shore. The seamen claim they are Spanish, but I'd wager a year's pay they're Moorish. Too damn coincidental to have a ship like that off the English coast, and el-Daibul missing at the same time."

At last! Geoff's planning, plotting and baiting had yielded results. Excitement coursed through his veins. He hadn't been able to reach el-Daibul in Algiers or Tangier, but he'd finally succeeded in luring the son of a bitch to England by checkmating his every move! "Where is the ship?"

"Towed to Dover. The crew is under lock and key. Do you want me to go down and question them?"

With a couple of changes and fast horses, he could be to Dover and back within two days. "It isn't that I don't trust you, Harry, but I've come this far. I want to finish it. I'll know the questions to ask. I'll know if they're lying. And I know how to make them tell the truth."

"Christ have mercy on them. When do we leave?"

"In the morning. Get some sleep. It's going to be a long ride. Meet me at the White Lion at dawn."

"That's scarce six hours away."

"You don't have to come, Harry."

"I'll be there."

Harry was a good friend and a trusted confidant. Geoff clapped him on the shoulder on his way out the door. It should be safe to go home now. Dianthe would long since have been snoring softly in her bed. Now, for a deep sleep and an early start.

Dianthe saluted her reflection in the mirror, thinking how odd it was that the fencing blade was almost becoming a part of her—like an extension of her right arm. Now she understood the need for all the mirrors. Watching her form helped her to see her weaknesses and figure out how to improve them.

She did not like her weaknesses. She hated being wrong. And she'd been so terribly wrong. About—well, about everything. It bothered her worse that Geoffrey Morgan had been so aggravatingly right.

She *was* a snob. Oh, not in the traditional sense. No, in a much more insidious way. In a way that had allowed her to deceive herself about the fact. It wasn't that she'd ever thought herself inherently better than others—she didn't. But she *had* been judgmental, deciding a person's worthiness based on gossip and appearances. How could she have been so shallow, never looking beneath the surface, and letting others shape her opinions?

She'd lived a sheltered life, despite that her family had to scratch and save to keep body and soul together. They'd clung to their gentility with tenaciousness. Somehow, she'd believed that everyone made the choices they wanted to make. But now, when she thought of her cousin and Flora Denton, she realized they'd become courtesans because they'd had no alternative. And Dianthe was scarcely a breath away from a like fate. The same society that had touted her as a reigning beauty was now judging her based on gossip and a single unfortunate incident. The wheel of fortune had turned, and she was paying the price for her ignorance.

She moved through the exercises again and again, thinking how unfair she'd been to believe Mr. Munro over Lord Geoffrey. The latter had been nothing but good to her. And, she had to admit, patient with her insults. He'd taken her in when she was stranded, and saved her life that night on Curzon Street. To her knowledge, he'd never lied to her. Then why hadn't she believed him until he'd said those fateful revealing words? *I tried to protect her and the others, but it was not enough! It's never enough.*

No wonder he had an abhorrence of being responsible for her. No wonder he'd insisted upon the fencing lessons. Well, she'd make him proud there, at least. The best way she could repay him was to not add to his burdens. And, perhaps, to see if she could get to the bottom of Charlotte's death.

Geoff let himself into his office through the garden door and dropped his key on the desk. He was still too tense, too unsettled, by his argument with Miss Lovejoy to do anything but toss and twist in his sheets. A little physical exercise would be just the thing to relax him.

At the door to the ballroom, he paused and stepped back into the shadows. Miss Lovejoy, in her trousers and shirt, was moving through the various postures and positions, fencing with her reflection. Prescott must have taught her that method of improving one's form.

She'd tied her glorious blond hair on top of her head with a green ribbon, and he was amazed anew by how different she looked without the dark wig. As Lizette, she was exotic and seductive, but as Dianthe, she was fresh and innocent. God help him, he wanted them both.

She lunged at the mirror, her trousers tightening over her buttocks and legs in a way that left nothing to the imagination. A slow fire kindled in his loins. When she straightened and rolled her shoulders, her breasts pushed against the fluid drape of her shirt, and he gritted his teeth.

He started to retreat, but her voice, a wistful sigh, stopped him.

"Oh, you've been such an idiot! How are you going to unravel this knot?"

What knot? He glanced back into the ballroom. She was speaking to her reflection.

She sensed him there and turned to meet his eyes. He expected her to accuse him of peeping, but she smiled instead. Here was an opportunity sent from God to begin unraveling that twisted knot.

"Lord Geoffrey." Raising her blade, she saluted him, then bowed. "Have I thanked you for the fencing lessons? I'm finding them quite helpful, especially when I cannot sleep."

He gave her a wary smile. "I usually come here before going to bed."

"Shall I leave?"

"I think you need the practice more than I."

"Come, then. Teach me what you know, sir. I could benefit from your…instruction."

Something almost humorous flickered in his hazel eyes, Dianthe noticed. "Are you suggesting a match?"

"Oh, I see. You are rusty and need time to hone your skills?"

The corners of his mouth twitched. He shrugged out of his jacket and vest and tossed them over the lone chair. He went to the rack to consider his choices. He glanced back at her foil and chose one for himself.

She smiled, flexed her blade in a challenge and moved to the center of the room to face him, waiting for him to join her.

"Would you rather use blunts?" he asked.

She shook her head. "I haven't used blunts since my second lesson. Mr. Prescott says it is cheating. He says you must always fence as if your life depends upon it."

"Very well. Let me secure a button—"

"Not necessary. I trust you."

He studied her for a long moment. "You are using a button."

"I do not trust *me*."

He laughed as he came to face her. They stood in the center of a large circle drawn on the marble floor with chalk. "Mr. Prescott has been teaching you the Spanish Mysterious Circle method?"

"He says it is the quickest route to perfection."

Morgan nodded and stretched his arms over his head to loosen his muscles. Coming back to the *en garde* position, he nodded that he was ready. "*Veney?* A practice bout to three? Shall we see what my money has bought me?"

She grinned and returned his nod. They crossed swords and she quickly pressed her button to his heart. "Hit," she called. She stepped back and bowed, knowing she'd caught him completely off guard.

He laughed and spread his arms. "Your point, Miss Lovejoy. I'll be better prepared next time."

She slashed her blade to the side flamboyantly. "Do not underestimate me, Lord Morgan."

"What happened to Lord Geoffrey?"

She shrugged, circling him. "You are the one insisting upon formality. Have I not invited you to use my given name? I think you prefer the formality to keep distance between us. Your choice, sir."

They crossed swords again and this time Lord Geoffrey was ready. He parried her thrusts and scored a hit by slapping her upper arm with the side of his blade. "Hit," he called.

"Aye," she conceded, stepping back.

"I am bound to say, *Dianthe,* that you exceed my expectations."

Her heart skipped a beat and she warmed with pleasure. She loved the sound of her name on his lips—drawled with a hint of softness. A cautious heat crept through her.

The next encounter forced her to pay closer attention.

She managed to hold him off nearly three minutes before he scored a hit. When she conceded with an "aye" and a bow, he smiled.

"Enough practice, Dianthe? Are you ready for a competitive match?"

A few wisps and curls had escaped her ribbon, and she blew them out of her eyes. "To five." She nodded. "*En garde,* Geoffrey."

His mouth curved in a delicious smile as he lifted his sword to the *garde* position. He was obviously pleased that she'd used his name. After a strenuous exchange of blows, Geoffrey traversed and, before she could turn to face him, she felt a tug at the top of her head. Her hair tumbled down around her shoulders and she spun about to find her green ribbon dangling from the point of his foil.

She grinned, knowing the degree of skill that had required. She liked this playful side of him. She'd seen flashes of it before, but she'd managed to crush it rather quickly. "Your point," she conceded.

They crossed swords and moved into the next bout quickly. She focused on his rhythms and began to anticipate his moves, pleased to see the look of surprise and approval on his face. She feinted to the left, then slipped her sword under his, pressed the button to his neck and moved close to his chest to deny him an opening.

"Hit," she panted.

He froze, obviously unwilling to risk injury, but his eyes shifted to meet hers. They were filled with something akin to pride. "Aye," he acknowledged.

But Dianthe did not disengage at the concession. She smiled and slid the button down the side of his neck to the bottom of his cravat. Very carefully, she pushed the button between his neck and the fabric. At last he flinched.

"Tsk-tsk, Geoffrey. Don't breathe yet. I have never done this before." With an upward slicing motion, and just missing his earlobe, she cut the silk folds, and the cravat slipped to the marble tiles.

His chest started to rumble and she realized he was trying to contain his laughter. She grinned and stepped back before he could retaliate.

"Your point," he acknowledged. "One each." He saluted her and resumed the *en garde* position.

She crossed his sword and they were engaged. She realized he had merely been amusing himself with her when he applied himself to the attack. It was all she could do to defend herself, parrying his thrusts, but he gave her no opening for a riposte.

He lunged in a lightning move, his sword drawn back and his left hand extended toward her to stop her advance into his blade. As it was, the foil's point dimpled the skin at the V of her shirt. Very slowly, he lowered his foil, flicking the buttons off her shirt one by one. The fabric gaped, but the way it was tightly tucked into her trousers kept it in place.

Heat washed through her, but she resisted the impulse to look down to see if she was still decent. Instead, she looked up, into Geoffrey's eyes. His expression was guarded, as if he were waiting for some reaction from her. Given their prior relationship, he would be expecting anger, indignation or an accusation. Instead, taking heed from Miss Osgood's lecture on a woman's power, Dianthe ran her tongue over her lips and smiled. Something glimmered in his eyes, and she knew she'd scored a hit of her own.

"Will you call it?" she asked, reminding him of his privilege.

"Hit," he muttered, his voice thick with emotion.

"Aye," she replied, agreeing to his claim. He was going to kiss her. He was leaning toward her, his head tilting ever so slightly to cover her mouth. She lifted her chin to meet him halfway.

He blinked and shook his head as if he'd forgotten himself, then stepped back into *en garde* position.

Oh, shame! *She* wanted *him* more than he wanted her. From the night he'd brought her to Salisbury Street, she'd fought her feelings, tried to keep distance between them, afraid of what loving a man like Geoffrey Morgan would do to her reputation and marriage prospects. She'd only wanted to find Nell's killer and regain her place in society. Now she didn't care about society. It was Morgan's good opinion she wanted. Reputation and eligibility were nothing balanced against a moment in his arms.

Trying to forget her gaping shirt, she raised her foil and traversed to the left. Geoffrey followed, keeping in step with her. After exchanging a few blows with their blades, she took the initiative to score a hit, and lunged. The button at the tip of her foil pressed into his navel. He spread his arms wide in a gesture of surrender.

Peeved, instead of calling the hit, she drew her foil downward, cutting the fastening of his trousers. He scarcely breathed. She used the button to lift a corner of his shirttails out of the waistband. Only then did she step back and say, "Hit, Geoffrey."

He cleared his throat. "Aye. Match point?" he asked, his sword angled toward the floor.

She brought her blade up, in position, and concentrated on his face, looking for a blink, a shift in his gaze, anything that would betray that he was preparing to advance on her. *Concentration, calm, detachment.* But, in the end, it did not matter. Nothing of Geoffrey's icy calm betrayed his intentions. After a moment of unnerving stillness, he lunged and flicked his unprotected point upward, slicing the tapes of her waistband. He stepped back, as lithe as a panther, his blade back to *garde,* making it clear he would not call the hit.

She parried with a blow against his blade and he executed a blinding riposte, sliding his foil the length of hers as he continued his advance, causing her arm to come up until their hilts locked. At that exact moment, his chest landed against hers and he grabbed the wrist of her sword arm, rendering her helpless.

With her arms upraised, her chest pressed to his, he looked down at her and said, "I can think of quicker ways to do this, Dianthe."

Was he waiting for her to demur? She'd wanted this, invited it. But could she go through with it? There was only one way she'd ever find out. She came up on her toes and placed her lips against his, waiting.

With a hungry growl, he released her wrist, dropped his sword and pulled her tightly against his chest to deepen the kiss. Her foil slipped from her hand and clattered to the floor as she wrapped her arms around his neck. The heat of his mouth, the greedy demand of his tongue, the stroking of his large hands on her back brought her to a fever pitch.

She was breathless with yearning, straining to feel his body pressed to hers. All the days of denial and resistance were swept away in that flood of desire. She wanted more. She needed more.

Chapter Thirteen

A deep shudder passed through Geoffrey and he loosened his hold on her. "Dianthe," he whispered. "Dianthe. I feared this would happen if I ever said your name."

He was right. Without the defense of formality, all their carefully erected walls were crumbling. But she didn't care. She wanted more of the wild yearning he awoke in her.

"I'm not one of your society fops," he warned in a low voice. "You cannot play with me like this and think I will take it in good grace. Do not expect nobility from me, Dianthe. You know me for the libertine I am. I know right from wrong, but I don't give a damn."

She closed her eyes and took a deep breath. "Whatever this is, it doesn't feel wrong."

He tangled his fingers in her hair and cupped her head, bringing her mouth up to his. "Reckless Dianthe, to tempt me so," he whispered against her lips.

"It may be that I am a libertine, too." She smiled.

He lifted her off her feet and carried her up the stairs. Her room! It would have to be her room. Giles and Hanson would never open that door uninvited. He kicked her door closed behind them before carrying her to the edge of her bed and setting her on her feet.

He tugged at her shirttails, freeing them from the snug fit of her trousers. With nothing restraining it, the front of her shirt fell completely open and he skimmed it over her shoulders. God save him! No stays. No chemise. Just long tendrils of liquid gold tumbling over her breasts and curling around her firmed nipples. Her breasts were perfect for her slender frame, full, lush and in proportion to her figure. His hand shook, actually *shook,* as he cupped one breast and bent to nibble the beckoning tip. "Beautiful," he sighed.

She emitted a tiny gasp and made a feeble effort to cover herself with her hands. "Geoffrey! I cannot—"

"I can," he murmured against the soft swell. "You needn't do a thing."

She dropped her hands, surrendering to him with a small groan. God! She was so fresh. So ingenuous. All that he'd hoped for. More than he deserved. He fumbled with his own buttons and pushed his shirt away, desperate to feel the heat of her skin against his. Her fingers, featherlight, brushed over him—teasing, enticing, arousing. He doubted she even knew what her touch was doing to him.

He curled his fingers over her waist, easing the trousers and drawers over the soft curve of her hips and down her firm thighs and calves. Thank God the Hessian boots he'd ordered for her had not arrived. He had only to kneel and slip off her buckle shoes to complete his removal of her trousers.

"Geoffrey," she sighed, placing one hand on the top of his head to keep her unsteady balance. A virginal blush covered her entire body and he couldn't imagine what she must be thinking. Geoff prayed fear was not a part of it.

"I won't hurt you, Dianthe." He came up on his knees and kissed her belly. "If you trust nothing else, trust that."

She made a sound in the back of her throat and chill bumps rose on her flesh. "None of this hurts, Geoffrey. 'Tis just so…so brazen."

If she kept saying his name like that, he'd lose what self-control he had left. "You are perfection," he whispered, wanting to reassure her. Moving lower, he kissed the curly thatch of nether hair, reveling in the scent, taste and texture of her.

Women were exotic creatures, to be cherished, respected and appreciated for what they were. For him, making love was not mere copulation. Not just a steady mindless drive to orgasm. It was a journey, full of discovery, subtleties, experimentation and shared delight. And with Dianthe, it was more. His senses were heightened, attuned to hers. He was experiencing the act through her. He was lost in her, helpless to resist her slightest wish, driven and directed by her sighs, her moans, her gasps.

He held her hips steady as he deepened his kiss, moving subtly lower. She swayed, and he knew her knees were about to give way. He stood quickly and caught her, laying her back on the plush pillows and cool velvet counterpane. Her eyes had deepened to a midnight hue and her cheeks were flushed with passion. She was Venus on the verge. And she was reaching out to him.

Heel to toe, he pried his boots off and kicked them away. He finished the job of unfastening his trousers that Dianthe had begun in the ballroom, and rid himself of those, too. Finally naked, he joined her on the bed.

He needed to slow this down, to be certain she was ready, that she had shed any trace of virginal reticence and had no reservations about going forward. He had to know it was him that she wanted, and that she hadn't just been caught up in a moment of madness.

He nibbled her earlobe, then kissed his way to the hollow of her throat. She smelled of lilies and musk, both innocent and luxuriant. She made a sound that was half moan, half sigh, and reached for him.

"Shh," he whispered. "Easy, Dianthe. I have plans for you. Things I've dreamed of doing to you since the day I met you. Do not speak. Do not think. Only feel. And trust that I will not hurt you."

She settled back against the pillows and a surge of possessiveness swept through him. He had a sudden desire to mark her as his. He found the tender dip of her collarbone and kissed her there, applying gentle suction. She made a mewling sound that tickled along his nerve endings, and he lifted his head to look at her.

Long dark lashes fanned against her flushed cheeks, and her teeth bit into her lower lip as if to prevent an outcry. She was lost in a world of sensory pleasure, aware only of him and what he was doing to her. The edges of the little love bite he'd left on her collarbone blurred into the fevered flush of her skin, and he smiled with satisfaction before moving lower.

Her breasts, aroused and peaked with firm rosy nipples, were like berries ripe and ready for plucking. He nipped at one, savoring it. The firm beaded texture teased his tongue and he cherished first one and then the other until her sighs deepened to moans. Ah, he couldn't leave them. They were too enticing, too responsive, to abandon yet. But Dianthe's passion was growing apace and she would demand more before long. He continued his kisses, increasing the pressure as he slipped his hand downward and found the small bundle of nerves he had so recently been denied.

One tentative touch with the soft pad of his thumb sent Dianthe into trembling gasps. She clutched at his shoulders, her fingernails biting into his flesh. And now she'd left her mark on *him.* Her reaction had been just what he'd wanted. All he'd hoped for.

When she'd caught her breath and her trembling ceased, he pushed his hand lower, finding the entrance of her passage. Ah, sweet Jesus! She was hot and slick—responsive beyond his dreams. She shuddered with shock when he probed the shallow entry with one finger.

He clenched his jaw, drawing on his reserves for whatever strength he could still find. This was Dianthe's initiation. Her attitude toward the sensual arts was dependent upon what he did tonight, and he wouldn't rush, and risk ruining her or losing her trust. He couldn't. She'd become far too important to him. This was his gift to her—the awakening of her sensuality.

He eased his finger out, then back in, beginning a rhythmic stroking, and drew forth a sweet whimpering. Instinctively, she lifted one knee to give him better access, then began moving in concert with his stroking. She was Aphrodite, Venus and Diana. She was meant for making love.

Dianthe's breathing grew rapid and shallow as she neared her completion. The end was sudden and shattering. She arched, clutching the counterpane, with her fists and crying out *"Geoffrey...!"* and *"Yes. Yes. Yes."*

As her inner muscles closed around his fingers, hunger hammered in his brain, thundered through his blood, threatened to ruin everything by inciting a blinding urge to bury himself inside her and find his own satisfaction. He'd never experienced passion so intense before. Nor would he likely ever again.

He moved upward, gathering Dianthe into his arms,

stroking the curve of her back, smoothing her hair out of her eyes, kissing away her tears of release, murmuring praise and endearments. She clung to him as her ragged breathing evened and she surrendered to sleep. And that was enough.

The few scruples he had left had prevented him from taking her virginity and thereby her future. His pride would not allow it. But never again would he lie with Dianthe without taking her in full. That would surely drive him mad.

"Lost them *all,* miss?" Giles frowned as he looked down at the shirt in Dianthe's hand.

"No, not lost. They…they came off." She was still feeling lazy and luxurious from the night before, and she couldn't seem to make her brain work. "I need to sew them back on. Please make my excuses to Mr. Prescott and tell him I shall be prepared for our lesson tomorrow."

"I see," Giles said, clearly not "seeing" at all.

Fearing she would blush, she struggled to set her mind on anything at all besides the events of last night. Giles would certainly suspect something, if he didn't already. She glanced at the ormolu clock on the narrow sideboard in the small sitting room. "But I will see Miss Osgood when she arrives. Please do not bother announcing her. Just send her in."

"Yes, miss." He picked up her luncheon tray and made his way to the door.

She cleared her throat. "Oh, Giles? Have you seen Lord Geoffrey today?"

"Yes, miss."

Curse the taciturn man! Would he volunteer nothing? "Is he about?"

"No, miss."

"Did he say when he'd be back?"

"Not until tomorrow evening, miss."

"He left town?" Did he regret the night before so much that he'd fled?

"At dawn, miss." Giles sighed, as if realizing that he would have to volunteer information if he did not want to be here all day. "On business, he said."

Or was he simply trying to avoid her? Dianthe looked down at her fencing shirt and heard the soft click of the door as Giles closed it behind him. She attacked the shirt with needle and thread as she tried to sort out the jumble in her mind.

She'd woken to find herself alone beneath the velvet counterpane. She was country bred, had spent her first twenty years observing animal husbandry, and knew enough about the physical aspects of mating to know that she was still a virgin. Despite the breathtaking things he had done to her last night, Geoffrey Morgan had left her intact.

Had she been so dreadful as to send him running out of town? Lord! Was he laughing at her? Appalled by her na-iveté? *"Gauche,"* he'd told Miss Osgood. "Daunting." Had he been so disgusted that he could not even face her?

Oh, but Dianthe should have known. He'd told her, warned her several times. Virgins were a novelty, but not worth the trouble. They soon grew tedious, he'd said, and experience was far more alluring. That even a homely woman willing to put puritanical morals aside was more seductive, more attractive to a man than a reigning beauty. Like she had been.

She put down her sewing and went to look at her reflection in the mirror over the sideboard. She appeared much the same as always, but her newly critical eye saw more this time. She noted a prim little pinch between her eyes, a slightly haughty lift to her chin, a studied composure that betrayed little of what was going on beneath the surface— all the things she'd been told were ladylike and desirable in the ton. Pleasant. That was it. She was pleasant looking. But there was nothing about her that spoke of acceptance or warmth or welcome. High-minded and judgmental, Geoffrey had called her.

But when she'd been Lizette, she'd put on a more flirtatious personality. She'd tried to look open and approachable, because she'd needed to inspire confidences. And men, attractive, powerful men like Lockwood, who'd never even noticed her at soirees and balls, were drawn to her. Inspired to flirt with her and even suggest alliances, however unsuitable.

Geoffrey's words when she'd asked what men found attractive in courtesans came back to her in a rush. *Freedom to be themselves. Release. Peace, if only for a moment. Pleasure beyond description. Gratification without guilt. Acceptance without judgment. Comfort in a cold world. Give it, and a man is your slave. Withhold it, and he becomes surly and resentful.*

Now she understood. A proper sort of woman, even a wife, would not have permitted the liberties she'd allowed Geoffrey last night. And would never reciprocate. Was that what he wanted from women? From her?

The sitting room door opened and Miss Osgood entered, divesting herself of her bonnet and gloves. "*Bonjour,* Miss Deauville. Mr. Giles said you were expecting me."

Dianthe turned from the mirror, still reeling from her revelations. "Miss Osgood, I must learn everything you can possibly teach me, and as quickly as possible."

"Heavens! I thought you were somewhat reluctant."

"Not any longer. I want to know all."

Miss Osgood laughed and sat on the sofa opposite Dianthe's chair, waiting for Dianthe to join her. "Perhaps you should tell me what you'd most like to know, and we can start from there."

She sat, took a deep breath and folded her hands in her lap. "I would most like to know how to make a man wild with desire."

"You certainly know a part of that," Miss Osgood said with an arched eyebrow. "You've captured the attention of Lord Geoffrey."

"I fear that was…accidental. We were thrown together by circumstances. Our relationship just…well, happened. I think it surprised us both."

"Lord Geoffrey would not take you to his bed just because you were convenient. But I gather you mean that he did not woo you, or court your favors."

Dianthe looked down at her folded hands. "No. I mean I think it was entirely unintentional. If he thought I was desirable, why would he have hired you to tutor me?"

"My dear," Miss Osgood said, leaning forward to touch the little bruise on Dianthe's collarbone, "this is quite intentional. He put that there so that others would know you belong to him. And he hired me to instruct you in regard to what is expected from a woman in your position. He would not throw his money away on lessons if he did not intend to keep you around for a bit."

She looked Miss Osgood in the eye and confessed, "I have been most recently connected to the ton. An unfortunate incident has…has ruined my prospects. I fear I know little more than what any young lady of similar background would know. Which is to say, nothing."

Miss Osgood laughed so hard she had to dab at her eyes

with a corner of her handkerchief. "Oh, but this is rich! To think that Geoffrey Morgan has been brought down by a debutante! Well, no wonder then that you know so little. But do you know anyone who has been accused of 'very fast behavior'?" She waited while Dianthe nodded. "Well, that is what I intend to teach you. Very fast behavior."

"Men find that attractive?"

"Very, because he does not intend to marry you. You must learn to balance it. You must value yourself or a man will not. You must make promises with your eyes and body, but deny the prize until you have reached agreement as to your compensation. *Then* you will be able to drive a man wild with desire."

"Yes! How do I do *that?*"

"Shed all your former conceptions of what constitutes acceptable behavior. You must learn how to use your gifts shamelessly. Men are really quite easily pleased. They want only to be accepted and encouraged in their pleasures. Encouraged, Miss Deauville. Think of that. If you are more than merely willing, they will adore you for it. If you can take the initiative, so much the better.

"Come," she said, grasping Dianthe's hand and leading her to the mirror. "Look at that woman."

Dianthe saw only what she always saw. She was afraid Miss Osgood's subtleties were lost on her. She gave the woman in the mirror a curious look.

"Your chin is too high. Lower it so that you will not look haughty and unapproachable."

She did, but Miss Osgood then lifted her chin a fraction with her finger. "Not so low that you look like a shy school-girl. Directly, as one would look at an equal. Frank. Un-afraid. Confident. Sure of your own worth."

Ah, Dianthe saw the difference.

"Now, moisten your lips and give a tiny smile. Say, 'I am the most desirable woman in the world. If I choose, I can give more pleasure than a man could bear.' And, 'I can please a man in bed better than anyone ever has.'"

Dianthe coughed. "Can you mean it?"

"But of course. And you must say it as if *you* believe it. You must think it, live it in your mind, every time you meet a man. Add to it. I promise if you do, men will follow you wherever you go. And Lord Geoffrey will be your most devoted servant."

Somehow, she doubted that. Nevertheless, she gave herself a little smile in the mirror, licked her lips, and said, "I am the most desirable woman in this room. I can give a man more pleasure than he could bear. I am Venus, Aphrodite and Athena. I am every man's desire."

"Well done! Say it each time you pass a mirror until it is natural and a part of you. Now come, Miss Deauville. I think I should teach you a little about the interesting physiology of men, and what they like. I have brought some diagrams. We shall discuss technique tomorrow."

Stepping down from her hired carriage in front of Thackery's, Dianthe smoothed her emerald-green gown, the most recent in the deliveries from Madame LaFehr's shop. She had followed Miss Osgood's advice and had not worn jewelry that would call attention away from her breasts, which Miss Osgood called, "Adequate, and actually quite charming." But the pronouncement had left her feeling altogether *in*adequate. Scarcely an eighth of an inch of black lace kept her aureoles hidden.

Painfully aware that she was alone and unprotected, she opened her black lace fan and carried it in front of her, as if she were too warm, even in the chill of evening. Now that the doorman knew her, he merely nodded and held the door as she entered. She did not stop to view the main salon, but hurried up the steps to the mezzanine, where she knew she'd find the ladies of the demimonde.

Almost the moment she entered, Miss Tucker spied her and separated herself from a group of raucous men to come to her side. "Have you heard?"

"I've only arrived," she said, marking the woman's agitation. "Heard what?"

"Elvina Gibson has been murdered!"

Everything inside Dianthe stilled. What horrible insidious forces were working in the demimonde? How could two popular courtesans be killed within a few weeks of each other? It *had* to be more than coincidence. Had Elvina been murdered for what Nell had told her? Had she told anyone else?

"Miss Deauville?" Miss Tucker took her arm. "Are you unwell? You've gone quite pale."

"*Je m'*… Two murders in the same circle. It is too… terrible."

"Quite," Miss Tucker agreed. "Why, I'd just had the nicest visit with Elvina earlier yesterday."

"*Oui?* And she suspected nothing?"

"She did not seem unduly concerned about anything. But, now that I think of it, she was a little flighty—as if she could not concentrate."

Dianthe took a deep breath and lowered her voice. "Miss Tucker, 'ave the police interviewed you?"

The woman smiled. "Of course not, Miss Deauville. And I do not suppose they will. They will ask questions of whoever found her, the proprietor of the Blue Moon and anyone else who might have been around at the time."

"Can you think of something—anything at all—that

Miss Gibson might 'ave said that would indicate a secret? Or a fear that something might 'appen to 'er?"

"Goodness, Miss Deauville, you are quite earnest. Did you know Miss Gibson well?"

"Not at all," she admitted. "But if the police will not ask, we must tell them."

"Thank you, my dear. But I do not have conversations with police or runners. Disaster always follows."

And that was the reason courtesans and prostitutes were such easy prey for unscrupulous men. Dianthe sighed. "Then tell me, Miss Tucker, and I shall tell Lord Morgan. 'E shall converse with the authorities. But we simply cannot do nothing."

"You are quite passionate about this, Miss Deauville."

"Stop him…" Nell had said. Dianthe fought back the horror of that night. She couldn't give in to it now. *"La justice tout est moi,* Miss Tucker."

The woman's demeanor changed just then and she shrugged indifferently. "Everything to you, eh? Very well. If I should learn anything, I shall tell you at once." She was staring at a point over Dianthe's left shoulder.

She smiled and turned, thinking the woman had spotted Lord Geoffrey. Unfortunately, it was Mr. Munro who approached.

"Ladies," he acknowledged. "Where is Geoff this evening, Miss Deauville? He is usually hovering somewhere around, but I do not see him."

Dianthe tried to keep from looking disappointed, then hesitated, deciding it would not be wise to admit she was alone. "Temporarily engaged elsewhere. I expect that 'e will be along presently."

"Ah, well, he can have no objection if I keep you busy at the tables whilst you wait." He took her arm and led her toward the hazard table, leaving a bewildered looking Miss Tucker in his wake.

Remembering Geoffrey's suspicions of his brother-in-law, Dianthe wondered if they could be true. What harm could a little gentle questioning do? She'd begin with a mixture of ignorance and guilelessness. "Mr. Munro, Miss Denton tells me that you are a widower. Then Lord Geoffrey said you were 'is former brother-in-law. Were you married to Lord Geoffrey's sister?"

He sighed deeply and squeezed her hand on his arm. "Yes. Dear Charlotte. How I miss her."

"Lord Geoffrey never speaks of it."

"Likely because he was not present when it happened. Yes, he had gone off on some business or another. I recall that she sent for him, but he never came. Mail was sporadic, you see. Perhaps he never got her letter."

Or got it too late? "Then she'd been ill?"

There was a long pause, as if Munro was deciding what to tell her. "She'd been having fainting spells, as a result of her delicate condition. She'd never been a particularly graceful girl in the best of circumstances."

Not what Geoffrey had said. "An accident, *oui?*"

Munro hung his head dramatically. "Tragic. Devastating. I was the first to find her. I doubt I shall ever recover—finding her there, at the bottom of the stairs. Awful."

"Oh, dear. You were not there at the time?"

He shook his head. "I was in my library, tending to correspondence. I heard her scream, and then the tumble."

"Oh, you poor man! Were there no servants about?"

"Alas, no. 'Twas the middle of the day. Everyone was engaged in their work. She'd been resting in her room and was coming down to find me." He glanced sideways and

Dianthe caught something speculative in his expression. He was trying to gauge her reaction.

"And you 'ave not remarried," she sighed. "You must be very lonely, Mr. Munro."

"Lonely, indeed, my dear. That is why I come out so often. Looking for companionship. Looking to bury my sorrows, if only for a moment."

Heavens! Was she supposed to offer herself? The man was using his wife's death shamelessly. "I sincerely 'ope you will find everything you deserve, Mr. Munro."

He stopped in the center of the room and gave her a puzzled look. There was a hard glint in his eyes now.

He reached out to touch the little bruise—love bite, Miss Osgood had called it—and he gave her a salacious smile. She loathed this part of her masquerade. That men— virtual strangers—felt free to touch her without her consent. It was a violation of her person and an assumption of familiarity. They assumed consent by her mere presence.

"As Lord Geoffrey is not here, Miss Deauville, would you consider coming upstairs with me for a short period? You will be well compensated."

So he'd decided to make it a business transaction? "*Mais non,* Mr. Munro. Lord Geoffrey 'as required that I keep myself only for 'im. I could not dishonor 'im so."

"I'd never tell, Miss Deauville. And you will have a chance to make a tidy little sum on the side."

"Thank you for the compliment, sir, but no."

"I will be brief," he said, unable to disguise the anger in his voice. His hand tightened on her arm, the fingers biting into her flesh. That small gesture told her all she needed to know about Munro's true nature. He was not to be trusted.

She glanced around the room for anyone who could

help her. Alas, only Senor Ramirez, who had been watching them from nearby, caught her eye and came forward. "Munro, Miss Deauville," he said, bowing sharply at the waist. "Are you sporting tonight?"

A chill went up her spine. She knew he hadn't meant games of chance.

"We are going upstairs, Ramirez. Care to join us? Miss Deauville, being French, will surely know how to keep us amused."

"I am loath to refuse such a tempting offer, but…" Ramirez left the thought dangling and gave a continental shrug. "So you are no longer Morgan's woman?"

"I am, but Mr. Munro—" Her protest fell on deaf ears as Munro pulled her out of the salon to the mezzanine, with Senor Ramirez following. Munro intended to take her, use her, regardless of her refusal! She glanced around, her desperation rising, and saw Lord Lockwood coming up the stairs. Munro, she suspected, did not want a scene any more than she did, and she called to him.

"There you are, Lord Lockwood! I thought you 'ad forgot your promise."

It took him only a fraction of a second to understand her predicament. He came to them and nodded to her companions while disengaging Munro's hold on her. "How could I ever forget, Miss Deauville?"

"*Pardonnez-moi, Messieurs,* but I 'ave a previous commitment."

As Lord Reginald led her away, he asked, "What was that about?"

"Could you escort me downstairs and stand with me until a coach is summoned?" She bit her tongue when she realized she had forgotten her French accent in her eagerness to escape Mr. Munro.

"Where's Morgan?"

"'E is out of town at the moment."

"Spare me the accent, Miss Deauville. I know you are not French. I haven't the faintest notion what you are up to but be warned. Morgan is not easy to deceive, and will not like being played for a fool. And men like Munro and his foreign friend will look for opportunities to get you alone." Lord Lockwood inclined his head toward that infernal love bite on her collarbone. "As you plainly have discovered."

She was speechless as he hurried her down the stairs and out to the street. He sent the doorman to hail a coach, and when they were alone again, she asked, "What are you going to do?"

"Do? Why, nothing. Unless your purpose is to bilk Morgan or the others."

"I am not a…bilker, Lord Lockwood. And I am not playing Lord Geoffrey for a fool."

"See that you don't. That would be an unwise endeavor. I would not like to think what he would do to you."

"He knows what I am about."

The coach arrived and Lord Lockwood handed her up and slammed the door. "Stay on Morgan's good side, Miss Deauville. He has had enough trouble with women," he called after her.

Chapter Fourteen

Geoff swung his leg over the saddle and urged his horse to speed, leaving a disgruntled Harry Richardson to stare after him. He was well aware that Harry was not pleased, but someone had to stay in Dover and clean up the mess. They'd found no answers here—only more questions, a hard hunch and a tight ball of anxiety gnawing at Geoff's innards.

By the time he and Harry arrived in Dover yesterday to question the crew of the captured ship, the insurrection was over. To a man, the prisoners had been killed and buried mere hours before. The commander of the garrison claimed that a simple misunderstanding in language had caused the riot, but from the description of events, Geoff surmised it had been more like suicide.

He'd asked to see the prisoners' effects and board the captured ship. The commander reported that the crew had thrown many items overboard before surrendering, rather than have them confiscated. Harry searched the vessel with his meticulous attention to detail and reported the results. Any item of a personal nature—letters, books, diaries, religious items and currency—were gone. There was nothing left to identify the origin or nationality of the ship. They'd sailed under a Spanish flag, but that was easy enough to come by.

Geoff and Harry agreed that such odd circumstances could easily mean that the vessel was a spy ship. The commander had shrugged indifferently and concluded that they'd never know.

But there was one thing that could betray the crew, even in death. Geoff demanded the soldiers exhume the prisoners' bodies. To a man, they'd been circumcised. Lacking any known band of Jewish pirates, that left only one possibility.

"Berbers," Harry had muttered.

But el-Daibul's body hadn't been among them. There was no trace of his distinctive long beard, the red-and-white checked *kufiyah* and the slash above the left eyebrow that Geoff had made years ago.

The mere possibility that el-Daibul could be somewhere close at hand made his skin crawl. Geoff needed to get back to London, because if he'd come for Geoff, that's where he'd be. But Geoff had learned from bitter experience that el-Daibul would not be satisfied with killing him. First he'd kill anyone Geoff loved, destroy anything that gave him pleasure. And that meant he had to stop el-Daibul before he found and destroyed Dianthe.

He should have known better than to love her. Ruin always followed. It was no protection for her that he'd managed to keep from taking her virginity. He hadn't left any part of her undiscovered to his touch, to his tongue, to all his senses. He'd been without conscience in the way he'd utterly seduced her, used her to slake his need for something good and untouched. *For something he could hold in his heart and memory, if not his arms.* Knowing her like that, and not having her in full, had been his punishment.

But hardest of all, almost impossible—he'd have to stand by when Dianthe was finally acquitted of the murder charge, and watch while she found a proper husband, the sort she'd always wanted. He'd have to see her belonging to, *possessed* by, another man.

He'd have to leave town to keep from doing murder.

Dianthe had been so caught up in her investigation and Morgan's insistence on fencing lessons, courtesan lessons, fittings and evenings spent traipsing about London that she forgot entirely about contacting Mr. Renquist and Madame Marie. They would be beside themselves by now.

She opened the shop door to La Meilleure Robe and winced as the little bell rang. She glanced at her disguise in the foyer looking glass as she tugged her gloves off and removed her bonnet.

"I am the most desirable woman in this room," she recited by rote. "If I choose, I can give more pleasure than a man could bear. I am Salome, Delilah and Helen of Troy."

She turned around to find Madame Marie behind her, a look of pure astonishment on her face. "Salome?" the dressmaker asked as she closed the distance and pulled Dianthe into her arms, nearly weeping with relief. "Oh, *chère!* François 'as been looking for you for days! We thought…we feared you were in trouble and could not come to us. Where 'ave you been?" She dragged Dianthe to the back sitting room and closed the door.

"I am so sorry, *Madame,*" Dianthe began, a rush of guilt sweeping over her. "I've been busy investigating. I didn't think Mr. Renquist would have much to report. Has McHugh come to fetch me?"

"Mais non, chère." Marie turned and went back to the door. "Wait 'ere while I fetch François. 'E will be so relieved to see you."

Tears welled in Dianthe's eyes and she wiped at them impatiently. She was not a schoolgirl. She should be strong in the face of adversity, and she was so tired of intrigue and drama.

Geoffrey. She sighed. When had she started to care what he thought? She suspected it was sometime after the incident on Curzon Street. He'd always seemed so strong, so invulnerable, that she'd thought he hadn't any feelings at all. But when he'd blurted that he couldn't be trusted to protect her, she finally saw the depth of his emotions—a pain so deep that he'd shut everyone and everything out.

Mr. Renquist hurried into the dressing room and closed the door. "Marie is with a client. She will be along in a moment. Where have you been, Miss Lovejoy? What the deuce have you been up to?"

"It would be better if you didn't know that, sir," she said. "But please believe that I've been quite safe. I am sorry I haven't been able to contact you before, but—"

"Precisely why you must tell me now how to reach you when your sister arrives. We cannot have you floating about London with no means to find you."

"Afton is *enceinte.* McHugh will likely come alone."

"All the more reason to be able to find you. He is not a patient man. And there are *things* that could happen to an innocent girl."

She sank into a chair and shook her head. "I promised I would not divulge my whereabouts, Mr. Renquist. I could arrange to meet you each day, if you wish, but I simply cannot tell you where I am staying."

Mr. Renquist's mouth tightened to a thin line. "Every day, Miss Lovejoy?"

She nodded.

He looked far from satisfied when he sat on the little fitting stool and regarded her somberly. "I have not had much success in the investigation, Miss Lovejoy. Everyone is suddenly close-mouthed about it. Little bits and pieces show up, but they all seem to incriminate you."

"You've heard that they found my calling card amongst Miss Brookes's effects?"

He nodded. "Where were you night before last?"

Gambling, then in Geoffrey's arms. "Why, sir? Is something wrong?"

"Another courtesan was killed. A woman by the name of Elvina Gibson. Would you know anything about that?"

"I heard about it. Do you think it has anything to do with Nell?"

He nodded. "She'd been asking questions. And she was the last to admit having a conversation with Nell."

Dianthe suddenly remembered that Miss Denton had known about Elvina's conversation with her cousin. "Have you interviewed Miss Denton, the woman from the funeral?"

"I haven't been able to find her."

"Something isn't right." Dianthe frowned. "Nell and Flora were best of friends. If Elvina was killed after talking to Nell, and Flora talked to Elvina, then Flora may be next. You must find her, Mr. Renquist, and warn her to leave town until this is over."

"Advice we've all tried to give *you,* Miss Lovejoy. It seems to me you know more than you should about the demimonde. And last time we were together, you were asking me questions about…" His eyes grew round and his eyebrows shot up. "Say you are not involved with those people."

"None of them know who I am. None but Flora, and she will not tell."

"Good God!" he exclaimed. "Have you gone mad? How will you ever explain this to your sister? To your suitors?" He groaned. "To McHugh."

"'Twas that or Newgate. They will not judge me, sir."

"Marie and I—"

"For the last time, Mr. Renquist, I will not compromise anyone I care about, nor will I taint them with scandal or put them in conflict with their superiors. And that is an end to the subject."

He gave her a disgruntled look but took a different direction. "Our leads regarding Nell have revealed nothing. I will locate Miss Denton, and meantime I could turn my attention to Elvina Gibson. There may be something in her background or in her last days that will give us a clue if the two deaths are linked."

Dianthe sighed, glad she would not have to argue further. One tiny niggling thought had been troubling her since her conversation with Mr. Munro. "Have you also investigated Lord Geoffrey Morgan?"

"Morgan? Yes. I wondered if he plays into this. He was in Vauxhall Gardens when you discovered Nell. He was at her funeral. And I learned Nell had been his mistress."

She had always known they had been involved but she hadn't stopped to consider how that affected her. Geoffrey and…her cousin? Had he made love to Dianthe because he missed Nell? Could she bear to be a pale substitute in his eyes? But they'd been at odds of late. Miss Denton had said so. Lockwood, Munro and Mr. Renquist had all warned her of Morgan's temper.

"Do you think he is the murderer?"

"I know he's capable of it. I've had dealings with Morgan before—a case of Lady Annica's several years ago. He's a dangerous man, and involved in some very nefarious schemes. Anyone with a care to their life would do well to avoid him."

"Did you turn up anything specific?"

"Only that he's known for his coldness and detachment. And that he has a long fuse before he snaps. He's never been known to harm a woman, but that does not mean he is not somehow involved."

"I see," she said, a headache beginning to hammer at her temples. She couldn't believe it, but caution and good sense warned her to be wary.

"Why should it matter to you, Miss Lovejoy? You have nothing to do with Lord Morgan."

She looked down and fumbled with her reticule, hoping he wouldn't notice she hadn't answered his question.

"Good God, Miss Lovejoy. Say you have not—"

The door opened and Marie hurried in, looking harried and breathless. "Thank 'eavens I 'ave caught you before you left, *chère*." She pulled an envelope from a pocket in the sewing smock she wore. "In case you need it."

Dianthe took the envelope and smiled. Cash. Dear practical Marie! Dianthe tucked it into her reticule and stood to leave. "Thank you, *Madame*. I shall pay you back every pence."

She glanced at Mr. Renquist and knew he had not forgotten about Geoffrey Morgan. She went to the dressing room door and said over her shoulder, "I won't keep you, Mr. Renquist, *Madame*. I really must be going. Wouldn't want to get caught out after dark alone. I shall come again tomorrow."

"But—"

"Tomorrow." She waved as she hurried out the shop door.

* * *

Geoff arrived home to be told by Giles that Miss Love-joy was preparing to go out that evening. He ordered a bath to wash away two days of hard riding, sleeping in his clothes and digging up graves, then dressed quickly. He wanted to see Dianthe, and prayed she would speak to him without denouncing him for the cad he was.

The swish of fabric and soft footfalls on the upper landing warned him that she was coming. He went forward a few steps and saw her pausing on the landing to check her appearance in the mirror. Strangely, she began talking to her reflection, though he couldn't hear the words. Her pause gave him a moment to collect his wits. He'd never experienced such trepidation about facing a woman he'd lain with.

She was dressed in a gown they'd selected together. Of a pale lavender hue with an embroidered hem of gold metallic fleur-de-lis, it flattered both her natural blond coloring and the brunette wig she wore now. Her neckline left nothing to the imagination, and he cursed himself for selecting such scandalous gowns. Had she become inured to the temptation she presented?

She turned away from the mirror and began her descent to the foyer. When she saw him, her steps faltered and she took a deep breath, then gave him a smile so sultry that his blood rose immediately. He was no school lad in the flush of his first crush. He was a well-seasoned man who could hold his passions in check. But Dianthe Lovejoy was making him feel eighteen again.

"Geoffrey!" She greeted him in a low, throaty purr. "How nice to see you. Giles did not tell me you'd come home. Were you waiting for me?"

"I thought we could go together. I assume you are still in the process of your investigation?"

"I am, amongst other things."

"Dare I ask what other things?"

"Best if you don't," she laughed. She had been trailing a matching lavender shawl, and she handed it to him to drape around her shoulders.

My God! Whatever he'd expected, it wasn't this cool sophistication. It was enthralling, but he wasn't sure he liked it. When she turned, his gaze snagged on her décolletage. Lord, there they were, those virginal, rose-tinted crescents peeking above the lavender satin banding. His mouth literally watered when he remembered how they'd tasted, how they'd felt beading against his tongue.

Was it his imagination, or was the scent of warm lavender trailing in her wake as she went around him to the door and waited for him to open it? No, it was real…and very seductive.

He chose the seat facing her. As the coach started off, he cleared his throat and tried to remember his rehearsed speech. "Um, Dianthe…Miss Lovejoy, I cannot tell you how deeply I regret the events of the other evening. I know you would prefer to ignore it, but I believe we should clear the air, just so that we know where we stand. And I would like to give you my assurances that it will never happen again."

"Hmm," she said, fiddling with the fringe on her shawl. "I really prefer not to discuss it, nor to make promises we cannot keep. It happened. It is over. Shall we leave it at that?"

"But you were innocent, relying upon my goodwill. I was unconscionable—"

"I have no expectations, if that is what concerns you, Geoffrey. I am grateful for all you've done for me, and grateful, too, for your…restraint the other evening. Though it was somewhat disappointing for me, I would not have your remorse on my conscience."

Disappointing? Her reaction was very unlike most of the women of his acquaintance. Most would be expecting an expensive gift, or to be installed in their own residence as his mistress. He'd been prepared to offer her all of that, and more, along with the promise never to touch her again. Had the incident meant so much less to her than it had to him? Disappointing? Even the notion was maddening.

She arranged her skirts to avoid wrinkling and gave a deep sigh.

"Melancholy?" he asked, hoping she would confess to being at least a little affected by their night together.

"Elvina Gibson. She was murdered night before last. Is being a courtesan fatal?"

He watched her through the dim light. "Not ordinarily," he admitted, "but these are extraordinary times. And circumstances no one could have foreseen." But he should have when he began baiting el-Daibul out of Tangier.

She frowned and tilted her head to one side. "What circumstances?"

Perhaps it was time for the truth. Nothing else had worked as a restraint on Dianthe's determination. "Women have been disappearing."

"Disappearing? Not murdered, but just…gone?"

"Just gone," he confirmed.

"Perhaps they've gone home, or decided to quit being courtesans. Or perhaps they've had to leave for a time to, um, cover an untimely birth?"

He gave her a rueful smile. "All those things have happened before, but not all at once, and not without signs. These women would have packed bags, bought passage on a coach, left a letter for friends or lovers. Something, Dianthe. Anything."

"How do you know they haven't?"

"I've asked. They've been leaving empty-handed in the middle of the night, taking no bags, belongings, jewelry or keepsakes. I've searched lodgings. I've looked for them in their home villages."

"What is happening to them?"

"Kidnapped, we think."

"Kidnapped? But who will pay ransom for a courtesan?"

"There have been no ransom demands. We suspect they've been abducted for the slave trade."

Dianthe's mouth dropped open in astonishment. "God in heaven! How do you know all this? And why have you troubled yourself over a few courtesans? Have they *all* been your mistresses?"

So someone had finally told her. Well, it was bound to happen. "Only Nell. I know, Miss Lovejoy, because I have been investigating this case for years."

She sank back against the leather squabs and narrowed her eyes. "Years? You've been investigating all this time, and you haven't said a word to me?"

"I couldn't be certain Nell's murder was linked to my investigation. I thought it might have something to do with you."

She blinked and looked out the coach window. "I did not murder her. I'd never heard of her before that night."

"It does rather stretch the imagination, does it not? Your resemblance to one another, the fact that you were dressed alike, your card found in Nell's possession, your hand holding the knife."

"That is why I am in this predicament, Geoffrey." She frowned and rubbed her temple.

Her insistence on using his given name was driving him wild. Every time she said it, a nerve tingled somewhere and his memory flashed on her pale form against the velvet counterpane. *Geoffrey...yes, yes!* He shifted his weight, easing the pressure of his trousers against his sudden erection.

"So you know about the card? And you knew about Miss Gibson, too? Is there anything you didn't know?"

Was there a hint of annoyance in her voice? "I had no idea that Elvina was upset or might know something about all this until you told me, Miss Lovejoy. But by then, it was already too late."

She nodded and folded her hands in her lap. He could not tell from her expression what she was thinking.

The remainder of the ride was made in silence and, when he helped her down from the coach in front of Thackery's, he was hard pressed not to tug her neckline up to cover more of her. As if she sensed what he was thinking, she gave him a provocative smile and preceded him through the wide glass doors.

Dianthe hadn't been certain she'd have the courage to venture into the hells again after the debacle with Mr. Munro, but she felt safe with Geoffrey beside her. His mere presence in the same establishment was a deterrent. His brother-in-law would not importune her again.

Screwing up her courage over the state of her décolletage, she allowed him to take her shawl and hand it to a footman. *He* had chosen this dress; he could deal with the consequences.

"Do you mind if I look around and see what games are in play?" he asked.

Another surprise—asking her permission, almost as if he were a suitor. "Certainly, I'll just look for some of the... ladies."

He glanced down at her décolletage and hesitated. Oh,

this petty vengeance was every bit as delicious as Miss Osgood had said it would be! Dianthe waited while a myriad of emotions passed over the usually unreadable face. Discretion won, and he merely nodded and turned away. She wondered what that decision had cost him as she began her ascent to the mezzanine, pushing her aureoles into the scandalous neckline. She would have to remember not to breathe deeply.

Nell. Geoffrey and her cousin. How could that suddenly hurt her so much?

Flora Denton was the first person she noted. Dianthe hurried to her side and drew her apart from a circle of admirers. "Where have you been? Have you heard about Elvina Gibson?"

Miss Denton nodded. "It is awful. I cannot conceive what is happening."

"You must leave town at once. Go to the countryside, or anywhere safe, until this is over."

"I have nothing to do with all this. No one would wish to harm me."

"But you talked to Elvina just before her death. The murderer may think you know something. And that is all that matters."

Flora looked down at her fan and murmured, "I thought someone was following me earlier today."

"There! You *must* go. Your life may depend upon it."

"But I haven't any money."

Dianthe thought of her meager hoard, down now to three pounds and the five Madame Marie had given her this afternoon. She'd lost the money Geoffrey had given her at the tables. She didn't know how long it would be before this was over, but she could ill afford to be penniless. Still, there was another possibility. "Miss Denton, I have a fare for a post chaise to Scotland, and I can give you the names of friends there who will take you in and care for you until this is over."

A tremulous smile curved Flora's lips. "You would do that for me?"

She nodded. "Meet me tomorrow on the north side of Leicester Square at one o'clock. I shall have the ticket with me. Bring your valise so that you will not have to return to your rooms. Do you have any cash at all?"

"A few pounds. I could scrape together another few," she said.

Dianthe breathed in relief. "Once there, your needs will be provided. I will bring the names and addresses for you to contact tomorrow. It would be best if you'd go home now and pack."

"I have…an appointment with Mr. Munro later this evening. Surely that will be safe enough?"

Dianthe suppressed a shudder. She pitied anyone whose sustenance was dependent upon Mr. Munro's goodwill. And anyone who must sell themselves to a man who would hurt them. Munro. "Is he here tonight?"

"Yes. At the vingt-et-un table. He was not coming home with me. We agreed only to go upstairs. He was to arrange for a room."

"Flora, I cannot emphasize this enough. You must go now, and you must be very careful." Dianthe steeled herself for the next offer, gaining courage from the fact that Geoffrey was present. "I shall speak to Mr. Munro for you. I shall tell him you've come down with a stomach malady and have gone home."

"But he will expect you—"

Bile rose in her throat. The very thought of Lewis Munro touching her where Geoffrey had made her blood run cold. "Munro will expect nothing. Nor will he bully me. Lord Geoffrey is here, and he would never permit it."

"How will I ever repay you, Miss Lovejoy?"

"You needn't. But, if you have one, I'd like a key to Nell's lodgings."

"The police have already searched there and have left it in shambles. If there were anything to find…"

Dianthe shrugged. "They may have overlooked something. Something that would only catch a woman's eye."

"Then you shall have it, and a key to mine, as well."

Miss Denton gave her a quick hug, and Dianthe went down the stairs with her, determined to see her into a coach. But she waved Dianthe off as she exited the building, turned left and disappeared into the night.

Squaring her shoulders, and checking to make certain she was all tucked in, Dianthe headed for the vingt-et-un tables. She wasn't looking forward to her encounter with Mr. Munro.

She found him rattling his counters in his hand as he watched a game in progress. She reminded herself to be pleasant and not show her fear before she tapped him on the shoulder and stood back. When he turned, his eyes lit with a feral gleam.

"Ah, Miss Deauville. Have you changed your mind?"

She waved his words away as if they were insignificant. "Actually, Mr. Munro, I've come on be'alf of Miss Denton. I fear she is suffering the debilitating *mal à l'estomac*. She 'as gone 'ome."

"Are you prepared to take her place?"

She smiled and tapped his cheek with her fan, wishing she could stuff it down his throat instead. "We 'ave 'ad this discussion, sir. I am under obligation to Lord Geoffrey."

"Why you bother with him is beyond me, Miss Deauville. You could do so much better."

"With you, sir?"

"Precisely. You are wasted on a scoundrel and libertine the likes of Morgan."

"Nevertheless, *M'sieur,* I would not violate our understanding. That would be unethical, would it not? And 'ow would you ever trust me if you thought I 'ad no more regard for my word than to break it? No." She shook her head and moistened her lips as Miss Osgood had taught her. "Because, should we ever 'ave the arrangement, I would want you to be able to trust my word, just as I'd want to trust yours." She wondered again if she could cozen him into admitting complicity in Charlotte's death.

"Hmm. I see your point, m'dear. Then is there a chance for me when your fascination for Morgan has waned?"

She smiled again but said nothing.

"Yes," he mused, "I can see there would be an advantage to an ethical mistress. Are you as discreet as you are ethical?"

"You 'ave no idea the secrets I am keeping, *M'sieur.*"

"'Lo, Morgan." Reginald Hunter, Lord Lockwood, took a place beside Geoffrey at the hazard table.

"Lockwood," he acknowledged. He placed his bet and turned to look at the man.

Lockwood laid his counters alongside Geoff's and fastened him with a hard look in his eyes. "How long have we been friends, Morgan?"

Geoff shrugged. "Five, six years?"

"It would be a shame if anything ruined that."

"What could ruin it?"

"A certain woman, whose name shall not be mentioned in this company, has come to my attention. I would just like to say that I would take it amiss if anything, ah, untoward should occur as a result of her placing her trust in you."

Good God! He knew about Dianthe Lovejoy! "Did she ask you to speak to me?"

"She has no idea that I know who she is. I recognized her voice when she forgot her accent last night."

Keeping his expression neutral, he called Lockwood's bluff. "If you know all that, you know her circumstances. Would you like to take her off my hands?"

"Hell, no!" Lockwood gave a short laugh and shook his head. "She's more than I could handle. She'd have me wrapped around her finger within three hours."

"Then you see my problem."

"Yes, and I don't envy you. Nevertheless, she is of some importance to my sister. I would have much to answer for if Sarah found out I knew about this and did not put a stop to it."

"Then we shall not tell her."

Lockwood lifted his glass in agreement. The croupier called the numbers and pulled the winnings away. Once more, Geoff was on the losing end. This was becoming a habit.

"Looks as if she is testing her boundaries again," Lockwood said, tilting his head toward the vingt-et-un tables.

Geoff followed his line of vision and winced when he saw Munro running his hand up and down Dianthe's arm. Geoff handed Lockwood his glass and tried to keep from clenching his hands into fists as he went to them.

"Here you are, my dear," he said, taking Dianthe's arm. "Having any luck at vingt-et-un?"

Dianthe gave him a look he could have sworn was relief. "Alas, my luck 'as run out."

Munro laughed and turned away.

As he led her away from the table, Geoff asked, "Was I just the target of your jesting?"

"Only Mr. Munro thinks so." She looked up at him and

there was a softness in her eyes that made him catch his breath. "I want to go home, Geoffrey."

He retrieved her shawl and had her to the coach before she could change her mind.

Chapter Fifteen

"Was it Munro?" Geoff asked when they were halfway home. "Did he say something, do something to upset you? Did he lay so much as one hand on you?"

She smiled at him. "Be careful, Geoffrey. That sounds very much as if you are protecting me."

He bit his tongue and stared out the window at the passing lamplights. It was true. He was nearly desperate to keep Dianthe safe and untouched by the ugly, dangerous part of his life. He glanced down at his boots and said nothing, neither admitting nor denying her charge. He couldn't even look at her for fear that she would see the truth in his eyes.

When she spoke again, it wasn't what he'd expected. "Why did you not simply fire into the ground?" she asked. "If you had not wounded Lord Grayson, he and Mr. Lucas would be alive today."

Geoff crossed his arms over his chest and studied her. Was she still brooding over that debacle of a duel months ago? Would he ever make her understand that there'd been more at stake than winning or losing? "Firing away is considered an admission of guilt, Dianthe. It is taken as an apology. Deloping, some call it."

"Then—"

"I did nothing wrong. I did not cheat Grayson, and I could ill afford to have anyone think I did. Every young cub in town would be challenging me if they thought there were no consequences. I'd be caught in an endless cycle of duels, and even more men would die. A slight wound was the best Grayson could hope for, and that was all he got at my hand."

"My cousin said you stood still, allowing Lord Grayson the first shot. He said you had real 'bottom.' He also said you could easily have killed Lord Grayson."

Geoff shrugged and looked out the window again. "The affair should have been over after that. And Lucas, as his second, should not have gone so far…" There was no sense in going over that again. She believed Lucas was *his* victim, and nothing would persuade her otherwise.

"Mr. Lucas behaved dishonorably," she said in a soft voice.

He glanced at her and she offered him a small smile. "There was no way for you to know that my cousin would be wounded when he had to kill Mr. Lucas in order to protect you, or that Lord Grayson would then commit suicide in shame."

"Do not make me a hero in all this, Dianthe. I have oceans of regret for the things I've done in my life, but that isn't one of them."

"Tell me something you *do* regret, Geoffrey, besides the other night with me."

He sighed, wondering what she wanted to hear from him. That he wasn't the devil she had accused him of being? Very well, he'd humor her. "I regret not warning Constance Bennington that there was danger abroad in London. I regret leaving Charlotte at Munro's mercy. I regret—"

Dianthe sat forward in her seat. "Did you receive a letter from Charlotte just before her death?"

"That is another of my regrets—that I did not communicate with her more often. That she did not feel she could ask my help."

Dianthe's eyes narrowed and she sat back, tapping her fan with one fingernail.

"You don't believe me?" he asked.

"You are not the one I don't believe," she said cryptically.

"Are you keeping secrets again? I thought we were through with that."

"Have you told *me* everything, Geoffrey? I think not. You were in Vauxhall Gardens the night Nell was killed, but you haven't said why. You are looking for someone, but you won't tell me who. Tit for tat."

The coach pulled up with a lurch and he threw the door open. Somehow, Dianthe had managed to corner him again. But this was a case of too much knowledge being dangerous. Any woman but Dianthe would have listened to him and stayed sensibly at home until the matter was resolved. But she'd step into the fray without a second thought. "I've told you all I am going to, Dianthe."

She stormed past him, then paused at the door for him to catch up. "*Protecting* me again, Lord Morgan?"

"I am *not* protecting—"

"Of course not. How silly of me. You are simply treating me like a brainless twit." She opened the door herself and stomped into the foyer.

"Only when you act like one!" he shouted. How could she drive him to distraction so easily?

"How, prithee, have I acted like a brainless twit? I thought we were getting on quite well."

"Damnation, I—"

"Pas devant les domestiques," she hissed.

Not in front of the servants? Good God! When had they begun to sound like a married couple? There was a hurried scuffle in the vicinity of the hallway behind the stairs. Giles or Hanson had made a quick escape. Whoever it was wouldn't be seen again tonight.

She tossed her shawl, fan and reticule on the foyer table and headed toward the ballroom. She was glorious in her fury—flushed with indignation and high emotions. How could he be both amused and furious at her?

"Come back here, Dianthe," he called after her. "We are not finished with this discussion."

"I am."

He followed her into the ballroom and watched while she selected a foil and slashed the air. "Prescott will be here in the morning and—"

Facing the *segno,* the wall target, she executed a few nearly perfect lunges, striking principle organs. "As you've so often reminded me, you will not protect me, so I must be ready to do the job myself."

He crossed his arms over his chest and observed her technique. She wielded the blade as if her life depended upon it. He was impressed. But target practice was different than a bout or a fight. "Knowing technique does not mean you are able to defend yourself."

She turned to him and narrowed her eyes. "Do you think you can teach me something I don't know?"

He removed his jacket, tossed her a pair of fencing gloves, retrieved his favorite foil from the rack, turned her toward the mirrors and took a position beside her. "There are a few techniques that Prescott will not teach you. They are dangerous. The sort you'd encounter on the street."

He walked her through the *botte de paysan*, demonstrating the technique of gripping one's own blade to make a two-handed stab at one's adversary. Her movements were somewhat impeded by her gown, and he offered to wait while she changed her clothes.

"If I am challenged, do you think my attacker will wait for me to change?"

It was on the tip of his tongue to tell her that she would only need to defend herself over his dying body, but he couldn't allow her to count on him. "Watch, then, and follow me."

When she had memorized the technique, he turned to face her and brandished his sword. He brought his sword down in slow motion, giving her time to grip hers and hold it out to deflect his descending blade.

"Good," he said. "Again." He continued with a variety of attacks and postures until she understood the timing.

"Now, *passato sotto*—the pass under. This technique will use your size to advantage. Take the initiative, Dianthe. Attack me. Hard, as if you mean it."

Starting at the *en garde* position, she stepped into an aggressive riposte. Geoff ducked under her attack and dropped onto his free hand to deliver an upward counter thrust by tapping her side sharply. Her look of utter confusion changed to wary respect.

"Again," she said, and made him demonstrate again and again.

When she tried the move, her satin slippers went out from under her and she landed on her bottom. She stood and turned her back to him, lifted her skirts and removed her slippers and stockings. She shed the dark wig and ran her fingers through her blond strands. By the time she turned to him again, he was completely aroused. Pale lavender stockings were puddled beside her slippers, and he recalled how those bare legs had felt against his hips, his cheek.

She held her sword out in an invitation and beckoned him forward with the other hand. He obliged. This time, Dianthe completed the drop flawlessly, and he marveled that she could do so in a dress. He could have easily evaded her sword, but he held his ground, wondering if she would complete the technique.

She did, tapping his side rather harder than she'd intended with the unguarded side of her blade. Though it barely stung, a thin red line appeared on his shirt, and Dianthe's eyes widened.

"Oh! I didn't mean to—"

"The fault was mine for not protecting my flank."

"But this was not a bout to first blood. I was too aggressive. I…"

"There is no such thing as 'too aggressive' when you are fighting for your life. And no such thing as fair play. Do not expect it. Not even from me."

Dianthe's eyes glistened and she blinked rapidly as she stepped back and raised her sword again to the *en garde* position. Was she crying? How uncharacteristic of her.

He crossed her blade and exchanged a few blows before taking the advance. She successfully held off his attack with the two-handed technique, but he could not force her into the pass-under again. His scratch had frightened her and now she didn't trust herself.

Seeing her fear, Geoff was suddenly tired of the games, the subterfuge, the secrets. He stepped across the distance between them and grabbed her blade. Her lips parted in a tiny gasp and her eyes shifted up to his.

"That is called seizure, Dianthe. It is a desperation

move. Never do it to catch or deflect a descending blade or you will lose half your hand, and never do it without a glove."

"Seizure," she repeated, tears welling in her eyes.

"Best, but not always, done by seizing the hilt rather than the blade."

She released her sword to him and he tossed it aside, slipped his hand around her waist and gathered her close. He dropped his own sword and cupped her cheek. "Dianthe," he whispered on his way to her lips.

Her eyes closed when he made the contact, and her waiting tears slipped beneath the dark fan of lashes and spilled over her cheeks. His stomach twisted to think of her being so vulnerable. He ended the kiss and she settled her cheek against his chest with a shaky sigh.

"Why the tears, Dianthe? I am not hurt. And we have argued before. We've always been at sword point in one way or another."

"I did not love you before."

He held his breath. "Do you…love me…now?"

She shivered and her voice caught on a sigh. "Yes."

She loved him? But how could she? He'd been so careful to keep her at a distance, to shock her and make her life difficult. He'd flaunted her as a courtesan, warned her she could not trust him, refused to protect her, and treated her like an annoyance. He'd reminded her over and over again that the only reason he was helping her was to repay his debt to her cousin.

But he'd never admitted that she'd taken his breath away the first time he'd ever seen her in her aunt's parlor, and that when she'd cursed him for a devil, she had cut him to the quick. He'd never told her that he was often gruff with her because he wanted her so desperately and couldn't have her, or that he dreaded the empty days and nights when she reclaimed her rightful life.

"Dianthe," he said, his voice cracking over the force of his emotions. "I…not a single one of your kin would thank me for loving you, and a few would call me out. And they'd be right. I want nothing more than to despoil you. The effort not to do so has cost me more dearly than you can know." He held her closer, burying his face in her hair and breathing in her scent. "I am not accustomed to being noble."

"Do not try," she said. "Finish what you've begun."

He groaned. "My sanity is too tenuous to lie with you again without taking you, and while you are in my keeping, no harm will come to you through me."

She was silent for a moment, nuzzling against his chest, then she pulled back a little and looked up at him. "I quite understand, and I would not ask you to compromise your principles. Then whom shall I choose for the task? Lord Lockwood has expressed an interest, as have his brothers. Or Mr. Munro or Senor Ramirez. Would they be better fit for the job?"

An uneasy feeling tweaked him. "What job? What are you talking about?"

"Deflowering me. If you will not, then who should? And once I am deflowered, will you have me then?"

He nearly choked on his reply. "I'll kill anyone who touches you."

"And I am determined it will be you. What will that take, Geoffrey? What will I have to do?"

God! How could he fight her when he wanted her more than life and breath? But how could he dishonor her and betray her cousin's trust?

In his split second of indecision, Dianthe came up on her toes and lifted her mouth to his to give him a series of soft but insistent kisses. "I know you fear I will regret this tomorrow. I won't. Tomorrow may never come, Geoffrey," she said against his throat. "If I am found out and taken to Newgate, what do you think will come of me there? Will all I know of love be what *they* teach me? I cannot bear to think of it happening that way. I want *you*. I want the memory of you to be my sanctuary in whatever dark times are to come."

He moaned and tightened his arms around her. After a moment, he lifted her and carried her across the great room to the stairs. Slowly, savoring every step, he climbed the long, curving stairway and walked down the hallway to his room. Yes, *his* room, just as she would become his tonight. He would lock his door and shut out the world. And he'd know true love for the first time. All the other women, all the other times, were merely a prelude to Dianthe.

Wavering between desire and doubt, Dianthe took comfort from the memory of Miss Osgood's words. *Embrace your sexuality and men will find you irresistible. Lord Geoffrey will find you irresistible.* Oh, pray he did! Pray he would not be put off by her inexperience. Pray she had the courage to go through with her brazen seduction.

A single candle on his night table cast a dim light in the room. He laid her carefully on a bed of deep evergreen velvet before returning to lock the door, and she looked around at Geoffrey's private quarters.

Leaves and graceful vines were carved into the cherrywood bed, and the feather mattress was as soft as a cloud. Four corner posts supported a canopy draped with evergreen hangings. The clean scent of his shaving soap wafted up from the down pillows and made her almost giddy. She felt strangely safe and content on that bed.

On the facing wall, a large fireplace held a heap of barely glowing embers, kept banked lest the night grow cold. A leather chair flanked by a table bearing a lamp, a book opened facedown to hold its place, and a decanter and glass gave evidence of quiet evenings in solitary pursuit. How odd that she'd never considered he might not go out every night. On the wall opposite the door, three tall windows framed by damask draperies.

She watched as he poured a deep red wine from the decanter into a glass and brought it to the bed. Placing it on the bedside table, he caressed her cheek.

"Are you frightened, Dianthe?"

She shook her head, but could not find her voice.

He smiled, seeing through her lie, and sat beside her. Slowly, with infinite sweetness, he met her lips and hovered there for a moment, barely making contact. "If you trust me, Dianthe, I can make this painless for you."

She nodded. She'd heard there was pain at first, but she'd always thought it was unavoidable. In truth, it wouldn't matter if it were agony. She would trust him, and she would take whatever came with it. How odd that she was now so ready to surrender the prize she had guarded for so many years and saved for her wedding night. A night that might never come if she were arrested.

He lifted the glass to her lips and she tasted a deep rich burgundy. Almost immediately, she felt her muscles release their tension and her breathing even. He took a sip and kissed her again. The flavor was on his tongue as it met hers, but it was more intoxicating coming from him.

He moved his hand from her cheek, down the curve of her neck to the slope of her shoulder, pushing her gown down her arm. But Miss Osgood said she should undress for her lover to give him pleasure. She shrugged his hand

away and stood, praying that her knees would support her
and that her courage would not fail. Silently, she repeated
her mantra: *I am Salome. I am Delilah. I am Aphrodite.*

Geoff's breathing sped up when she untied the ribbon
beneath her breasts and unhooked the clip that held her
bodice closed. Freed of the tight constraint of the fabric,
her breasts swelled above the top. As he watched, a deep
blush swept from her breasts to her cheeks. He was hard
and ready, and he ached to touch her.

She paused, as if waiting for a sign that he did not want
this. But he wanted it. Wanted it more than he'd ever
wanted anything in his life. He could not take his eyes from
her, and he gripped the bedpost so tightly he thought it
might snap.

Pushing the sleeves of her gown down her arms, she
stood still as the fabric made a lavender pool at her feet.
All that remained were her chemise, French drawers and
garters.

She lifted her chemise, slipped her fingers beneath the
waistband of the drawers and unfastened the tapes. They
slipped to the floor and her chemise dropped to cover her,
gliding over her skin and clinging to her curves.

Geoff stood and went to circle her, bending so close that
he could feel the heat from her body, though he forbade
himself to touch her. Anticipation was a powerful aphro-
disiac. A slight trembling began in her limbs and a little
shiver indicated he'd been right. She was anticipating his
touch, craving it, needing it.

His breath fanned her cheek as he whispered a single
word. "Breathtaking…" Another shiver caused a little gasp.

He stopped behind her and tugged the tapes at the shoulders of her chemise. The fabric slid over her skin in a whis-

per as it fell atop the other discards. Her head fell back as if she were intoxicated with the boldness of it all, and he prayed that the violence of his passion would not repulse her.

She turned to face him and lifted her arms to work at the knots of his cravat, but her fingers were cold and she fumbled with the unfamiliar task. He gave her a tender smile and she returned it. He made no attempt to help her, nor did he betray any sign of his impatience or the lust surging through his veins. This was important to her, and he would not let his eagerness ruin it for her. When, at last, she removed the stubborn knots and freed the cravat, he leaned down and kissed the top of her head, whispering, "Thank you."

He pulled his shirt over his head and dropped it atop her things. Her gaze lifted to his and he realized that she was as anxious as he. Oh, but he would give her the chance to accustom herself to this intimacy, and to become comfortable with the texture and heat of his skin, his scent, and to trust the strength of his self-control. Pray God it held.

She trailed her fingers from his shoulders downward, tracing the ridges of his muscles and finding the ragged rhythm of his breathing. She swayed forward and rubbed her cheek against the matting of hair on his chest. When she moved her hands downward, his nipples beaded against her palms and he shuddered. God, she was insanely erotic. Her curious blend of innocence and experience was a powerful stimulant.

She paused and touched them more carefully, and he knew she was wondering if they were as sensitive as hers. She surprised him by kissing him there, scraping her teeth across the hardened nub. He groaned and brought his hands up to cup her shoulders. Could she possibly be as aroused as he? No. She was too innocent of what came next to appreciate the nuances and the slow, steady rise of passion. Oh, she was coming to a simmer, but she was far from a boil. How long before she learned that he'd never say no? Never stop her, no matter what she wanted to do with him?

He couldn't recall how many times had he done this, and with how many women. Countless. Yet this time was different. This time he was filled with a tenderness he'd never known before. This time he would trade his soul to make it perfect for Dianthe.

She paused in her exploration again as her fingertips traced the raised welt she'd inflicted when practicing the *passato sotto*. The cut was shallow and thin, no more than a sting, but she was distressed. Her tender conscience bothered him. Would she ever be able to defend herself if she was not willing to inflict damage?

But his thoughts were lost as she continued downward, hooking her fingers into the waistband of his trousers. He groaned, but remained steady, hoping she would have this part done quickly. She fumbled with the buttons of his waistband and he covered her hands with his to guide her through the task. One fumble, one misplaced touch, and he'd snap. He was already so hard that he could scarcely bear it.

Once his trousers were unfastened, he pried off his boots, then let her have her way.

She smiled and began to push the trousers down his hips, and when she tugged them lower he doubled his hands into fists at his sides. His self-control had never been so tested, so tenuous. And he was still not certain he'd pass this test, when all he wanted was to ravish her.

She came up on her toes again to kiss him, and her aroused breasts scraped against his skin. She was trembling even more and he knew she'd be nearly ready for the next level. When she parted her lips for him, he took her tongue hungrily and pulled her so close that he could feel every inch of her burned into him. *Every inch.*

He moaned and lifted her, laying her on the bed. Within seconds he had finished the job she'd begun and was beside her. The delicate intimacy of her bare silken skin against his was wildly sensual. She stroked his chest, his back, his sides, and lifted her knee to skim her heated inner thigh along his leg and hip. Her core was vulnerable to him in this position and it was all he could do to keep from claiming it now.

He wove his fingers through her hair and held her head still so that he could kiss her. She parted her lips and sighed, whispering, "Such heaven…can it be real?"

He kissed her eyes, her nose, her throat, her chin, and finally came back to her mouth. Against her lips, he said, "*We* are real, Dianthe, and we will make our own heaven." And then he cherished her lips with a dozen soft kisses.

For a moment, she gave over to him, allowing him to set the pace, deferring to his needs. He used the time to cool his burning hunger. She was closer than she knew to being ravished. He kissed her tenderly and moved lower to the irresistible lure of her breasts. He gave them exquisite attention, caught up in the taste and texture of her, and the wildness of her response. She whimpered, her hands clutching fistfuls of the velvet beneath her. She was incoherent, murmuring single words like *please, now, heaven, dear God,* and his favorite—*Geoffrey—oh, Geoffrey.*

Soon she would be ready, nearly frantic to have him inside her, and he slipped his hand down to test her response. Her hips lifted and her knee crooked as she turned toward him. Lord, she was like a passionflower in full bloom— lush, damp, opening to him, glistening on his fingers, and soon, his tongue. Little sobs began to escape her and her head thrashed on the pillow as he pushed one finger, then two, into the entrance to her deepest being. He stretched her, readying her for him. She was so small, so snug, that he wondered if he could keep his promise not to hurt her.

He found the barrier and tested its strength, and she pushed up against his hand. She was gasping now and clutching his shoulders. It wasn't pain that drove her; it wasn't fear. It was blind desperation. He'd need to ease her, take the edge off the driving need. He nibbled his way downward, on his way to her mons. He couldn't wait to taste her, to feel her inner vibrations against his tongue.

But suddenly she seized his hair and dragged him upward. "No," she panted. "No. You won't cheat me again tonight."

"That wasn't my intention," he said.

And she pushed him over on his back. "You are taking charge again, turning me into your mindless slave. *My* turn, Geoffrey."

He was so taken by surprise that he could only grant her what she wanted. He lay back while she began a tender assault on his body. Her fingers raked over his chest and abdomen, leaving little trails of tingling nerves in their wake. His own immediacy had waned as he gave attention to her, but now it was back, aching, throbbing, demanding. She could not know what she was doing to him, how she was testing the limits of his endurance. He reached for her again, wanting to feel the length of her body pressed against his.

She seized the initiative before doubts could set in. He made a sound like a strangled laugh. She had not shown much finesse. "I am flattered by your enthusiasm, my dear," he said as he nuzzled her ear, "but as I have more experience, perhaps you will allow me—"

She shook her head and pursed her lips against his ear. "Shh," she said, "or all Miss Osgood's expensive lessons will go to waste."

He groaned. He'd meant to shock her into quitting her charade, and now it had come back on him. "This wasn't what I had in mind."

"Too late," she murmured against the column of his throat.

Her lavender silk garters, still fastened above her knees, slipped off easily and then she straddled him. She had them fastened about his wrists before he realized her intent. "No," he groaned. "No, Dianthe."

"Do you trust me?" she asked, her lips moving against his ear.

There was a long pause, then a faint reply. "Aye, I trust you."

She reached over him and tied the silk ribbons to the bedposts, fastening them with simple knots. She sensed his tenuous surrender in the relaxing of his muscles as he settled against the mattress. She was surprisingly aroused by the freedom to do as she pleased to this strong, solid body.

She kissed her way down his throat to his chest, running her hands over his laddered flanks, amazed at the strength and muscles that had been hidden beneath his elegant clothing.

She moved down to his diaphragm, her nipples abraded by the crisp matting of hair on his chest. The sensation was arousing. She lay atop him and she could feel the hard swell of his manhood against her belly. Her breathing quickened and she wondered if she should…if she dare…

She trailed her hand downward, found that uniquely masculine appendage and closed her hand around it. Geoff gasped and twitched.

"Easy," he urged her.

The smooth glide of the velvet skin over the thick stiffness of his erection intrigued her, and she slowly moved it up and back down, eliciting a deep groan and a shudder. She marveled at the power such a thing had over him, and tried it again.

"Dianthe, love…be careful how you test me," he moaned. But even as he said it, his hips jerked, pushing his shaft further into her hand.

Her courage soared with the deep vibration of his voice, the heady mix of control and desire. He was so powerful, always in command, and yet she could make him quiver with need. That knowledge fascinated her. With each new and daring thing she'd done, Geoff had praised her, begged her for more, just as she'd begged him. Dare she do to him what he'd done to her?

She moved lower, kissing the ridged muscles of his abdomen and trailing her tongue down a faint line of hair toward her destination, gripping his hip with one hand and his erection with the other.

He convulsed as he realized what she was going to do. Did she instinctually know what would drive him insane? Such play was not new to him, by any means, but that Dianthe would attempt such a thing was completely beyond his wildest fantasy. He didn't know whether to curse Miss Osgood or to praise her.

The garters binding his wrists had never been tight, and he pulled his hands free, still gripping the ribbons so she wouldn't know he'd done so. He'd hold on as long as he could, but the end was imminent.

Her breathing was ragged and her touch was unsteady. Her damp inner heat brushed against his thigh. He ached to touch her there, to bury himself deep inside her, hear her welcoming sighs, feel her contracting around him. Ah, but he had vowed there would be nothing forbidden between them. Nothing. How could he forbid her this?

He clenched his jaw as she moved relentlessly lower. How could he both want and dread the same thing? The mere stirring of her breath against his flesh caused him excruciating agony, and he'd never known a passion so potent. At the merest touch of her lips, his control snapped as violently as if it had never been. He released the lavender ribbons and pulled her upward.

"Geoffrey," she whispered in a thick voice.

He rolled with her until she was on her back and he was nestled between her thighs. Dianthe clung to him, wrapping her legs around his hips, knowing that, somehow, this was what she should do.

He kissed her deeply, and with an urgency she hadn't felt before. Her skin was on fire, her breathing now shallow and rapid as she gripped his arms to steady herself. He slipped his hand—his strong, talented hand—between them and entered her again, opening her, stretching her, making her ready.

"Please," she whimpered, rising to him, certain she would die if he didn't do something quickly.

With a deep groan, he cupped her bottom, easing her upward as he came down to meet her. When she felt him at her entrance, she had a fleeting moment of panic, but he moved to touch, to stroke, that small bud of flesh and nerves he had cherished with his tongue, and her doubts evaporated on a sigh.

His thickness pushed into her, a slight burning, a little pinch, no more. Chill bumps raced along her skin and she bit her lip to hold back a sob of relief. He strained above her, shaking with control as he eased downward again. His face was a study in restraint. A fine sheen dampened his forehead and the dark hair around his face. He started to withdraw and she feared he was going to leave her.

"No!" And she lifted with him, trying to keep that thickness within her.

He grinned and dropped back to the mattress with her, kissing her and smoothing the hair back from her face with a tender touch. "Your turn to trust *me*," he said, lacing his fingers through hers and holding them against the pillow.

He began moving his hips again, rocking into her, demonstrating the rhythm of love. The friction was unbearable. The more he gave her, the more she craved. She moved faster, demanding, understanding now that the short separations were temporary and that he came back to her with added pleasure. They were rising inexorably to some unreachable summit, leaving her trembling and increasingly desperate.

And then, just when she feared she could bear no more and would die of this strange wanting, she was washed in a shimmer of electricity, every nerve ending tingling and screaming with joy. Her own voice sounded distant as she spoke from her heart.

"Geoffrey...oh, Geoffrey. Thank you."

He sank into her one last time and, with a sound that was half moan, half laugh, gathered her close. "My pleasure, Dianthe."

Chapter Sixteen

Geoff tied his cravat as he watched Dianthe sleep. The bedsheet was tangled around her, exposing a length of leg here, the curve of her back there, and the delicate flush of a cheek through the tousled blond hair. She sighed deeply and turned, reaching out to the space he had vacated a few minutes ago. Wild, sated, completely untamed. That was the new Dianthe. His love. His match.

God, how he longed to be with her there, responding to that touch. He couldn't get enough of her. Long after she'd fallen into an exhausted sleep, he'd lain awake, wanting her still, stroking her arm, the length of her spine, the soft curve of her hip. He'd watched her sleep, as fascinated as if she'd been dancing or fencing.

And now, the longer he stood there, the more he was torn between rejoining her and his need to insure her safety. Now that he was involved with—*in love with*—Dianthe, she had become a potential target for el-Daibul. Geoff was too wise in the ways of gossip and subtleties to believe they could keep their affections secret for long. Even if his true feeling were never known, he had taken the public role of her lover. Thus, his need to find el-Daibul had gone from urgent to critical. If harm came to Dianthe because he had dared to love her, he would not be able to live with himself.

He pulled a sheet of paper from the drawer of the small escritoire near the fireplace and dipped a pen in the open inkwell.

Dianthe my dear,
    Thank you for a lovely evening....

He crumpled the paper into a tight wad and threw it onto the hearth. Good God! That sounded as if they'd had a trivial encounter at the gaming tables. He could not dismiss her passion so easily. He tried again.

My darling Dianthe,
    I wish I was waking with you, but business calls me forth. Pray, rest today and restore your energy. I shall return by evening and see you then. We have much to discuss and settle between us.
    Always, Geoff

He folded the note and placed it on the bedside table so that she would see it the moment she woke. He needed to know her wishes before he tried to untangle their predicament with her cousin or the McHugh. Both of them were likely to kill him for what he'd done last night.

Dianthe turned her face up to the sun. She hadn't wanted to venture beyond his bedroom, but now she was glad she had. Still feeling luxurious and languid from Geoffrey's touch, she'd decided that an outing would be just the thing to clear the cobwebs from her mind and renew her energies.

But sitting on a bench on the north side of Leicester Square at quarter past one o'clock, she tried to still her unease. Miss Denton was fifteen minutes late. Dianthe opened her reticule for the third time to make certain the ticket voucher was there, and the slips of paper with her sister's and Charity MacGregor's addresses. She'd left nothing to chance—nothing but the fact that Miss Denton might not come. Or…or that she *couldn't* come.

That thought sent chills up her spine. What sort of monster was abroad that preyed on vulnerable women? Such a thing took a singular kind of villainy. Could it be as Geoffrey said?

"Miss Lovejoy? Are you unwell?"

She looked up to find Flora Denton standing in front of her, holding a small valise. "Oh, Miss Denton! Thank heavens you've come. I was worried that something might have happened to you."

Flora took the seat beside her on the bench. "No, but I nearly changed my mind. This life is all I've ever known. To change it all now…"

"Your very life may depend upon it." She fumbled through her reticule again, removing the voucher and addresses. With barely a hesitation, she added the last of her little hoard of cash and handed the lot to Flora.

"I do not know how to repay you, Miss Lovejoy. You cannot know what this means to me."

Dianthe smiled through her tears. "There is enough to see you to Scotland and for a few days at an inn if you cannot reach the persons on the list immediately. Simply tell them that I sent you, and they will take you in."

Miss Denton looked through the documents and put the money in her reticule. She removed her glove and shook out two keys. "One is Nell's and one is mine," she told her, then handed her a torn scrap of paper with the address written on it. "I have left something for you, Miss Lovejoy. Something you may find useful. Please be very careful. I fear what might happen to you if you are found there."

"And I fear what might happen if you stay. I'll walk with you to the coaching house and see you safely off."

"Please, Miss Lovejoy. That is not necessary. It is just a few streets away and it's the middle of the day."

Dianthe glanced around. There was nothing unusual, nothing to cause alarm, and she realized Flora should be perfectly safe as long as she was out of town by nightfall. "Do you promise you will be on the very next northbound coach?"

"Yes, of course. But before I go, I must give you a warning, as well."

"Me? Whatever for?"

"You think you know everything, Miss Lovejoy, but you are dreadfully naive. Dabbling in the demimonde has exposed you to certain…unsavory elements. While my income was dependent, I could not say anything, but now, well, now I must speak out. You must stay away from Mr. Munro, and also Senor Ramirez. They are very dangerous men. Stay close to Lord Morgan. He will keep you safe if anyone can."

Dianthe's pulse pounded. Did Miss Denton know something about Munro? "What has Mr. Munro done? Why do you warn me against him?"

"He has a sudden and violent temper. Some of the girls have borne marks after entertaining him, and I, as well. I believe he is threatening them, Miss Lovejoy. I know he threatened *me.*"

The very things Munro had accused Geoffrey of! "What sort of threat can he make that would require them—and you—to remain silent?"

Miss Denton looked into the distance, refusing to meet Dianthe's eyes. "That we could end up like his nosy wife. That he would be forced to hurt both us and whomever we told. And that women who crossed him have been known to disappear."

Her heart skipped a beat. His nosy wife? Was this the key to discovering if Mr. Munro had killed Charlotte Morgan? "Did he say anything else about his wife?"

"I have said too much already, but you should be warned. Stay as close by Lord Morgan's side as possible."

"Miss Denton, do you think, given the nature of the warnings, that Mr. Munro or Senor Ramirez have anything to do with the disappearance and murder of our friends, or do you think Mr. Munro was merely using the circumstance to frighten you?"

Flora stood and lifted her valise. "I believed precisely what Mr. Munro said. Take that as you will."

Dianthe looked at the torn scrap of paper again and then back at the building. Yes, the address was correct. She had not expected it to look so, well, respectable. Only its location in a back street off St. James proclaimed it a place for disreputable women. But, knowing the address was nearby, she had wanted to finish this much at least before unburdening herself on Geoffrey.

She had to do it now, before she told Geoffrey the whole sordid truth about Nell's death and what she'd said before she died. Confessing that she and Nell were cousins would risk losing his regard. But she wouldn't tell him what she'd learned about Charlotte until she could offer him proof.

She climbed the three steps to the door and wondered if she should knock. As she hesitated, it opened and a young man exited, straightening his cravat. He gave her a grin and left the door open for her as he skipped down the steps. Thank God for her disguise. She'd never have found the courage to come here without it.

She entered a dim hallway with doors along both sides, each labeled with a number. After a brief search of the main floor, she hurried up the stairway, hoping she would find numbers thirteen and fourteen quickly.

The doors were midway down the corridor and across from one another. Her first key, marked with a tag that said "Miss Denton," unlocked number thirteen. She closed the door behind her, went to the window and opened the draperies to admit the late afternoon light. The room was clean and neat, but unremarkable. Another door opened to a bedchamber, and the decorations made Dianthe blush. Paintings hung in a tidy row all around the room, each depicting a different sex act or position. Each was flagrantly explicit, and Dianthe wondered if the collection had served as a sort of "menu" from which clients could choose. They were quite similar to the engravings Miss Osgood had shown her to explain her lectures.

A search of the bureau drawers told her that Miss Denton had taken some personal belongings in her valise and left the rest behind. Dianthe opened the single drawer of a writing desk and found a small leather-bound book about the size of her palm. It contained handwritten names followed by dates and short notations regarding preferences. Dianthe grew warm as she scanned the lines.

She knew some of these men! Would she ever be able to face them again? She was about to return the book to the drawer when the thought occurred to her that this was what Miss Denton had *meant* her to find. Dianthe slipped it into her reticule and closed the drawer.

A quick search of the other room revealed nothing out

of place. No one would know that Flora Denton was gone, nor would the landlord miss her until her rent was due.

Dianthe locked the door behind her and stepped across the hallway. The sound of raucous masculine voices carried from the ground floor, and she slipped through Nell's door quickly, turning the latch and leaning her forehead against the wood panel. She held her breath until the voices diminished, as the men continued up the stairs to the next floor.

When she turned, she was shocked at the condition of the room. Belongings were scattered everywhere, as if the place had been searched many times. How would she ever find anything in this mess? The draperies were open, and sunlight flashed off broken shards of colored glass and blue-and-white porcelain. She felt the shock as a violation of Nell's very memory. How intrusive! How degrading to have one's belongings gone through and strewn about like garbage.

Dianthe knelt and began sifting through the mess, but the chime of a distant clock reminded her that she would have to be home before dark. As she started to rise, she caught sight of a small enameled frame beneath the settee. When she turned it over, she caught her breath in surprise. The frame enclosed a miniature portrait of two young girls, both blond, both beautiful—and one was Dianthe's mother. Tears sprang to her eyes to think of these two sisters, both gone now, who had been torn apart by circumstances. Dianthe had no doubt that Nell's claim was true, but this was hard proof.

She pushed the miniature into her reticule, knowing it had been left behind because it had no significance to the investigation. Dianthe's calling card had been found in this mess, and other evidence that had been taken away.

She went to the bedchamber, though she doubted

there was anything left for her to find. Clothes and personal items were strewn across the bed. The contents of Nell's bureau had been dumped on the floor, and her jewelry box lay empty and overturned on top of the heap. So little was left as testimony to so heartbreaking a life.

The room was directly lit by the setting sun, which illuminated a portrait of Nell on the far wall. As she turned to go, Dianthe caught sight of herself in the dressing table mirror, the portrait of Nell behind her. Yes, without her dark wig and beauty patch, they'd looked startlingly alike. They'd had the same taste in clothes, had both been poor, had loved the same man, but Nell had not had the advantage of family and love. They had not known she existed, and she had found them too late. How impossibly tragic.

Clearly, Dianthe would have to tell Geoffrey that Nell had been her cousin. But, oh, how she hated the thought. He had been so tender, so considerate, last night. And once he knew the same blood that ran through Nell's veins also coursed through hers, that tenderness would vanish, along with any notion that they could have a future together. Someday, Geoffrey Morgan would need to marry for the sake of his title, and a woman tainted with scandal and low family connections would never do as a wife.

The sun had dropped beneath the horizon and dusk was falling rapidly. Dianthe tucked her reticule under one arm, locked the door and hurried down the stairs.

Geoffrey seemed preoccupied on the ride to Thackery's, though he sat beside her, holding her hand and stroking her palm with his thumb in an absent manner. She was content to sit in silence, still trying to comprehend the things she'd discovered earlier at the lodging house. And the things she'd read in Miss Denton's little book, still tucked safely in her reticule.

"Geoffrey?" she ventured.

He glanced at her and smiled the same way he'd smiled at her last night. Her body remembered the feel of him and responded instantly with a longing to be touched. She glanced away and cleared her throat. "I have Miss Denton's, um, client book. There is something I think you should see. I trust you will be discreet?"

He stroked the line of her cheek and an invasive languor seeped through her. "Where did you come by it, Dianthe?" He leaned down to nibble her earlobe, and yearning kindled low in her belly.

"I went to Nell's apartment and…"

"You are in more danger than you know, Dianthe. You will not go there again, will you?" he whispered against her lips. "Because if you do, I shall have to lock you up. And do not doubt I would do it, my dear."

"Never," she conceded as he deepened the kiss.

"Then I will look at it tomorrow morning. I have other plans for tonight."

"I must talk to you, Geoffrey. Now. I haven't been completely honest, and I—"

"My dear," he said as he smoothed a dark curl back from her cheek, "at the moment I don't care if you assassinated the king."

She opened her reticule and removed Afton's letter. Dianthe hesitated, trying to justify not telling him the truth. But her conscience won, and she unfolded the paper and handed it to him.

He leaned toward the window, catching the light of passing streetlamps, and began scanning the lines. She held her breath and watched his face for any sign of anger or disgust. When he finished, he returned to the first page and read again. Finally, he refolded the letter and gave it back to her.

"This explains your resemblance to Nell and how she came to be in possession of your calling card. It also accounts for what she told her friends about discovering something that could set her up for life, and why she went to Vauxhall Gardens that night. She was looking for you. She must have intended to take your sister up on her offer of a new life."

"There is more," Dianthe said, returning her gaze to her lap. "Nell was not dead when I found her. She talked to me."

There was a long pause before he spoke again, his voice considerably cooler. "What did she say, Dianthe?"

"She knew who I was. She knew my name. She was very weak, and I could not decipher what she was saying." Dianthe stopped and cleared her throat, dismayed by the break in her voice. "I cannot recall her exact words. I was so frightened I could not think straight."

He reached across the distance and took her hand in his. "If this is too difficult, we can wait—"

"I want you to know everything, so that if something happens to me—"

"Hush! Nothing will happen to you." His voice was brusque.

But Dianthe was caught up in her story, her gaze fixed into the darkness, remembering. "She said thank heavens it was me. She entreated me to stop 'him' and made me promise not to let him get away with it—with murdering her. And she warned me to be careful, because he had seen me, and that I'd be next, and that he had killed others. But when I asked her who 'he' was, she…she died."

Tears were rolling down Dianthe's cheeks and her hands

were trembling. "No wonder you've been so driven to find the murderer. Enough, Dianthe. That's enough."

"There was a man on the path. He was wearing an absurd scarlet cloak and I could not make out his face, but he seemed startled to see me. Then he was gone and a few moments later I stumbled over Nell. Then…I forgot everything else."

Geoff gripped her shoulders. "A man in a scarlet cloak? *That* was how he slipped through the gates. He was the man who broke into the house and attacked you on Curzon Street. What did he look like, Dianthe?"

"I didn't see him clearly," she repeated. "The hood shrouded his face in Vauxhall Gardens, and it was dark in the library. Is he the killer? Do you know such a man?"

"Let me worry over the man on the path. I shall find him and deal with him. But you must go home, out of harm's way. I do not want you putting yourself in jeopardy again."

"I cannot stop now. I promised Nell."

"You are as stubborn as your cousin. Why didn't you tell me all this? How long have you known?"

She lowered her eyes, unable to watch his face and see his disgust. "I learned the night on Curzon Street, when you came to my room. I couldn't tell you because…well, I am from a courtesan's family. I…I have become a courtesan. Knowing that, do you wish me to leave your house?"

Geoffrey lifted her chin with the edge of his hand and whispered, "Later, Dianthe. We shall discuss this later when there is time enough for me to show you just what I want of you. Tonight I have business. And perhaps you will be safer where I can keep an eye on you."

The coach drew up at Thackery's and, when Geoffrey exited and offered his hand, she took it and laughed at his frown at her décolletage.

"Di—Miss Deauville, I believe you are wearing your gowns too low. Shall we ask Miss LaFehr to add trim?"

"If you think it necessary," she said.

"It is. To my sanity, at least." Inside, he took her wrap and handed it to a footman. "I must have a private word with someone, my dear. Stay close until I am done."

She turned to him and straightened his cravat, wondering why he still wanted to add trim now that he knew that courtesan blood ran through her veins. *"Mais oui, chéri,"* she whispered. "I will find Miss Tucker."

"See that you stay to the main rooms," he warned.

She smiled and patted the folds of the cravat as she stepped back. *"Oui, chéri."*

She glanced around to take her bearings, and a slight movement near the staircase drew her attention. Ah, it was Senor Ramirez. Geoffrey had said he'd never met the man, and this might be the time to introduce them. It would not hurt Senor Ramirez to know that her protector was not a phantom.

She caught Geoffrey's hand and whispered, "Just a moment. I'd like to introduce you to Mr. Munro's friend."

As they approached, Senor Ramirez turned his back and began to climb the stairway. Was he trying to avoid her? But with Flora's warning fresh in her ear, she thought it would be best if Geoff knew the man.

"Senor Ramirez," she called, putting on her French accent. "'Ow nice to see you this evening."

He paused, one hand on the banister. She could tell by his stiffened posture that he did not want this meeting. He turned, his expression impassive, his eyes flat.

Though standing on the stair below, Geoffrey was still taller than Senor Ramirez. His hand tightened around her arm, but he said nothing.

"Senor Ramirez, may I present Lord Geoffrey Morgan? Lord Geoffrey, Senor Ramirez comes to us from Barcelona."

The silence between the two men dragged out a fraction too long to be comfortable. Did they already know one another? Neither man offered his hand or even the courtesy of a perfunctory bow. Seeking to fill the void, she murmured, "Senor Ramirez is a friend of Mr. Munro."

"How…interesting," Geoffrey finally said. "Have you known him long?"

"Since my arrival," the other man stated.

"When was that?"

Ramirez shrugged. "A month ago."

"When last we met, Senor Ramirez said he will be returning to Spain before long," Dianthe prompted, wondering what it would take to start a conversation between the two men.

"Have you completed your business?" Geoffrey asked.

"I do not believe I said I was here on business."

Dianthe frowned. What was behind their antagonism? It was palpable.

"Pleasure, then?" Geoffrey persisted.

She looked up at him. She'd never seen him quite so intense. Quite so focused.

A thin smile lifted the corners of Senor Ramirez's mouth and a hint of a challenge edged his voice. "I always find pleasure in my business, Lord Morgan, and business in my pleasure."

She felt the muscles in his Geoffrey's arm tense, and wondered in horror if he was going to hit the man. This meeting had gone considerably beyond her intentions.

Then it was over as quickly as it had begun. Senor Ramirez nodded and continued up the stairs. The moment he disappeared, Geoffrey turned to her.

"Stay away from him, Dianthe. I'll have the coach brought 'round to take you home."

"But I must talk to Miss Tucker. If it will ease your mind, I promise not to speak with him further. Before tonight, he has always been quite attentive to me."

"How *much* have you had to do with him? What have you told him about yourself or me?"

"I…you have not been a topic of conversation. And Miss Denton already warned me against him before she left town."

"Damn! I should have left you home. If I didn't have to meet— Avoid the man at all costs. If he bothers you, or if you even think he might, find me at once."

"Where will you be?"

"Lockwood should be here tonight, and Richardson. One of the private rooms downstairs. Just keep looking until you find me or scream and I'll find you. It is urgent that I speak with them at once. When I'm done, I'll take you home."

She nodded and waited until he disappeared down one of the dim corridors before continuing up the stairs. She said a silent prayer that Miss Tucker would be in attendance.

All the rooms were crowded tonight, and the windows stood open to catch errant breezes and to allow the smoke from cheroots and the smell of overheated bodies to escape. She nearly missed Miss Tucker in the crush. She was standing in conversation with a mixed group, and Dianthe drew her aside and linked arms with her.

"Come walk with me, Miss Tucker. I 'ave to ask you something." When they had woven their way out to the mezzanine, Dianthe broached the subject that had been on her mind since reading the journal.

"Is Mr. Munro a regular with the ladies, or does 'e 'ave the mistress?"

Miss Tucker chortled. "Mr. Munro is too penurious to support a mistress, Miss Deauville. He would rather buy his pleasures on a transient basis."

"*Oui?* And are 'is needs great?"

"Of late," she said. "Flora left him dangling last night. He came to me, but I had made other arrangements for the evening. I am to meet him later tonight, though. Why do you ask? Are you not Morgan's woman?"

Morgan's woman. But for how much longer? "*Oui.* But I 'ave been warned 'is attentions are short, and if that is so, I would like to know the lay of the land."

Miss Tucker fell silent for a time as they strolled along, looking down over the main salon. Finally she heaved a sigh and replied. "Miss Deauville, I would recommend against Munro. I have already discerned that you are new to the sisterhood, but you appear to be fairly canny. A few of us have learned to deal with Munro. Those who haven't have suffered for it."

"But you told me 'e is the gentleman. And 'ow respectable 'e is. I misunderstand, yes?"

"No, Miss Deauville. I believe I also mentioned that discretion was important to survival. And, once you learn to manage the man…"

Ah, then Miss Denton had been telling the truth, and had meant her to find the little journal as a warning. The demimonde had engaged in a conspiracy of silence because their income depended upon it. "*C'est vrai?* 'E killed 'is wife?"

Miss Tucker glanced around as if afraid they might be overheard. "Hush!" She dropped her voice to a soft whisper. "Yes, I believe it is true. He has a violent nature with women, and a temper. I cannot say if the murder was planned, or simply the result of the heat of an argument, but I am certain he was responsible."

"Do you 'ave proof?"

"Heavens! What would I need proof for?"

"To…per'aps to keep 'im from 'urting you?"

"Blackmail Munro?" Miss Tucker laughed. "I am not that desperate, Miss Deauville. Such a thing would invite his wrath, not temper it."

"Should proof be available?"

"I would not chance it."

Dianthe took a deep breath. "I would."

Miss Tucker halted in her tracks to regard Dianthe with astonishment. "But why?"

"*C'est bien simple.* Men like Munro should not be allowed to 'urt women."

Gripping the rail and looking downward at the hazard table where Lewis Munro was placing a bet, Miss Tucker whispered, "I have heard there is a letter, or some sort of papers, that could incriminate him. A letter that was intercepted by Mr. Munro."

The letter that Geoffrey said he'd never gotten? That was all she needed to hear. "*Très bien.* I will tell Lord Geoffrey. 'E will demand the letter from Mr. Munro."

Miss Tucker glanced over her shoulder and pulled her a little farther along the railing. "He will destroy it before he will give it to Lord Geoffrey. And if he gets wind of your suspicion, the letter will be ash before dawn. You and Lord Geoffrey must fetch it at once."

Miss Tucker's urgency was contagious. "I do not know 'ow much longer Lord Geoffrey will be occupied," she said.

"I shall help you, Miss Deauville, for all the women he has hurt, and to keep us safe from him forever. I know just how to keep Munro busy, and I will do it gladly."

"*Mais non!*" Dianthe protested. "I cannot ask you to put yourself at risk."

"He and I have arrangements for later this evening, Miss Deauville. He will not think it unusual that I would entertain him early. And with me to watch him, you will be quite safe."

Dianthe hesitated. She glanced out over the floor below. Geoffrey was nowhere to be seen, nor was Lockwood, and opportunity was slipping away by the second. She couldn't be certain what Geoffrey planned to do with her. If she was to have any chance at all to keep her promise to Nell and discover if there was, indeed, a missing letter from Charlotte, she would need to do it now. With Miss Tucker to keep Mr. Munro busy, surely she would be safe enough for the half hour she would be gone.

She nodded uncertainly. "I will look through 'is papers and be back before anyone knows I am gone."

Chapter Seventeen

Dianthe knew Mr. Munro's address from the little journal. It was no more than a few streets away from Thackery's, and she was there within five minutes. The small town house, flanked by larger ones, looked shabby next to its well-kept neighbors. The trim was in need of paint, the windows were dirty and the steps had not been swept in weeks.

She knocked and glanced over her shoulder. She did not want to be seen standing here. People would think she'd come for an assignation.

An elderly man with only a few tufts of gray hair opened the door and hitched an eyebrow at her. "Madam?"

She prayed Munro was in the habit of entertaining women in his home, or her ploy would not work. "Mr. Munro has sent me ahead," she announced, shouldering her way into the house.

"Er, ah, he…he sent you ahead?"

"Told me to wait in his office."

"Office? Mr. Munro does not have an office."

"Library. I meant his library," she improvised, wondering where he would keep his private papers.

"When he returns, who shall I say has arrived, madam?"

"Charlotte," she said, imagining Munro's horror at hearing that name.

The man, who appeared to be the sole servant, turned and led the way down a short corridor, opening a door on the left. She edged around him, dismayed to find the room dark and not even an ember on the hearth. "Is there a light?" she asked.

The man sighed, walked past her and took a tinderbox from the fireplace mantel, and lighting the lamp on a small desk and another on a table beside a settee. "Will there be anything else, madam?"

"No, thank you. I shall be quite content to wait."

He shrugged as if he knew better than to ask too many questions, and left the room. She counted to ten, closed the door and surveyed the room.

Her best hope was the desk. She sat in the stiff wooden chair and studied the four drawers, wondering if there were any hidden springs or secret compartments. She pulled at each of them. Drat! All locked. If Munro guarded secrets or had something he wanted kept private, it would likely be there. But she had never picked a lock.

Fighting a sinking feeling, she shifted her attention to the single bookshelf with a few shelves of dust-laden tomes—far too bare to hold any hiding places. Or perhaps one of the books was a hiding place. She had read, once, of a book that had been hollowed out to hold valuables, both papers and jewels.

She crossed the room, an uneasy feeling settling around her. This was not going to be quite as easy—or as quick— as she'd thought. A noise in an upper room made her hold her breath for a moment, afraid someone was watching. When the silence returned, she began to remove the books, open them and riffle the pages, one by one.

Nothing! She had wasted time and had nothing to show for it. Defeated, she returned to the desk. She only had one choice left. She would have to pick the lock.

She slipped her wig off and removed the hairpins from the little knot on top of her head, shaking the loosened curls out of her face. She'd tuck her hair back in the wig when she was done. Breaking the tortoiseshell pin at the bend, she inserted it into the lock.

A mantel clock struck the hour and Dianthe jumped. She'd wasted too much time searching the bookcase. Geoffrey would be looking for her soon. And what if Munro decided to bring Miss Tucker home? Heavens! Dianthe would be trapped in the library, caught red-handed!

No matter how she twisted and poked, she could not turn the tumbler inside the lock. Defeated, she seized the brass letter opener from the pen tray and forced it into the gap between the drawer and the desktop. She slid it along the edge until it hit the bolt, which still didn't yield. If she pried, she would damage the desk and betray that she had been there. Ah, but the valet would tell Munro in any case, and even describe her.

With nothing to lose, she used the letter opener as a lever to separate the latch and the bolt. The sound of a crack followed by splintering wood made her cringe, and she turned toward the door, half expecting the manservant to come rushing in, demanding to know what she was doing. She held her breath, waiting. After a moment she exhaled in relief. No one had heard.

The middle drawer opened silently and she tested the ones on either side, relieved to find that the single lock had controlled all the drawers. The middle drawer was shallow, allowing for a deep knee well. There were several sheets of stationery, a few pens, a stick of sealing wax and some blotting paper.

The two drawers on the left were equally innocent, containing unopened bottles of ink, envelopes, more stationery, a small box of sand for drying ink, and other supplies. The top drawer on the right was more interesting. It held several long envelopes containing legal documents. One appeared to be a deed to Munro's country home, another his marriage license to Charlotte Morgan and a contract detailing her dowry, and yet another envelope contained Charlotte's burial papers. Dianthe lifted a small locked metal box and shook it. She recognized the rattle. Coins. This would be Munro's supply of ready cash.

An ornate leather case held a stunning necklace of emeralds and pearls, a gold ring, earbobs of jet and gold, and an emerald pendant strikingly similar to the sapphire one Geoffrey had given her. Had he chosen it for his sister? She replaced the box with a sigh of reluctance. She would have liked to return Charlotte's things to her brother.

Saying a small prayer, Dianthe opened the last drawer. Her heartbeat accelerated when she saw three oilskin packets of the sort in which her father had kept his important documents. She pulled them all out and placed them on the desk. Unknotting the leather thongs that secured them, she emptied their contents on the surface of the desk.

The first pouch contained a miscellany of correspondence. She leafed through it quickly and only stopped when a single name caught her eye. *Senor Juan Ramirez.* The letter bore a months-old date and made a veiled reference to Munro's relationship to Lord Geoffrey Morgan. Oh, how she would have loved to read Munro's reply to that. But hadn't Senor Ramirez told Geoffrey that he'd only made Munro's acquaintance after his arrival barely a month ago? Given Geoffrey's sudden and intense dislike of Senor

Ramirez, she had suspected a history between them, and this letter confirmed it.

Another letter, dated in mid-July, informed Munro of Senor Ramirez's imminent arrival in England, and requested a meeting. So Senor Ramirez had sought an alliance with Geoffrey's enemy. But for what purpose? Dianthe leafed quickly through the remaining correspondence from that pouch, but could find nothing more. Whatever else had passed between them hadn't been trusted to the written word.

The contents of the second pouch were startling and incriminating. The fabled letter from Charlotte to Geoffrey was on top of the stack. Dianthe unfolded it and scanned the lines. Here was news of her pregnancy, her fear of her husband, his abuses and infidelities, and her plea to her brother to come and take her home. This was the letter Nell had written about. The letter Munro had intercepted. The motive for both women's murder. If Charlotte left Munro, Geoffrey would have demanded the return of her dowry and would likely have filed a suit for divorce on behalf of his sister. Heaven knew she had grounds enough.

Dianthe refolded the letter and slipped it into her bodice, along with the letters from Senor Ramirez that mentioned Geoffrey's name. They were not proof, but they were incriminating.

"Nell?"

The voice startled her and she stood, whirling toward the door, the wig on her lap dropping beneath the desk. Against all odds, Lewis Munro stood there, his eyes bulging and his mouth agape. Miss Tucker was supposed to have kept him occupied!

"My God, Nell, I thought you were dead. What the deuce is going on? Fredricks said Charlotte was waiting."

With her blond hair exposed, and in the dim light of the library, Munro thought she was Nell! Dianthe gave him a nervous smile. "Are you surprised to see me?" she improvised. "Or did you know I would turn up?"

"How did you… There was a body. A funeral."

"Some innocent from the ton. Her family was out of town, so she has not been missed yet. Lovejoy was her name, I think." She waited, praying he would betray himself in some way.

"I told you to keep your nose out of what doesn't concern you, Nellie. But you wouldn't listen. Always poking around where you don't belong."

He came closer and she edged around to keep the desk between them. "I thought it was because of something I already knew."

Munro laughed but it was a harsh sound, almost cruel. "Are you hinting at my dear wife, Charlotte? Vulgar, Nellie, not to mention dangerous. I thought I taught you better than to bait me."

Her heartbeat sped. Despite the threat implied in his words, she needed just a little more to condemn him. "Why so coy now? 'Tis just between us."

The first sign of wariness showed in his narrowed eyes and a slight tilt to his head. She couldn't let him come too close, or he'd recognize her as Lizette. She had edged to the front of the desk as he'd come toward her. Now, with the desk between them, he looked down at the papers scattered across the surface.

"Looking for something, Nellie?"

She shrugged. "Was it you, Munro? Were you the one who killed the little chit in Vauxhall Gardens, thinking it was me? I thought pushing was more your method."

"You really don't know, do you?"

Again, she remained silent. He shuffled through the papers and then looked up at her again. "Charlotte's letter? What do you hope to do with that? That's no proof that I killed her. Did you think you could use it to blackmail me?"

Her heart was beating so fast she feared she would faint. She summoned all her courage to stand her ground. "Blackmail was not my intention."

"Yes. I can see that, Nellie." A thin smile slashed Munro's face and his eyes took on a sly look. "Why, you're trembling. Afraid, little pigeon? You should be."

"The letter may not be proof, but *I* am," she bluffed.

"My word against yours? Do you think anyone will believe a little whore over a respectable member of society?"

"Some might."

"Geoff Morgan?" He sneered. "His reputation is as bad as yours, Nellie. He's stolen too many fortunes at the gaming tables to have won any friends in high circles. No. 'Twas just a little shove. Impossible to prove. I'll get away with it, and there's nothing you or Morgan can do about it."

A confession! "Was it deliberate or accidental?" she asked, just to be certain.

"As deliberate as your 'accident' is going to be. And as impossible to prove. After all, everyone already thinks you are dead." He stepped away from the desk to come toward her, but his foot snagged on her wig. He looked down, then back up at her, narrowing his eyes to focus in the dim room as she backed toward the door. "Lizette? What the hell?"

She lifted her skirts and bolted for freedom.

Geoff watched the door of the private back room. The last thing their small group wanted was an interruption. Events were rapidly coming to a head, and they could ill afford distractions.

Lord Lockwood paced as he reported his progress, his hands behind his back. "We found the house down by the docks where he was keeping the kidnapped women, and they've been removed. We're holding them in a cottage outside the city for their safety. We can't find el-Daibul, but I've got a man watching the house for anyone who turns up."

"Are we sure it's el-Daibul behind the kidnappings?" Harry asked.

"Him or one of his henchmen," Lockwood said.

"I just met a man from Barcelona named Juan Ramirez. I can't be certain, but he could be el-Daibul," Geoff told them. "Can you verify his identity, Lockwood?"

"Ramirez? Damn, I've never met the man," he replied. "How can you not be sure?"

"He speaks English with a Spanish accent, he's clean shaven and wearing European clothes. But there is an indentation on his brow, as though a scar has been covered with cosmetics."

"Did you test him?"

"Nearly did, but we could ill afford a public scene. Time is essential. We must verify as quickly as possible, because if he learns we're onto him, he'll escape on the fastest transport to the coast."

Harry laughed. "If it's him, he'll have one hell of a surprise. It's the garrison at Dover that's waiting."

"He won't get that far. As soon as we verify, we'll take him into custody."

Geoff expected Lockwood to argue with him, but the man was silent for a long time. Finally he said, "I met el-Daibul when we were negotiating the release of hostages before the bombardment. I might recognize him, Geoff."

"I want him, Lockwood. You cannot know the havoc that man and his partners have wreaked in so many lives."

"Oh, I think I have an idea," Lockwood murmured. He took a generous swallow of brandy and slammed his glass down on the sideboard. "Shall we go see what's been under our noses, gentlemen?"

Harry opened the door and they stepped into the corridor. They hadn't taken more than a few strides when Emma Tucker spotted them and came running with a soft exclamation.

"Lord Geoffrey! You must come at once! I couldn't stop him, and now he's gone!"

"Stop who?" he asked. The woman looked harried and was sporting a swollen lip and a bruise high on her left cheekbone.

"Munro! He's gone after Miss Deauville."

Not Dianthe! Dear God, his greatest fear had come true! Geoffrey sprinted for the stairs.

"No!" Miss Tucker called after him. "She's gone to his town house."

He checked his momentum and turned back to the group. "I told her to wait for me."

"I confessed that I thought Mr. Munro had killed his wife, and that he had letters that would prove it. I said I could keep him occupied here so that he would not interrupt her. But he suspected something was wrong and…I could not stop him, Lord Geoffrey!"

His mind reeled. Munro and Dianthe, alone in Munro's town house. He turned to his companions. "Detain Ramirez. I'm going after Munro."

"Senor Ramirez left," Miss Tucker said. "At least a quarter of an hour ago."

Bloody hell! The son of a bitch was going to slip through their hands again. "Harry, go to Bow Street and have them send someone to Munro's. Then go to the house by the docks. El-Daibul will go there first. Lockwood—"

"I'm coming with you. Someone's got to stop you from doing murder."

As they rounded the corner and sprinted up the steps to the door, Lockwood cautioned him again. "Easy, Morgan. If she isn't here, we leave quietly. Understand?"

Geoff didn't answer. He'd tear the place apart before he'd leave quietly. He knocked hard several times and stood back. No one answered. He knocked again and looked up to see the quick flash of an elderly man duck behind a curtain of a third floor window.

"Something's wrong," he muttered.

A soft thump sounded somewhere inside and he shot Lockwood a worried glance. Of a single mind, they stepped back and then launched themselves at the entry. The doorjamb gave way with a sharp crack and the door rebounded off the inside wall from the force.

Geoff rushed through and nearly tripped over Dianthe, who was lying prone on the floor, half entangled with Lewis Munro.

Munro released her legs and scrambled to his knees. "What the hell?" he exclaimed. "You cannot just break in here and—"

Lockwood drew a small pistol from his boot and trained it on the man. "Shut up," he warned.

Geoff lifted Dianthe into a sitting position and searched her face anxiously. "Are you hurt?" he asked.

She shook her head. "Just…just had the wind knocked out of me," she said in a faint, breathless whisper.

Now that he knew she was safe, he wanted to shake her. "Why the hell did you come here? I told you to stay away from Munro."

"Miss Denton's journal said…well, I needed proof that

he murdered Charlotte. He was at Thackery's. He wasn't supposed to be here. Miss Tucker was keeping him busy. But all I found was this." She pulled several folded papers from her bodice and gave them to him. "Charlotte's letter to you, Geoffrey—the letter Mr. Munro intercepted. In it, she says she was afraid of him and that he'd struck her and threatened her, and that now that she was expecting… And there are other papers that mention your name. Letters from Mr. Ramirez."

Geoff glanced through them quickly, but when he saw Ramirez's name he handed the letters to Lockwood. Munro began decrying the violation of his home and privacy, demanding the return of his property as Lockwood scanned the lines.

But when Lockwood looked up, his eyes were hard. "Where's el-Daibul?" he shouted over Munro's protestations.

"I do not know anyone by that name."

"Ramirez, then, you bloody idiot," Geoff said. "Do you mean us to believe you were his pawn? That you knew nothing of his machinations, his years of murders, kidnappings and white slavery?"

"I don't know what you're talking about."

"It's all here, Munro," Lockwood said, waving the letters. "Letters from Ramirez to you, asking about Morgan, about where he was and what he was doing." He glanced at Geoff. "I think we have the verification you needed."

Looking more frightened now, Munro turned to Geoff. "He knew everything already—that you thought I'd killed your sister," he admitted. "He hinted that he knew a way to make you leave me alone."

"Murder me?" Geoff sneered. "Is that what he was going to do in exchange for your help? He used you to get to me, and if I know my enemy, he has no intention of leaving you alive to tell the story."

"No! You're wrong!"

Geoff stood and helped Dianthe to her feet. She swayed unsteadily and his blood burned in his veins when he thought of her at Munro's mercy. Lockwood had been right to come. Without him there, Geoff probably *would* have killed Munro where he stood.

"There's enough here to hang you, Munro," Lockwood said, tucking the papers into his jacket. "A pity they don't draw and quarter anymore."

"It's her!" Munro accused, pointing at Dianthe. "She's trumped up the evidence to help her lover get rid of me."

Dianthe shook her head, releasing Geoff's arm now that she was steady. "I don't know anything about Senor Ramirez. But when Mr. Munro found me going through his desk, he thought I was Nell. He admitted that he'd pushed Charlotte down the stairs."

"She's lying!" Munro screeched. "She broke into my house and was thieving. Arrest her, Lockwood."

Lockwood glanced between Dianthe and Munro, a look of utter disgust on his face. "Is there an ounce of truth to his claim, Miss Lovejoy?"

"Lovejoy?" Munro squinted in the dim hallway. "Not Lizette? Not Nell?"

"Nell is dead," Lockwood said.

Astonishment showed on Munro's face as he staggered to his feet. His mouth drew back, exposing his teeth in an angry snarl. "You tricked me!" he shouted.

Dianthe turned to look at Lockwood. "I will testify, Lord Lockwood. He won't get away with this. I could not make him admit to killing Nell, but I'm certain he did— because she knew what he'd done to Charlotte."

Geoff was furious that she'd endangered herself just to help him. He could have lost her, too.

"I didn't kill Nell! That was Ramirez. He killed Elvina Gibson, too. They knew too much." Munro suddenly lunged for Dianthe, and the two went tumbling to the floor.

A flash of light reflected off an unsheathed knife alerting Geoff to the man's intention, and he leaped into the fray, seizing Munro around the neck with one arm and attempting to grasp the hand that held the knife with his other. Dianthe screamed, and a stranger appeared, dragging her away from the struggle, then lifting her to her feet. A rush of fury surged through Geoff and he pulled back sharply when Munro tried to lunge for her again. Munro went limp.

Dropping his adversary and leaping to his feet, Geoff pulled Dianthe from the stranger's arms and ran his hands over her back and sides, trying to reassure himself that she was uninjured. Though she was shivering so hard that her teeth chattered, there was no trace of blood or injury. Thus assured, he held her tightly and murmured, "My God, Dianthe, what would I have done without you?"

"Renquist from Bow Street, isn't it?" Lockwood asked the stranger. "Did Harry Richardson send you?"

"Aye. I am a close friend of Miss Lovejoy's family," he said. "Are you all right, Miss Lovejoy?"

Dianthe nodded. "Thank you, Mr. Renquist."

Kneeling beside Munro, Lockwood shook his head. "Damn! His neck's broken. Do you have any idea the paperwork this will entail?"

Dianthe buried her face against Geoffrey's chest. He hadn't wanted this part of his life to touch her, but it had—in the ugliest possible way.

Lockwood nodded toward Munro's body. "I'll deal with

Bow Street on this. Meantime, we've got bigger fish getting away. You or me, Geoff?"

He hesitated. He needed to get Dianthe home and safe. Renquist stepped forward. "I'll take her home, Morgan."

Dianthe looked up at him and nodded. "Go, Geoffrey. Mr. Renquist will keep me safe."

He looked back at Lockwood. "I'll go." He'd been hunting el-Daibul for nearly five years now. He wouldn't let him out of his grasp this time. He gripped Dianthe's arms and looked down into her eyes. "I shouldn't be too long. Wait for me. Do you understand?"

She nodded and tears welled in her eyes. "Please don't do anything foolish, Geoffrey."

He gave her a reassuring smile as he scooped her reticule off the floor and handed it to her. "Not when I have you waiting," he said. He intended to go to the holding house and see if Harry had seen el-Daibul, and failing that, home to pack a bag for Dover, where he'd wait until the man showed up. El-Daibul would have to get out of England somehow, and Geoff doubted he could swim all the way to France.

Chapter Eighteen

Numb from shock and fear, Dianthe couldn't stop trembling. She begged Mr. Renquist to let her see Madame Marie before going to the house on Salisbury Street. Only another woman would understand what she needed to ask. He agreed, but told her she could not stay more than a quarter of an hour. Morgan wanted her home, and home she would be.

When they arrived at the dress shop, they went around to the back, where the Renquists had their apartments. Madame Marie, tying a light cotton wrapper around her, joined them. "*Là! Chérie,* what are you doing 'ere at such an hour?"

Dianthe hugged her friend and collapsed onto a blue damask sofa. "Oh, Marie, I needed to see a friendly face. I am still trying to sort it all out. I thought Mr. Munro was Nell's killer, but he said it was Senor Ramirez, and now Senor Ramirez is missing and Geoffrey says he is someone named el-Daibul."

Madame Marie brought a cup of tea and pressed it into Dianthe's hand. "Here, *chérie.* Breathe deep and think calming thoughts."

"El-Daibul…" Mr. Renquist repeated. "I know that

name. After I take you home, I'll go back to the Bow Street office and have a look at my files, but first I have some very bad news for you, Miss Lovejoy."

Dianthe groaned. The last thing she needed at the moment was more bad news. "Can it wait, Mr. Renquist?"

"I am afraid not. You see, I've been looking for a connection between you and Miss Brookes, and found that—"

"She is—*was*—my cousin. Afton wrote with the news. She sent my calling card to Miss Brookes and told her to contact me. That is why my card was found at Nell's lodgings." She sipped her tea and shuddered. Madame Marie had laced it with something strong. Brandy? Whiskey? Did she really look that bad?

Mr. Renquist nodded. "And McHugh has arrived in town. I told him you'd be back tomorrow, but he mumbled something about your sister's peace of mind. I'd guess he is tearing through drawing rooms even now. He swore to be discreet, at any rate."

"Discreet?" Dianthe giggled. "McHugh? Well, the fat is in fire, as they say. When will he be here tomorrow?"

"He said he'd call at noon," Mr. Renquist said.

"Then I shall be back at noon. I must face him sooner or later, I suppose."

Madame Marie gave her a sharp look and raised an eyebrow. "Shoo," she said, making a brushing motion with her hands at her husband. "I think little Miss Dianthe wishes the private talk." When her husband disappeared into another room, she said, "Your friends will rally 'round, petite Dianthe. You will live this down."

"I am not certain about that. Even if the truth is known and Geoffrey finds el-Daibul, my reputation is irretrievably damaged." She sighed. "*Madame,* I have been living with Lord Morgan."

Marie's eyebrows shot up. "I did not suspect this, *chérie*. Did you not assure us all was proper? What will your sister say? And the McHugh?"

She finished her cup of tea and sat back with a tremulous smile. "Good riddance?"

Marie coughed and glanced away to compose herself.

"*Madame,* I was frightened. And I foolishly thought I could manage by myself. Geoffrey literally saved my life. I would be in Newgate now but for him. And, I fear, I've fallen rather seriously in love with him."

"What are you going to do about it, *chérie?*"

She gave the worldly smile Miss Osgood had taught her. "If he will have me, I shall become his mistress. 'Tis all that's left for me."

To her credit, Madame Marie did not even blink. "Is this what you wished to discuss, *chérie?*"

"I admitted I love him, *Madame,* and he has not said he loves me. But when he looks at me…" She straightened her spine and sighed. "I used to think Geoffrey Morgan was beneath me, and now I realize that he is far above me. It isn't just that *my* reputation is sullied, it is that *he* was never what I believed him to be. And now I do not know how to make it up to him, or even if I can. You see, he will never marry a courtesan, and that is what I've become."

Madame Marie lifted Dianthe's chin with her index finger and dabbed the tears from her eyes. "But I think he wants you, yes? He just needs a little encouragement. So repeat after me, *chérie. I am Salome, Delilah and Helen of Troy.*"

Dianthe choked back her tears. Madame Marie had suspected all along.

When the coach pulled up outside the house on Salisbury Street, Mr. Renquist escorted Dianthe to the door. It was late, and she knew Giles and Hanson would have retired to their quarters below stairs. She put her key in the lock and turned it, then said goodbye, with the promise to see him at noon tomorrow.

The open door to the ballroom spilled light into the central hall as usual, and she passed it on her way to the stairs. Voices stopped her before she had gone far.

"Your mistress is late, Morgan. Could it be she has another lover already?"

She recognized that voice with its faint Castilian lisp—Senor Ramirez. El-Daibul. There was a taunt in the voice, too, that warned her to proceed cautiously.

"She is not coming, el-Daibul. Do you think I allow my mistresses to live with me? Just finish with me and go."

"I've never seen a man so anxious to die. Very noble of you. But do you think I am a fool? I followed her here several nights ago."

She tiptoed closer and peeked around the open door. Geoffrey, his arms tied above his head, was dangling from a rope slung over a chandelier, his feet barely touching the ground. Trickles of blood oozed down his right cheek from his temple. He'd been hit over the head! Senor Ramirez must have been lying in wait for him. If *she* had come home first… She drew a quiet breath and evened her erratic heartbeat.

"She won't do you any good, you know," Geoffrey said. "She doesn't know anything about this. She's just another little demirep who has a dozen men on a string."

"It wouldn't matter if she did," Ramirez laughed. "What matters is that *you* want her. I intend to destroy everything of yours, just as you destroyed everything of mine."

"I did not fire the cannons. It was war, el-Daibul."

"It still is war, Morgan. Why did your government order

the Bombardment of Algiers? Your urging, was it not—you and Auberville? That cannon fire killed my family. The dey exiled me, blaming me for inciting the British. I lost everything, Morgan. And so shall you."

"The dey was holding the British consul. What did he expect would happen?"

El-Daibul made a sweeping motion with a curved sword. Dianthe was so consumed by fear that she could not tell if it was a scimitar or a cutlass. She ducked back behind the door, her heart pounding in her chest while her mind worked feverishly. Her every instinct urged her to flee.

"The reasons do not matter," Ramirez said. "My family is dead, and you will pay for it."

"What are you going to do? Knock Miss Deauville over the head when she comes in, too?"

A sickening slap carried to her, and Geoffrey groaned. Ramirez—el-Daibul—was torturing him! She thought frantically, trying to sort through her options. Go for help? Not enough time. Summon Giles and Hanson? They were afraid of their own shadows. It was up to her, then. But what could she do? What weapons did she have at her disposal?

"Nell…" Geoffrey gasped. "It was you…."

"Yes, Nell. And Elvina Gibson. And Flora Denton, when I find her. But tonight it will be Miss Lizette Deauville. And you."

Dianthe straightened her spine, put an innocent smile on her face and made a fair amount of noise as she walked into the ballroom.

"Oh! Senor Ramirez! My goodness. What are you doing here at such an hour?" She was careful to keep a distance between them as she edged toward the sword rack.

El-Daibul was holding an odd whip with multiple short

lashes, and the curved sword. There was one like it in the rack, but she'd never used it.

Geoffrey strained against the ropes that held him, but dangled helplessly, only tightening the knots. "Run, Dianthe!"

She did her best to look innocent and confused, but given the circumstances, she would have to be very simple indeed not to know what was going on.

"Come here, little Lizette," el-Daibul coaxed.

She laughed. "You recognized me without my wig. How very clever of you, sir."

"How clever are *you*, my dear?"

"Clever enough to realize you are very angry with Lord Geoffrey. What has he done? Won your fortune at gambling? Seduced your wife?" She edged closer to the rack as el-Daibul moved toward the door.

He laughed. "We haven't enough time to discuss it. I must finish up here and ride for the coast." He closed the door and turned the lock, a look of deep satisfaction on his face.

She glanced at Geoffrey and he nodded when she stopped at the rapiers. She drew one from the rack and kicked off her shoes.

El-Daibul covered his surprise by laughing and gesturing at her. "How very amusing, Miss Deauville. Can you really mean to challenge me?"

Do not allow your enemy to know your skill. Surprise will be your greatest asset, and if you follow surprise with finesse, you have a fair chance at victory. She shrugged and widened her eyes. "Have I any choice, sir?"

"Lay down your sword and come to me."

She smiled. "You are teasing me. I can see by what you've done to Lord Geoffrey what you intend for me."

"But you have no hope of prevailing. It will go easier for you if you just accept your fate."

"Easy? Hard? All I know is that I have no chance at all if I lay down my sword."

He smiled, and Dianthe wondered why she had never realized how empty his eyes were. "Very well, Miss Deauville. This could be amusing. I had not thought of slicing you into pieces, but that could be quite effective." He glanced over his shoulder at Geoffrey. "What do you think, Morgan? Will you enjoy seeing her pretty little head separated from her body? Shall I take select parts of her back to Tangier with me to show around as my English souvenirs?"

Geoffrey let out a strangled growl that chilled Dianthe's blood. She knew without a doubt that he would kill el-Daibul if he could just lay hands on him.

But she could not afford the luxury of anger. She needed calm. She needed detachment. *Perception, distance, timing and technique.* She was grateful, now, for the boredom that had led to countless hours of practice.

El-Daibul showed his contempt by approaching her with his sword lowered. He took her measure and found her lacking—no competition at all. Good. That was just what she wanted. He smiled and tried to frighten her by slashing the air between them.

Concentration. She tried to anticipate his next move and was ready when he lunged. She stepped to the side and el-Daibul faltered when his blade only found dead air. She assumed the *en garde* position and he gave her a wary look.

"You've had lessons, Miss Deauville. How have you fared at the ladies' competitions?"

"I just started lessons a short time ago," she answered, keeping her eyes trained on his blade. "I've not had time to enter competitions."

He laughed, and this time sounded as if he were enjoying himself. "I wouldn't have wanted this to be too easy," he said.

She knew she would have to launch an attack before he had time to measure her skill. Once he had, any advantage would be gone. But could she injure him? Could she kill him? "I promise you, I will not be as easy to kill as my cousin."

"Your cousin? Ah yes! Miss Brookes. I see the resemblance now. But you are right. She was easy to kill. No challenge at all. My knife slipped into her like butter."

She gave a sideways glance at Geoffrey and saw that his wrists were bleeding. He was twisting the rope, attempting to fray it. She had to keep el-Daibul from seeing him or he'd run Geoffrey through.

Holding her ground, she fended off one advance after another until el-Daibul was panting. He narrowed his eyes and asked, "Is that all you learned, Miss Deauville? How to deflect my blade?"

"It was you on the path in Vauxhall, wasn't it?" she asked, ignoring his taunt, hoping at least her words would put him on the defensive. "And at the house on Curzon Street?"

"Clever chit." He lunged, his blade grazing her arm as she spun away.

Geoffrey called out a warning, but it was too late. The sting and warm flow of blood down her left arm surprised her, and made it clear that her life was hanging in the balance.

El-Daibul turned, saw Geoffrey twisting the ropes, and started for him. Dianthe knew he intended to stab Geoffrey, and sprinted past him to stand between them.

El-Daibul laughed. "Touching. But you are both going to die. You first, Miss Deauville?"

He brought his sword up and assumed an aggressive stance. He was going to rush her.

"*Sotto*, Dianthe," Geoffrey whispered behind her.

Without thinking, she closed the distance between herself and her opponent, dropping to her injured arm as she reached him, passing under his arm and thrusting upward.

Astonishment registered on el-Daibul's face. Crimson stained his shirt as he raised his sword for a downward slash. She seized her blade in the middle with her left hand. The vibration of the contact passed through her as she blocked the mighty blow. El-Daibul staggered, clutching his side from the wound she had inflicted and the desperation of his attack.

She scrambled to her feet and slashed at the rope holding Geoffrey. He fell to his knees, his hands still bound, and started sawing his bonds on the edge of Dianthe's sword. She turned back to el-Daibul and found him advancing, slower, weaker than he'd been before, but all trace of amusement gone. There was death in his dark eyes.

"Geoffrey! Hurry!"

Sudden pounding, deafening in its intensity, startled her. The ballroom door burst open and Lord Lockwood rushed through, pausing to assess the scene. El-Daibul glanced at him and then redoubled his advance, focused entirely on Geoffrey now.

The ropes fell away and Geoffrey seized the hilt in time to bring the blade up and deflect el-Daibul's attack. As the two men faced one another, Dianthe knew one of them would not walk away. Lord Lockwood pulled her back from the fight, and she bit her knuckle to keep from crying out and breaking Geoffrey's concentration.

El-Daibul sacrificed form for sheer brutal strength, dealing one bone-jarring blow after another and forcing his opponent into the defensive. She saw the cold detachment in Geoffrey's eyes and knew he would not let his anger make him careless. But el-Daibul's reckless fury was his undoing. His hatred, pain and frustration took a toll and left him vulnerable. Geoffrey found the opening and launched his riposte, forcing the man backward.

In a single swift move, Geoffrey's sword found its mark. Surprise registered on el-Daibul's face. As Geoffrey stepped back to slide his blade from the man's chest, el-Daibul pushed forward, impaling himself to the hilt. Geoffrey released the sword, allowing el-Daibul to fall to the floor, his sightless eyes staring upward.

Lockwood went to feel his neck for a pulse, and Geoffrey, breathing heavily, came toward Dianthe.

She was shaking with reaction. All she wanted was to have his arms around her and to know that he was safe. When he reached her, he touched her left arm, where the blood had slowed to a trickle.

"A small cut," she said. "Nothing more."

He lifted her left hand to examine the faint red crease across her palm where she'd held her blade.

"Nothing there, Geoffrey," she sighed.

"Just my heart." He raised her hand to kiss it, and she shivered with the seductive gesture. "I love you, Dianthe," he confessed against her palm.

The unutterable sweetness of his words made her light-headed with joy. Tears filled her eyes and she blinked them back. "Even though I've become a courtesan?"

"Mine," he growled possessively. "Only mine."

Lockwood cleared his throat apologetically. "El-Daibul is dead. I think it would be best if he wasn't found here," he said. "Do you—"

"Leave him in the street outside his holding house," Geoffrey suggested.

Dianthe stepped into Geoffrey's arms, not caring who might see or what they might think. She only wanted to feel the warmth of his touch, the strength of his love.

Lockwood nodded. "I'll take care of it," he said quietly. "Are you coming to Bow Street?"

"Tomorrow," Geoffrey murmured, looking only at her. "Lock the door behind you."

Lockwood lifted el-Daibul and slung him over his shoulder. He turned to go and a moment later she heard the front door close. And still Geoffrey searched her eyes.

"You saved my life," he said as he lifted her in his arms.

She felt a blush steal up her cheeks. "I most certainly did not!" she retorted. "You saved mine." She did not want his gratitude. She wanted his love.

He carried her up the stairs. "You could have run, but you didn't. You placed yourself between me and danger. You *protected* me, Miss Lovejoy."

She stifled a chuckle. "You are mistaken, Lord Geoffrey. I would never do that. I...I always tend to my own business."

"I don't believe you," he said.

"Well, it is your fault. You insisted I take those fencing lessons."

He laughed. "It is those *other* lessons I'm curious about. Shall we see how well you've done there?"

"I am Aphrodite." She smiled. "I am Venus. I am more than you can handle, Geoffrey Morgan."

"There's no doubt about that, Miss Lovejoy. That's what I deserve for courting a courtesan," he said as he kicked his bedroom door closed.

Geoff poured himself a cup of coffee from the service on the tea cart, settled in the chair behind his desk and prepared for the worst. He glanced at Lockwood and Rob McHugh and nodded. Whatever came of this meeting, he would be certain Dianthe did not suffer for it.

"Sorry to come so early," Lockwood began. "McHugh

insisted that he assure himself of Miss Lovejoy's well-being at the earliest opportunity, and to know where matters stand."

"Where shall we start?" Geoff asked the others, rubbing the bandages around the rope burns on his wrists, and glancing at the clock to note the time. He needed to be at the Chancery Court as early as possible.

McHugh studied him with a wary narrowing of his eyes. "I'd better hear it all," he said.

"Let's begin with the night in Vauxhall Gardens," Geoff stated. "If you have questions afterward, I'll answer them."

A few minutes later, he paused to take a breath, and Lockwood took the initiative, with a cautionary glance in Geoff's direction. "Then, last night, Lewis Munro met with an unfortunate accident. His neck was broken in a fall down the stairs at his town house. When going through his papers, we discovered that he had been corresponding with a Spaniard by the name of Juan Ramirez, who subsequently arrived here in London. Upon investigation, it was found that Ramirez was actually a Berber—Mustafa el-Daibul."

McHugh sat forward, scarcely breathing. "Here? In London?" he asked. "Where is the ill-begotten son of a—"

Lockwood continued as if he hadn't been interrupted. "He'd revived his trade in white slavery, and had come for Morgan. Realizing that we had discovered his identity, el-Daibul came here last night to kill Morgan and anyone else he could. There was…a fight, and el-Daibul was killed."

After a long silence, McHugh stood and began pacing. "Dianthe? What has she to do with this?"

Lockwood studied his fingernails. "As you know, Dianthe was the primary suspect in the murder of a courtesan. She got it into her head to investigate the murder on her own."

Geoff sighed. "It does not stop there. She was determined to find Miss Brookes's killer, and hatched a plan. Common reasoning and bald threats would not deter her. Without going into details, let me just say that only Lockwood and I know the lengths to which she went. The upshot is that her investigation entangled her with the demi—with el-Daibul. He killed Miss Brookes, who was trying to find Miss Lovejoy at the time, and Miss Lovejoy innocently stumbled into the mess."

McHugh nodded and, after his initial surprise, asked, "But what is she doing *here?*"

Geoff wished it was not too early for brandy. He sipped his coffee and sat forward, resting his forearms on the desk. "I ran into her in Leicester Square the day after Nell's murder. She could not find lodgings. I put her up in my house on Curzon Street with my housekeeper and butler as chaperones. There was a break-in—el-Daibul, but we didn't know it then—and she was nearly killed. I couldn't leave her there, and I couldn't turn her out. She wouldn't take my money, so…"

McHugh's lips twitched as if he were fighting a grin. "That must have been uncomfortable for you, Morgan. I know how my sister-in-law feels about you."

Geoff glanced at Lockwood and back at McHugh. He wouldn't speak for Dianthe—that was her privilege. If she chose not to acknowledge him, he would live with that, and keep her secret to the grave. "Regardless of how she feels, I am very much afraid she has been seriously compromised. We have lived here alone for weeks with only Giles and Hanson to serve us. I stand ready to correct the error, of course. I would have done so already if I could have used Miss Lovejoy's name on a license without inciting arrest. Lockwood, I know you have connections at the Chancery

Court. If you will help me acquire a special license, I will have this taken care of by nightfall."

His guests stared at him in disbelief. "*Marry?* You and Dianthe?" McHugh asked. "Does she know your plan?"

"I have not informed her of it, but she must realize where this was headed."

McHugh resumed his pacing. "She can be a stubborn little minx. How will you persuade her when she dislikes you so?"

"She thinks he may just be redeemable," Dianthe said from the doorway. Her arm was swathed in bandages, but otherwise she looked stunning. "His reputation has been much maligned. And mine has been much exaggerated. You do realize, do you not, Geoffrey, that marrying me will be quite a comedown for you?"

Lockwood stood and headed for the door. "I'm off to Chancery Court. Meet me there in two hours, Geoff."

Dianthe rose on her tiptoes to kiss her brother-in-law's cheek. "Thank you for coming, Rob McHugh. I knew it was just a matter of time."

McHugh folded his arms across his chest, doing his best to look stern. "Not soon enough to keep you out of trouble, Dianthe. Now you will have to marry Morgan. And before nightfall." He waved his hand when she opened her mouth. "Tsk! No arguments, missy."

Dianthe looked at Geoff and her heart was in her eyes. "I wasn't going to argue, McHugh. I was just going to say that I'm exactly what he deserves."

"I remember the day you told me I deserved to be loved. Do you love me, Miss Lovejoy?"

"More than my own life, Lord Geoffrey."

"Then I am content, since you *are* my life." He held his arms open and she walked into them. "I love you, Dianthe."

"Well, you know the old axiom, Morgan." McHugh laughed. "Lucky in love, unlucky in cards, or something of the sort."

Ah, that made perfect sense! He'd been losing at cards steadily from the day Dianthe came into his life. And now he'd won the greatest prize of his life.

* * * * *

New York Times **bestselling author**

JENNIFER BLAKE

MIRA®

Lisette Moisant is a widow, courtesy of the swordsmanship of Caid O'Neill. He bested her loathsome husband in a duel, but now she is a target for schemers who wish to steal her fortune and see her dead. It is Caid to whom she turns for protection, and guilt leaves him no recourse but to agree to Lisette's request.

But soon New Orleans is flooded with rumors, suggesting the two plotted to kill Lisette's husband all along. In a society where reputation is everything, the scandal threatens Lisette and Caid with ruin…and the person responsible will stop at nothing until they have paid with their lives.

Dawn Encounter

"The first in Blake's new series evokes everything alluring about New Orleans."
—*Romantic Times BOOKclub* on *Challenge to Honor*